BYWAY TO DANGER

SPIES OF THE CIVIL WAR ~ BOOK 3

SANDRA MERVILLE HART

Sandra Merville Hart

WILD HEART
BOOKS

Cover design by: Carpe Librum Book Design

Author is represented by Hartline Literary Agency

ISBN-13: 978-1-942265-56-6

PRAISE FOR BYWAY TO DANGER

Several years ago I had the distinct pleasure of vetting Sandra Hart's first manuscript submitted to our publishing company. Her story was about the Battle of Lookout Mountain, and became her acclaimed first novel *A Stranger on My Land.* I was amazed then at her level of research and the small details she got right. Not to mention her intriguing story and her courage in offering a fresh look at a battle that had been covered many times before. Now, several books later, I'm delighted to say that not only has Sandra maintained her quality, but her level of research and attention to detail have only improved from what was already an impressively-high standard.

In her new book, *Byway to Danger,* the third in her Spies of the Civil War series, Sandra has taken her writing to new heights. She sprinkles awesome historical details throughout that enrich the story without over-powering it. I could almost smell the goodies cooking in the bakery that is our heroine Meg's base of operations.

Sandra Hart has crafted a wonderful story, with rich characters and a taut, rollercoaster of a ride through the streets of Confederate Richmond, Virginia, and the incredibly tense lives of the undercover Union spies who live there. Yet even in constant danger, love can grow like a flower through concrete, and this, too, Sandra nurtures with a fine and delicate hand. *Byway to Danger* is simply a delightful, wonderful read. I hated to see it end!

— KEVIN SPENCER, AUTHOR, NORTH CAROLINA EXPATRIATES

Award-winning and Amazon bestselling author Sandra Merville Hart brings us another Civil War sweet romance you will not want to miss. *Byway to Danger* combines her gentle storytelling style with a plot full of secrets, danger, and sweet romance that kept me glued to the page. This is the last book of the Spies of the Civil War series and stands on its own, but if you missed the other books, after reading this you'll want to read the other two books.

— CATHERINE CASTLE, MULTI AWARD-
WINNING AUTHOR

Byway to Danger is an intriguing look into the heroism of the men and women loyal to the Union living in the South. Sandra Merville Hart's novels always satisfy this history buff with details that bring the characters to life. The love story between Meg, a Union spy and former Pinkerton, and Cade Yancey, the baker she works for who is also a conductor on the Underground Railroad, is touching as they both overcome past heartache to find love together. I found myself transported back to a time when danger lurked everywhere, but also where joy still reigned.

— CINDY THOMSON, AUTHOR OF THE ELLIS
ISLAND SERIES AND THE DAUGHTERS OF
IRELAND SERIES

Dedicated with love to Megan, Amy, and Kelly,
Three strong women
Who continue to amaze and inspire me.

CHAPTER 1

Just outside Richmond, Virginia
Thursday, June 26, 1862

"Confederate pickets up ahead." Meg Brooks, keeping her voice low, rubbed her fingers against the reticule hanging from her wrist. The hard metal of the loaded pistol calmed her, though it was scant protection against half a dozen men. Trouble from the men was unlikely, and she had shown her pass on many occasions since accompanying her cousin Beatrice Swanson to Richmond in February. Good thing Bea wasn't here today, for Uncle Hiram would not be pleased if Meg dragged his daughter into danger. She sank back against the buggy seat behind her two companions as if she hadn't a care. How she wished it were true. Fighting had erupted nearby the day before, and another one seemed likely, if dust clouds from small groups of soldiers riding in different directions beyond those guarding the crossroad were any indication.

"I see them." Elizabeth Van Lew, a wealthy Richmond citizen with no love for the Confederacy, held back on the reins to slow the team pulling their buggy. She stared at the soldiers, absently patting her brown hair, which was arranged in a bun at the nape of her neck. As the oldest of the three women traveling on the Mechanicsville Turnpike, she had taken charge the last time they'd spoken to the guards on this road and seemed prepared to do so again. "Keep calm, ladies. Be ready to show your passes."

A slight gasp drew Meg's eyes to their companion, Eliza Carrington, a few years younger than Elizabeth, who was likely in her early forties. Mrs. Carrington's back stiffened. Meg wondered why Elizabeth's long-time friend had joined their errand when she was obviously fearful.

Pickets strode across the dirt road, blocking their path. "Halt." A soldier took charge and held up a hand while his other hand rested on the musket with the business end pointed downward.

"Whoa." Elizabeth stopped the open, two-seat vehicle. "Good day, gentlemen."

Meg eyed the blue chevron on the soldier's sleeve identifying him as an infantry sergeant. Her glance swept over the others—no insignia, so the rest were privates. Hot afternoon sun beat down on weeds and bushes beside the road that reached to a forested area just beyond. Lingering dust clouds flying from soldiers racing away on horseback moments earlier was the only sign they'd been in the vicinity. She didn't fool herself. With all the activity yesterday, more soldiers were certainly nearby.

"What's your business on this road?"

"We're visiting a friend in Hanover County." Elizabeth spoke with confidence.

Meg, admiring her friend's direct manner, maintained a calm demeanor. Elizabeth and Eliza were Southerners who lived in Richmond. Meg was from Chicago. Best to allow Elizabeth to answer the sergeant's inquiries and keep quiet unless directly spoken to.

"There was fighting at Oak Grove yesterday." The sergeant's glance flicked toward the east.

Meg figured the officer was younger than she at twenty-six, yet he spoke with authority. No novice here.

"Might be more fighting today." His gaze returned to sweep across the women. "Yankees are close."

It was a timely warning, for danger was near. Meg had faced a dangerous man before—not in battle but in her husband's family. Thomas's brother had been a menace to his whole family. As fearful as she was of getting caught in the crosshairs of battle, it was nothing to the danger she'd felt from her former brother-in-law. If she could handle Lance, she could handle Confederate pickets.

"We're not going to Oak Grove." Elizabeth handed him a slip of paper from her bag.

Meg extracted her pass from the reticule hanging from her wrist and gave it to the officer. Mrs. Carrington gave her pass to a waiting private.

"Everything is in order here." The officer returned them. "Not certain it's a good idea to go on."

"We're not afraid." Elizabeth gave him a nod. "You're a credit to your country. Our country needs more good men like you."

Meg, knowing Elizabeth's Unionist support, acknowledged that she actually hinted at a desire to see more men like him serving the *Union* army. Thankfully, he didn't know it.

He flushed and raised his hat at them. "Be careful, ladies."

The temporary blockade of pickets on the road cleared after his warning. Elizabeth, giving the officer a gracious nod, set the horses moving at a walk until they topped a small hill, where they picked up speed. On their right, the forest was farther away with a farmer's field of vibrant green cornstalks lining the road.

Meg, seated beneath the scanty cover provided by the vehicle's hood, immediately missed the shade the forest had provided. She swiped her face with a handkerchief. Blistering

3

June heat wasn't entirely to blame for her discomfort, for blood surged through her veins at interactions with armed enemies.

"Well done, ladies." Elizabeth spoke only loudly enough to be heard over the horse's trotting hooves. "There may be more encounters before we reach John Botts's home."

Suddenly, a rider rode toward them at full speed. Elizabeth quickly navigated onto the tall grass to get out of the soldier's way.

"Something's happening." Meg tried to discern movement ahead through the dust cloud left behind by the rider already past.

"Look to the right, over by the tree line. Soldiers are leading their horses toward that pond by the forest." Mrs. Carrington peered toward a break in the tall, mature trees about fifty yards away. "Watering them in this heat, no doubt."

"Look there." Meg stifled a gasp. Five cannons were nearly hidden amidst a field of thigh-high cornstalks surrounded by at least two hundred Confederates. Some studied their muskets. Some counted the ammunition in their cartridge boxes. Others watched the women riding by. This was information she could pass on to her Union contacts. Unfortunately, there was no indication of the regiment or division. How many others remained out of sight in the woods beyond the field?

"Isn't it thrilling?" Elizabeth whispered. "Perhaps we'll see a battle this afternoon."

A shiver traveled up Meg's back. It was one thing to view battle smoke from a distant hilltop, as she had done the day before in Richmond. It was quite another to drive beside the soldiers in the field doing the shooting.

Cade Yancey, her new boss at the bakery where she worked, had tried to warn her of the danger, but the opportunity to acquire first-hand knowledge to pass on to her fellow spies in Washington City had proved irresistible.

4

Beyond that, she needed something to occupy her thoughts on this, the second anniversary of her husband's death.

~

*W*iping sweat from his brow after drill practice in the sweltering heat, Cade Yancey stored his musket above the shelves on the hooks, which allowed it to rest horizontally. Most folks couldn't reach the weapon there without a chair, including his new baking assistant, Meg Brooks, yet Cade, a couple of inches above the six-foot mark, was taller than most folks he knew.

Floor boards rattled in his bakery. He sighed. Everyone in Richmond had become accustomed to the ground shaking, impacts from distant cannons. They all understood. Trouble was, recent battles had jaded their natural fear. Now, citizens watched nearby battles from hilltops and rooftops, ignoring the danger of having the Union army so near.

And Mrs. Brooks was out there in the thick of it, most likely. Cade blamed it all on Elizabeth Van Lew. She'd come by this morning and invited Meg—that was, Mrs. Brooks—to ride up the Mechanicsville Turnpike with her.

Cade had continued to knead his latest batch of bread as he'd listened unashamed to their whispered conversation in the front room, where all the baked goods were displayed for customers. His keen sense of hearing took in Miss Van Lew's excitement and Meg's less enthusiastic agreement.

At least one of them understood caution.

Still, she had agreed to go.

Worry gnawed at his gut. If fighting broke out in the widow's vicinity, she faced danger from stray bullets. If Confederate officers suspected her of being on a fact-finding mission, they'd arrest her as a spy.

For he knew that was her real purpose for living in Richmond.

His friend, Paul Lucas, had never told him Mrs. Brooks was a Union spy in so many words. No, the Unionists he knew in Richmond had learned to give such dangerous secrets indirectly. Hints. A certain look. A raised eyebrow in an individual's direction. Body language. So when Mrs. Brooks asked Cade for a job, Paul gave him a piercing look that said, "Trust her. She's one of us."

Cade might not completely trust Mrs. Brooks, but he did trust Paul. He had hired her nearly three weeks before. She had begun working in the bakery last week.

This morning, after Miss Van Lew left, he strode into the front room. "This isn't a good idea."

Meg's head jerked. "You heard?"

"Both armies are nearby." He propped his hand against the door jamb and leaned closer, searching her beautiful green eyes for some sign that sanity had returned.

"Yes, but three women should be safe enough traveling together." Her auburn curls, swept back with ivory combs, fell across her shoulders as she raised her chin. "Besides, we aren't heading in the same direction as yesterday's battle."

"Armies move around." Cade shook his head. Her courageous determination sparked a twinge of admiration.

"I know, but Miss Elizabeth is set on going. " Her brow wrinkled as she studied him. "I'm looking forward to a drive. For weeks, I've done little beyond..." Her cheeks blotched bright red. "Please don't tell my cousin where I went if she comes by the bakery looking for me. She'll worry."

"Never." She didn't completely trust him either, though Miss Van Lew must have vouched for his loyalty. Meg never gave details of her previous activities. That was good. He knew nothing about them. There was plenty she didn't know about him, and he planned to keep it that way. The less she knew, the less danger she faced. "We must protect one another."

They stared at each other. Meg's glance dropped first. "Yes, well, Miss Elizabeth will bring a buggy by for me. Is it all right if I leave early?"

Nice of her to finally ask. Businesses closed in Richmond at two o'clock for the time being to allow the home guard to drill. "I'll not stop you, if your mind is set on it. I'd accompany you if not for drilling practice."

Meg's eyes had widened. "I never thought... It's good of you to..." She looked down at her clenched hands. "We'll return by evening, so I will be here in the morning."

What was she not saying? That she hadn't expected him to be concerned for her safety? He had watched her go, wishing he had the authority to stop her. Yet didn't they all take dangerous chances?

Now, he strode to the big window and stared at the north-western horizon. Puffs of gray smoke showed the direction of battle. Deserted streets told him that many watched the battle from hilltops surrounding Richmond. Since nothing was in the oven this hot afternoon, he'd join them. Maybe he'd be able to figure out if Meg was in danger.

He strode outside. Childish laughter snagged his attention. That might have been his son, had God willed differently.

Cade shuttered his mind against the pain. He was almost thankful that Meg gave him something else to think about. *Be careful, Mrs. Brooks.* He didn't voice the words as he locked the door. He'd learned to remain silent.

Too dangerous to do otherwise in the Confederate capital.

⁓

*M*eg huddled near the window of the Botts's family farm with her companions. Sounds of the cannons roaring initially robbed them of a need for conversation.

The Richmond ladies had been invited into the Congressman's home, where they sat in the parlor with his wife and adult daughters. They all watched smoke billowing on the horizon. The gray-haired former Congressman Botts had been arrested in March for no greater crime than supporting the Union. That he had spent two months in solitary confinement both angered and troubled Meg. Such a fate might happen to any Unionist.

Artillery continued to thunder its murderous intent. Meg gripped the cushion of her chair and riveted her attention toward the sky, ready to bolt should a cannon rip toward them. The battle was within a mile or two of the farm—far too close for any sense of safety.

Yet the information Meg had gleaned might help the Union in upcoming battles, a sacrifice worth the danger for a childless widow. She kept a sharp eye on the horizon for soldiers in retreat, a bad sign for those watching at the window no matter the side running for shelter at the home. Thankfully, no one ran toward them.

Finally, the thunderous rumble slowed. Meg sat on the edge of her high-backed chair, watching the field for movement. Nothing.

No way to know which side was winning, yet the diminishing noise of battle released some of the fear palpitating in the room.

They spoke in hushed tones of what they'd heard, though all eyes were riveted toward the battle smoke creeping toward them.

"How thrilling to be so close to the fighting." Elizabeth's eyes gleamed.

Her excitement to be so near the fighting wasn't shared by everyone in the former representative's family. One of the girls, who all wore their brown hair gathered at the nape of their necks, jolted every time the window rattled from a shell's impact in the distance.

"I expect I could do with a little less excitement." The former representative patted his wife's hands, which were squeezed together in a prayerful pose so tight that her knuckles showed white.

"No doubt your family had enough worries this spring. How were you treated in prison?" Elizabeth scooted to the edge of her seat.

"They came without warning in the middle of the night." Sighing, he glanced at his wife, whose face tightened. "I was held at McDaniel's Negro Jail."

Meg, guessing that the Congressman was near sixty, shook her head at the indignity of the unwarranted arrest. Several other citizens were arrested without warrants around the same time, for no greater crime than being a Union supporter.

"The jail is now called 'Castle Godwin' after the prison's commander." Elizabeth stared at the gray smoke cloud billowing over the tree line. "I despaired of your release. How did it come about?"

"Captain Alexander told me he'd release me in exchange for my service as a brigadier general in the Confederate army." He waved his hand in disgust. "I'd not go against my own principles in such a manner. Finally, I agreed not to publish any more letters against the Confederacy in exchange for my release. It's good to be back with my family." He smiled at his daughters.

Mrs. Botts sandwiched his hand in hers.

Meg's heart constricted. Mrs. Botts still had her husband. While Meg... No, she wouldn't allow her thoughts to go there. It was the anniversary bringing her grief to the surface.

"The battle appears to be in the vicinity of Beaver Dam

Creek." Congressman Botts turned his attention to the northeast.

"Think we're winning this one?" His wife scooted her chair closer to her husband. Whether she sought comfort or gave it was unclear.

"I asked one of the pickets who stopped us how the battle was going." A look of derision crossed Elizabeth's face. "In his opinion, the Confederates are whipping up on us."

"Perhaps, in this instance, they are." Meg spoke in a soothing tone. "Yet I believe events will turn in our favor eventually."

"Is it my imagination"—Mrs. Carrington's brow furrowed as she stared out the window—"or is the fighting becoming sporadic?"

Meg realized she was right. The floor didn't shake. Nor did the window rattle.

"I believe you're right." Elizabeth's eyes widened.

"Ladies, if you are determined to return today, I believe you must take advantage of this lull." Their host rose to his feet. "Confederate soldiers are near, but the battle is not coming from the Mechanicsville Turnpike."

"Yes, let's do leave now." Meg pushed the drawstrings of her reticule further up her wrist. There had been no need for a shawl in this heat. "We'll be back in the city well before sundown."

"A wise suggestion." Mrs. Carrington touched Elizabeth's sleeve. "I don't feel comfortable remaining this close to the musketry."

Meg was ready to return to Richmond—now that she had information to pass on. She stared at Elizabeth, who had secured the vehicle for the day's travel, hoping she agreed.

"It's such a thrill to be close to the thick of things. I feel there's more to be seen." Elizabeth sighed. "Since you both want to leave, we will go."

Meg gave a crisp nod, fearing if she showed any sign of

faltering they'd be there overnight. She must be at work shortly after dawn.

They were on the road back within a quarter hour.

Canteens, bedrolls, and knapsacks lay in trodden-down fields where Meg remembered seeing soldiers a few hours earlier. The men might have advanced toward the battle, or they might be lined up, awaiting orders.

Lone riders on horseback cantered through the fields and along the turnpike at various points. A picket in high spirits checked their passes at an intersection. Was he happy to be near the battle? Or had the battle gone well for the Confederacy?

As they neared Richmond, she began to compose a letter in her mind.

Elizabeth turned onto Eighteenth Street, where Meg's boarding house was located. "Why, I do believe that landau belongs to Trudy Weston. I recognize her driver."

Meg craned her neck. Her cousin, Bea Swanson, stepped from the open carriage, her face tense and worried as she grasped her fiancé's hand. It was only then that Meg remembered an aunt of Bea's lived near Mechanicsville.

CHAPTER 2

"Bea." As soon as the wheels stopped, Meg alighted from the buggy to rush to her cousin, her junior by seven years. "What has happened?"

"My aunt Victoria has come with my cousin Carolina to Aunt Trudy's home today. Carolina's children are with her. That's a good thing." Bea tossed her head, and her blond curls held back by combs tumbled across her shoulder. "It's the reason they came."

"Today's battle." Meg patted her arm.

"We were there." Elizabeth, seated beside Mrs. Carrington, spoke from the buggy.

Bea gasped. Then, as if recalling her manners, she greeted Meg's companions, as did her fiancé, Jay Nickson, who stood beside her.

"You traveled to view the battle?" Jay's eyebrows shot up, nearly reaching the sweep of his brown hair across his forehead.

Meg flushed at his incredulous look. She liked him very much as her cousin's future husband—even if he supported the Confederacy—and didn't want to lose his good opinion by believing her foolhardy. "No, Miss Elizabeth invited me to accompany her to visit a friend. Yesterday's fighting happened more to the east, nearer your uncle Isaac's home in Seven Pines. That's several miles from Mechanicsville."

"Not as the crow flies." Jay's brow puckered in concern.

"We watched much of the fighting from my friend's parlor window." Elizabeth smiled, as if remembering the excitement.

"Not the combat." Meg hastened to explain as Bea's face blanched. "All we saw was smoke from the battle."

"Why didn't you tell me you were going?" Bea took a step back, her expensive yellow dress rustling against Jay's leg.

Because you would worry. "There was no time. Besides, we're safely back in the city." Meg wished they were having this conversation away from the pedestrians. One couple unashamedly slowed to listen.

"We must be going." Elizabeth's glance flicked across the strangers who stopped a few feet from her buggy. "Thank you for coming with us today, Meg."

"My pleasure." Meg uttered her goodbyes as they left and then turned to Bea. "Do you want to come inside? Mrs. Ferris allows us boarders to use the parlor."

"Aunt Trudy wants you to come to supper. Uncle Isaac brought Aunt Meredith yesterday, so we are quite a crowd with the two children."

"I'd welcome that." Meg was only related to Bea, as their mothers had been sisters. She had stayed with Trudy Weston when she and Bea arrived in Richmond in February and had grown quite close to the gracious, kind woman, so much so that she called her "Aunt Trudy" and considered her family. "Let me tell Mrs. Ferris I'll be out for supper."

While inside, Meg hid her pistol in her third-story room. No need to tote the weapon to Trudy's spacious home in the Church Hill neighborhood of the city. However, she did bring her pass that allowed her to move freely about the city. Otherwise, if General Clayton's men who enforced the curfew asked to see her pass and she didn't have it, the situation could become ugly quickly. She never went anywhere without it.

Once seated in the landau opposite the betrothed couple, Meg leaned toward Beatrice. "Tell me about your aunt Victoria. Why did she come?"

"Her servants noticed soldiers near their property. That was enough for Aunt Victoria to flee to Richmond. Good thing she came. We heard the cannon blasts from here." Bea glanced at a family standing on a landing at the base of a roof. "Lots of folks watched from roofs. I can only imagine what you saw."

"Let's just say I never want to be any closer to the fighting." She kept her tone light to ease Bea's worry. Her cousin was one of the few who knew of Meg's spy activities, which had escalated after she came to Richmond. She had been a scout at the Pinkerton National Detective Agency, until Allan Pinkerton released her in December, saying only that her services were no longer required. That didn't stop her from sending information to Washington City. She was just no longer paid to provide it.

"Do try to avoid it," Bea said. "When you weren't at your boarding house, we looked for you at the bakery. Your employer wasn't there either."

"He works long hours." Cade had impressed Meg in the nearly two weeks she'd worked for him because he knew how to keep his mouth shut and listen. "In this heat, most bread preparation is done in the morning and after sunset. Is your uncle Michael in town?"

"No. He remained at the plantation. Arthur—that's Carolina's husband—stayed with his own farm. It's significantly smaller than Uncle Michael's land but plenty big enough to provide a living, according to Carolina." Bea giggled. "Be warned. Carolina loves to talk."

Meg laughed. "I don't mind." Perhaps she'd discover something important to add to tonight's note to Ina Riggs, a former Pinkerton scout.

A distant rumble drew all eyes to the northwestern sky.

"It started again." Bea's blue-eyed gaze settled on wispy gray clouds on the horizon.

"Indeed." Meg pondered how they could approach the roar of cannons with such resignation when last month's battles had panicked citizens to such an extent that many packed their possessions into wagons and headed westward.

The answer must lie in the inevitable. Folks didn't want to live in a constant state of fear. Worse than the battles were the wounded they always brought to the city. Meg had held the hand of a twenty-year-old as he passed from his wounds. All he'd wanted was to make it back to Tennessee to marry his childhood sweetheart. He had been far too young to die.

Richmond's citizens had already seen enough war-related tragedy to last a lifetime.

~

*C*ade, watching Mrs. Brooks roll out buttermilk biscuits the following morning, feared that her baking skills weren't up to his father's standards. Had George Yancey still been alive, Cade figured Meg would already be gone.

So far, he had given her the easiest tasks. No yeasted breads after the first day's fiasco. Ingredients were far too precious at this stage of the war to waste them on teaching an employee how to bake, something he'd assumed she knew when she applied for the job. She had cooked for her husband. Perhaps they had purchased their bread.

"Did anyone ever tell you that you're a quiet man?" Meg set her rolling pin aside and crossed her arms, her beautiful green eyes searching his face.

He grunted. He'd heard that more than once. Evelyn had said the same at the beginning of their courtship, but she got used to it. Of course, he was happier back then. And he wasn't courting

Mrs. Brooks. She worked for him, so there was no pressure to make conversation.

"I've been here an hour, and all you've said is 'You can bake biscuits this morning.'" She brushed back a wisp of hair.

"Ten dozen." Meg sure looked pretty with a smudge of flour on her cheek.

"That's right." She gave him an impish grin. "I forgot. You told me ten dozen."

A woman with a sense of humor. He liked that. He checked the bread dough. Looked good. Poked it. "You got back last night in time to have supper at your aunt's home." He began the dough's final knead.

She paused, biscuit cutter poised over the rolled dough. "You saw my arrival?"

"Wanted to make certain you got home all right."

Her eyes flew to his. "Thank you. Knowing someone watches out for me helps."

Good to know she appreciated his watchful care—even if she'd ignored his advice to steer clear of the battle. He sighed. No need to dwell on it. "Learn anything yesterday?"

"Miss Elizabeth took us to former Representative Botts's farm. I learned why he was released."

He placed the kneaded bread into loaf pans for a final rise before baking and listened to her brief explanation about the Congressman's agreement to stop writing letters on the Union's behalf. Waited for more. In vain. So she knew how to keep her mouth shut too. He admired that trait, especially under current circumstances. "Have any trouble?"

She shuddered. "We were too close to the battle for my comfort."

"How close?" His protective instincts spiked at her involuntary shudder.

"Maybe a mile away." She explained where the former congressman figured the fighting took place. "I didn't see any soldiers fighting, yet the smell of gunpowder permeated the atmosphere."

"Encounter pickets?"

"Four times. No problems."

Good information to pass on to his Unionist contacts. It was also safe for him to travel on the Mechanicsville Turnpike to replenish baking ingredients, for news on the streets last night had been that the Confederates had pushed the Union farther from Richmond. He most often traveled in another direction anyway, but it was nice to have options.

Meg left out details she might have told a friend. Perhaps, someday, they'd trust one another. Miss Elizabeth trusted her, and Cade figured the older woman to be a powerful ally.

"I want to display either biscuits or muffins in the window every morning." Meg kept her eyes lowered as she cut another biscuit and placed it with the growing number on a greased baking sheet. "Can you leave them there until noon?"

A clue for someone. What did it mean? "Care to explain why?"

"I'd rather not right now." She picked up the baking pan. "I have to get these in the oven. Please don't sell whatever's on display until lunch."

"Is it anything to do with me?" He eyed her.

"No." She looked at him then, her green eyes clear and honest. "I'll never do anything to hurt whatever it is you do. We're on the same side."

He believed her. He rubbed his clean-shaven jaw, considering if the baked goods could be mistaken as a sign *he* was giving to someone. Under the leadership of Confederate General Clayton, a security force of men wearing shield-shaped silver badges stamped with "C.S. Detective" roamed Richmond day and night in search of spies and Union supporters. They were good at picking out the smallest changes. Their presence made it more difficult for them all.

Still, baked goods in the window were an advertisement to draw in customers.

"What do you say?"

The simple act could cause trouble for him if noticed by the wrong folks. "If we're out of biscuits before noon, we'll sell those. Otherwise, we'll try it a few days."

A light flickered in her eyes. "Understood."

He figured she did. "I'll get this bread into the oven."

"I'll follow you."

He led the way to the three-sided, roofed outdoor kitchen, which was outfitted with three ovens and as many worktables. Two he kept at a moderate heat for baking bread. Meg went straight to the last oven, the hottest one, and placed her tray inside it.

Delicious aromas of rye bread baking in one of the kitchen ovens struck him afresh when he strode back inside. He placed his hand inside the oven to check the temperature. Perfect. His mouth watered. This was his favorite type of bread, and he only made it two days a week. Cade kneaded a third batch of white bread dough, which should be ready to bake after the next loaves came out of the oven.

"Are you making cinnamon cakes?" Meg measured flour for more biscuits.

"Four of them. That's next." In the morning, something was always going into the oven as soon as something came out. It required planning. And silence for thinking. His new assistant must not appreciate the peace found in silence.

"I think we should slice them into generous squares to sell for a nickel." She waved a cloud of flour dust away from her face. "More customers could buy one."

"Make them a bit larger and sell them for a dime." It was something he hadn't considered. The whole cake had sold for twenty-five cents a year ago, before the cost of ingredients had escalated.

"Perfect." Her face lit up at his agreement.

Cade couldn't deny the extra set of hands allowed him to sell more goods. And when she wasn't talking all the time, it was nice to have her here. He could get used to her presence.

Four taps on the back door. In the middle of the day? This might be trouble.

"Take those baskets of muffins into the front and display them on plates already there." Sweat beaded on his forehead. "Stay there five minutes and then get your pan from the oven."

Her eyes darted to the closed door and back to him.

He feared she'd ask more questions, and he had no time to answer any.

Instead, she carried two baskets into the store area.

He shut the door behind her. Quick strides took him to the back door. Who needed help now?

~

The first cinnamon cake was warm from the oven when Meg swung wide the front door at eight o'clock that morning. The room smelled of cinnamon and freshly baked yeasted bread, making her long for a piece. Since she missed breakfast every morning at the boarding house to arrive here at six, Cade allowed her to help herself before they opened. She had devoured a hot biscuit before learning he planned to make the cake. If there was some left at the end of the day, she'd eat a piece. After all, he'd agreed to sell individual slices.

She sold two loaves of bread, a dozen biscuits, and five cake squares in the first half hour before there was a lull in customers. Her baking was done for the day. Since Cade hadn't emerged from the kitchen with more baked goods, Meg opened the door dividing the two rooms.

Cade wasn't there. Rounds of rye bread cooled on boards

next to two cakes. The man was a gifted baker, no doubt about it. Organized too. He had to bake in an orderly manner to produce so many baked goods daily.

She wondered who had been at the back door earlier. Cade had been coming down the stairs from his living quarters on the second floor when she reentered the kitchen. A sweep of dark brown hair across his forehead almost hid his furrowed brow. Shadows had darkened his blue eyes. His expression changed to his normal pleasant demeanor when he met her concerned gaze. When she asked who had knocked, he merely said, "A friend."

The back door now opened silently, giving her a start. "Oh, it's you."

"Expecting someone else?" Cade set two gem pans containing two dozen Graham muffins each on one of the empty boards covering a table.

"No." She sliced into a warm cinnamon cake. "It's simply that you move quietly for such a—"

"Big man?" He quirked an eyebrow at her. "And give those cakes another five minutes to cool before you cut them."

"Sorry." Meg held up a piece, brushing crumbs from her pink bib apron. "Want to share this one with me?"

He reached for his half and ate it in two bites.

"I didn't mean to imply you are heavy, by any means." Quite the opposite, she mused, staring at his broad chest and muscular arms. He'd be a tremendous support in a fist fight, not that she imagined too many picked a fight with a man his size. His strength likely pleased the Home Guard. She had no doubt he joined those protecting the city to mask his Unionist support. "Your step is light for such a tall man." He towered above her five-foot, four-inch slender frame.

"A skill I learned as a boy." His expression shuttered as he carried a tray of rye bread to the front room.

Her teasing smile died at a fleeting glimpse of some remembered pain. So, he had learned to walk as if on eggshells when a child. Was that also when he'd learned to keep his mouth shut? She finished slicing the cooled cake and carried it to the front room.

"That cinnamon cake smells delicious. And how nice to see it available in slices." A woman in a yellow calico dress followed Meg to the table where sweet treats were displayed. "How much?"

"Ten cents a slice." Meg hid a grimace at the price. Before the war started, she would have been ashamed to ask so much.

The stranger stared at it. "Wrap up three slices. The biggest ones, please."

Meg flushed as Cade glanced at the irregular pieces. She'd have to be more careful with her knife next time. "Of course."

"Did you hear the good news?"

Meg, in the middle of moving the cakes to a square of paper to wrap them, quirked an eyebrow at the woman.

"Lee's army pushed the Yankees further away from the city." The young woman's face lit with pride.

"In yesterday's battle?" Meg glanced at Cade on the far side of the large room. His hands stilled in rearranging a basket of muffins.

"That's right. Me and my young'uns watched from the roof. Must have been an impressive sight up close."

"Likely." It had been frightening to be so near the shot and shell. Meg could vouch for that.

"Some say that Stonewall Jackson marched his men to the battle to save the day, but it ain't clear they made it in time." She sighed. "Got a cousin in Jackson's army. I figure I'll hear it from the horse's mouth soon enough."

"It's good to have such strong, brave men serving our country." The talkative customer didn't realize Meg referred to the Union as she finished wrapping the woman's cinnamon cake.

"That's a fact. Well, that cake and the rye bread in my basket is all." She paid Meg. "Thank you kindly."

Grateful for the update though frustrated that the Union had been pushed back from Richmond, Meg dropped the money in the divided cash box behind the only glass display case. She reflected on how much information their customers unknowingly provided. Two notes with such tips had already been sent to Ina Riggs, her Washington City contact, since she'd started working at the bakery.

Other customers spoke of the nearby armies yet didn't provide new information.

Meg prepared sandwiches for her and Cade's lunch using rye that he held back for his own meals. Later, she stayed busy with customers while he cleaned both kitchens.

He counted the money after Meg locked the door. "It was a good day. Selling individual cakes insured it all sold. Good idea."

"Three Graham muffins, five corn muffins, and eight biscuits left over." She combined them on one plate. "Want to sell them tomorrow?"

"Nope. Leave them in the kitchen." He wrote some figures into a journal and then followed her to the kitchen. "I might go replenish supplies this evening. Here's the key to the bakery in case it's locked in the morning."

Rumbles sounding like distant thunder drew both of their eyes to the northwest sky. It could only mean one thing on the clear, hot summer afternoon. "Another battle."

"Likely. This one's farther away."

"Strange how much we've learned about such things in the past weeks."

He grunted.

She placed the key in her reticule and pulled the drawstring tight. "You must be traveling out of the city to obtain your supplies."

More distant rumbles.

"It's cheaper. I'll need you to start preparations immediately if I'm not down yet."

"Not … bread?" She put a hand to her throat. Her first attempt had been unsalvageable, and he hadn't asked her to try again.

"Not for a while yet. We'll serve other goods tomorrow." A spark of mischief lit his blue eyes and then was gone. "You've prepared biscuits, corn muffins, and egg rolls. Think you can do all those again? Same numbers."

Trepidation gnawed at her stomach. "What if I don't remember all the ingredients?"

"My recipes are over there." He pointed to some pages on the table lining the back wall. "Ever made a tea cake?"

She shook her head uneasily. How long did he expect to be gone?

"It's easy. Leave it until last." He eyed her with a touch of concern. "I'll probably return with flour and such by then anyway. Open at the usual time no matter what."

Meg took a step closer. "Cade, what will keep you away all night?"

CHAPTER 3

*A*s soon as Meg left for the day, Cade prepared a sandwich and carried it with a glass of milk upstairs to his three-bedroom quarters and sitting room that had once housed his family. He could still hear his pa's drunken slurs. "Spill that milk and I'll have your hide."

Closing his mind on those bad memories, Cade entered the middle bedroom on the back wall, the one without windows, remembering to shut the door behind him. His old room still had his childhood bed and dresser. He and Evelyn had planned to prepare it for their first child's room, once the infant no longer needed to nurse.

Sadness enveloped him. He avoided this room unless a runaway slave required its protection, as a young man did today. Setting the man's meal on the dresser, he rapped on the wall. "Jim. It's me, Cade."

He slid a slat of wood on the wall upward to reveal a latch. He lifted it, and a hidden door sprang open.

"Mr. Cade, I sure am glad to see you." A slightly-built black man of perhaps twenty emerged, rubbing his eyes.

"Remember to whisper." Cade maintained a light tone in an

attempt to lessen the fear in Jim's eyes. "There's no one in the bakery, but our voices mustn't carry outside. My neighbors know I live alone."

Jim's brown eyes darted toward the door.

"Daylight's no doubt welcome. Sorry you can't have light in that closet. Lantern light could alert a customer you're here. I tried to patch up all the tiny cracks in the floor and walls, but I never want to take a chance with a man's life." He pointed to the plate. "Go ahead and eat. We won't leave until nightfall. You'll ride in a hidden compartment in my delivery wagon."

"Glad I won't have to walk." Jim took a huge bite of his sandwich.

Cade explained every aspect of the escape the young man needed to know except where he planned to take him. With the armies in the vicinity, he might change course mid-trip, as he'd done on several occasions. No sense placing fellow conductors in jeopardy needlessly.

"Can you do all that?"

"Yessir, Mr. Cade." A determined glint lit his eyes.

"I have to be gone for a while." Dratted daily drill practice cut into what he was able to do for his fellow Unionists, but volunteering for temporary Home Guard service had shifted suspicion from him. That made it worth the effort. "You'll hide again until I come for you. We won't talk then. At all. Don't speak unless I speak to you. If I can, I'll sing a song while we're traveling. Listen to the words to know if the escape is going well or if you need to stay alert for danger."

"I can keep my mouth shut." Having finished his sandwich, Jim downed the milk in one long swallow.

Cade believed him. He'd come all the way from Georgia already on the Underground Railroad. "Need anything before I go?"

He shook his head. "Reckon you put everything I needed in my hiding place already."

"Good." Cade cleaned the room and washed the blankets and clothes left behind after each guest *traveled on*, as his ma had put it. "Since the customers are gone, you can stay in this room while I'm gone, but scurry into the closet if you hear someone coming. Close the door behind you until it clicks."

Jim nodded.

"I'll give you a sack of food tonight."

"Much obliged."

Minutes later, Cade strode along the streets to drill practice with his musket resting against his shoulder. He whistled as if he hadn't a care while he kept a sharp watch for anything out of the ordinary.

∼

*M*eg meant to return to her boarding house room only long enough to retrieve her latest carefully written note to Ina, which was nestled in the basket she carried with her for shopping. She was almost to the bottom of the stairs on the first floor when Mrs. Ferris, her talkative landlady, hailed her from the hall.

"Mrs. Brooks." The gracious Southerner, a childless widow like Meg, hurried down the hall from the kitchen. "Was that Miss Van Lew I saw last evening? You descended from a buggy where the driver greatly resembled her."

"Please, call me Meg." A request she'd repeated twice since moving here two weeks before. "I accompanied Miss Van Lew to her friend's home."

"Oh?" Bright blue eyes surveyed her, inviting her to elaborate.

Meg busied her hands with repositioning a cloth in her nearly empty basket.

"Where did you go?" The woman's blond hair, pinned into a

bun, shifted when she inclined her head. "A fair distance, I'll wager, since you didn't return until time for supper."

"Not too far. I came home and told you my aunt asked me to dine with her, remember?" Meg kept her eyes lowered. So Mrs. Ferris monitored her actions. Curiosity about her boarder from Chicago? Or for some other purpose? She'd best be careful to keep her correspondence on her person in the future. "I did hear the roar of cannons."

"It's all rather frightening, isn't it?" Eyes wide, Mrs. Ferris covered her mouth with her hand.

"It can be." Sights and sounds of the day had kept her awake during the night, but her landlady didn't need to know. "I've been told that General Lee pushed the Northern army back."

"Yes, a great relief it is."

"Pardon me." A pretty young maid, Delphine, hurried over. "Cook has a question for you."

"I was just on my way out anyway." Meg half turned toward the door.

"Will you return for supper?"

"Oh, yes. I will see you then." Meg stepped outside and shut the door without waiting for a reply.

She decided to take a meandering route to Main Street. Mrs. Ferris just let her know she was monitoring her comings and goings. Not knowing if there were others watching her, it seemed best to alter her route sometimes. This made for a long walk, and she already felt the effects of rising early after a tiring day.

Her thoughts turned to the pleasant supper she'd enjoyed last evening. Bea's aunt Victoria had peppered her with questions about the battle. The beautiful woman in her fifties with thin gray streaks in her brown hair wore it in a braid pinned around her crown. Her looks and poise reminded Meg of her cousin, Annie Finn.

On the other hand, Carolina, Victoria's blond-haired daughter, filled every lull in the conversation with chatter. Carolina had brought her children to the city's safety while her husband, Arthur, stayed on their farm. Gabby, her five-year-old daughter, could be heard playing with Daniel, three, in the parlor while the adults talked.

Since Miss Victoria planned to stay with her sister until the current round of battles ended, Meg looked forward to seeing them at church on Sunday. Aunt Trudy had also invited her brother and sister-in-law to lunch, should it be safe to travel, for they lived outside the city.

Chances were good Meg would learn some bit of information to pass on. She hoped her contributions had been helpful because it cost one dollar and fifty cents to send notes via mail carriers like Mrs. Jordan and her husband, the couple she planned to meet this afternoon. Miss Elizabeth also gave her information to pass on—without knowing or caring about her method. Unfortunately, the wealthy woman never offered money toward the expense, possibly not knowing a price was involved—a cost beyond the danger of discovery.

That was something all spies and Unionists feared.

Even Cade must fear it.

He had evaded her question that afternoon. Where was he going that required him to be gone overnight? Did it have something to do with the person who'd knocked on the door that morning? He had sent them away quickly. Perhaps someone had given him information that demanded action.

With troops from both armies within ten miles of the capital, it could be anything.

If only he trusted her enough to tell her. Yet she had her own secrets.

What would it take for them to trust each other?

A train whistle jolted her from her thoughts. Meg looked around, surprised to find she was at the Central Railroad depot on Broad Street, a train chugging its way out of the station. She should have taken a left already, on a side street leading to Main. No, this was fine. It was better to take different routes in case she was followed. She'd best keep her wits about her, for Mrs. Jordan didn't know she was coming today.

That was something she wanted to discuss with her.

A few minutes later, Meg spied Mrs. Jordan emerging from a milliner's shop, hatbox in hand. The woman in her forties might prefer gingham to silk, yet she always wore large fashionable hats. Today's wide-brimmed blue hat was decorated with white silk blooms and purple berries.

Meg gave a slight nod and then followed the older woman to a bench. Pedestrians across the street weren't close enough to overhear their conversation.

"Good day to you." Mrs. Jordan set her hatbox at her side.

"Good afternoon." Meg smiled as if they were mere acquaintances and not involved in passing secrets out of the Southern capital. "Lovely day for a stroll."

"If I hadn't ordered a hat, you would have missed me today."

"Yes, I have an idea to avoid that."

"Do tell." Mrs. Jordan rarely looked at her as she fanned herself with an elaborate ivory fan. Instead, she observed the people on the street with a pleasant expression.

"I will try to keep my correspondence to one or two a week." The high cost was already a strain. "Watch the morning display in my baker's window. Corn muffins means no letters. Biscuits are a sign that I'll deliver mail to you, and the number of them is the time I'll be on Main Street that day."

"I'll alert my folks. It seems a good plan." Mrs. Jordan pursed her lips. "But if Clayton's men start nosing around..."

"No more signals." Meg agreed. Cade would watch for trouble too. "If you see cakes and breads in the window, I had to abandon this signal." She pushed the basket close to the letter-carrier.

"Very wise." Mrs. Jordan lowered her fan to her waist,

managing to block her other hand fishing in the basket. The note and payment were whisked into a concealed pocket as the fan continued to sway back and forth.

"How is your dear husband?" Rising, Meg placed her basket on her arm.

"Tolerable." She arranged her skirts as she stood. "Mr. Jordan is away. I expect him in two days."

"Safe travels to him." No letters would be delivered until he returned. No need to deliver notes for a couple of days. "Good day."

Mrs. Jordan inclined her head and then scurried away.

Meg went inside a flower shop so that anyone watching imagined that had been her errand.

Little would they know her chore had already been accomplished.

～

*C*ade met the first pickets a mile outside Richmond around nine o'clock, beating the city's curfew by an hour. His pass was in order. The Confederate guards seemed too excited about something—possibly the nearby battle—to care why he was on the road after dark. They let him go.

Distant rumbles dwindled to a stop after he left the capital because the fighting was too far away. A conversation with his friend, Paul Lucas, after drill practice led him to believe the day's fighting was some thirteen miles east of Richmond in the vicinity of Gaines's Mill. Cade uttered a silent prayer that the mill hadn't been destroyed, for he acquired a fair amount of goods there.

Cade had traveled there several times that year, but he wasn't about to risk a trip there tonight. There were other mills closer to Isaac Pratt's homestead, which was his current destination. The first order of business was to get Jim safely to the next stop on his journey. Should there be sheriffs or military near Isaac's place, he'd drive to the next stop. Though Jim had food and water, it was best not to leave him hidden too long in the compartment large enough to hold two regular-sized men.

Woods lined the Williamsburg Stage Road, a familiar byway by moonlight. Yet Cade always kept a sharp eye out for unwelcome folks hidden in the trees and bushes and urged old Sam to a faster pace.

He wanted to let Jim know things were all right but to beware. Church songs worked best because others didn't usually see them as signals.

"*A mighty fortress is our God,*" he sang softly in his baritone voice. "*A bulwark never failing.*"

He continued singing. An owl hooted from a branch overhead. Crickets sang. After a mile, there was a small clearing with a cabin and then more woods continued for not as long a stretch.

Cade drove on, his enclosed delivery wagon rumbling over the road for all to hear. Allowing this everyday noise was better than sneaking about, at least it had been for him. So far. Most folks on this oft-traveled road were familiar with his wagon and baked goods. They didn't pay him much attention during daylight hours. He had an answer ready for being on the road at night should anyone ask.

Movement on the road ahead in the clearing. No time to sing an alert for Jim.

"Halt." A gray uniformed man swung a lantern.

"Whoa." Cade guided his faithful horse to a stop. "Good evening to you."

"Your pass." More men stood at the side of the dirt road. Seven in all.

Cade pulled it from an inner pocket, where it rested next to his pistol. His musket lay concealed under a blanket at his feet. He never looked for trouble, but he'd meet it head-on if necessary to protect the man hidden beneath the floorboards. Unfortunately, there was no way old Sam, while pulling the bulky wagon, was going to outrun a fit man running after them. Maybe Cade should think about getting another horse.

"Yancey's Baked Goods." The man held a lantern toward the painted side. "Business good?"

Cade shrugged. "Folks always need bread."

"Reckon so." He handed the pass back. "Where you headed?"

"To a mill to purchase supplies." Cade glanced at the blue chevron on the soldier's sleeve, showing he was an infantry sergeant.

"At half-past nine?"

"Work all day. Then drill as Home Guard." He scratched his head before replacing his slouch hat. "Makes for long hours."

"Ah. One of ours."

Not by a long shot. Cade didn't allow even the flicker of an eyelid to betray him.

"Then you guard the city." The sergeant handed him his papers and stepped back. "There's a place for you in our army when you've finished that work."

"Much obliged." Cade eased up on the reins and old Sam plodded off.

The Pratts lived off the road a mile from there. If Cade ran into more soldiers or if he was followed, he'd have to drive an extra eight miles to the next safe home.

Fifteen minutes later, he checked behind him. Nothing. Crickets sang. He always took that as a good sign.

"Were not the right man on our side," he sang. *"The man of God's own choosing."*

He wasn't a man who took unnecessary gambles. His spirit was at peace about getting Jim to safety, like it usually was when God let him know it was all right to proceed.

He'd go on as planned. Risky, but didn't everything he'd done since Fort Sumter hold an element of danger?

CHAPTER 4

*C*ade stirred at first light with a roaring hunger. His hiding place yards from the road had allowed him to sleep four hours after dropping Jim off safely with the Pratts. Isaac told him that he was skittish to take Jim further until the armies stopped moving around so much, so the man was to hide out with them. Cade believed Isaac had built a concealed room in the cellar, but he never asked particulars. It was better he not know details that didn't affect him.

Couldn't tell what he didn't know.

His father's pocket watch, one of the few things from his pa he really treasured, showed that it was five minutes past six. He devoured a biscuit that he'd held out from Jim's sack for his own breakfast. Not bad. Meg was learning. She would be at the bakery by now. He hoped she got the ovens heated to the right temperature without him, for he'd be pushing it to arrive in time to open the bakery for the day's business.

Raising the suspicions of those who might be watching him by opening late—or not at all—was the last thing he wanted. He'd best get started.

Harvey Ferguson no doubt was up and working, even if his

mill wasn't officially open for the day. Cade fed and watered old Sam and then hitched the horse to the wagon. The horse had been with him seven years now. Evelyn had made a friend of him by sneaking him apples the first year of their marriage.

Best not think of her now, not when there was so much to do.

The mill was less than five minutes away. Harvey might quirk an eyebrow at the early customer, but he'd accommodate Cade. The empty sacks on the wagon's floor would be full when he reached Richmond.

∼

eg brushed back her hair with floured hands. No time to redo the combs. She'd started the day with such high hopes, having unlocked the back door at half past five.

Heating up the ovens in the outdoor kitchen had been her first challenge. How did Cade make maintaining two ovens at moderate heat look so easy? The third one, which needed to be heated to a high temperature, got there much faster, probably because she'd added a generous amount of wood to the kindling straight away.

A person observing might think she'd never cooked or baked a day in her life.

Thank goodness she'd finished the biscuits, which filled two baking sheets. She shoved them into the hot oven and then pondered the other stoves. Waving her hand in despair at her lack of knowledge, she added more wood to them and then rushed to the kitchen to start the next batch.

Where was Cade?

Wait. He always had the two ovens in the kitchen heated and ready for use whenever the outdoor ones were full. She laid her hand on one, as if there was any hope it was already lit and

34

ready even though the owner was nowhere to be seen. Of course, it was as cold as the morning dew.

Not a moment to spare on building fires now. That task must wait. She had to have something to sell when the bakery opened. Biscuits were quick. After another batch was baking, she'd prepare corn muffins. What was next?

Ah, yes. Egg rolls and tea cakes. The easy things first.

Meg scurried outside with two pans of biscuits ready to bake and placed them on the table. A burning smell stopped her short. Was that ... smoke?

Her heart sank as she flung open the oven door. Gray smoke billowed out in a wave and then grew wispy. She covered her hand with a towel and rescued the overly baked goods. The biscuit tops were far past the golden color Cade favored but not yet charred. She flipped one over and gasped. Black.

This wasn't the way Cade sold them.

Near tears, she shoved the unbaked ones in the moderate oven. *Please, God, let these be better.*

Now for the muffins. And then she'd tackle the egg rolls.

She didn't know if she had enough courage to prepare tea cakes.

No time to wallow in remorse. A glance at the clock on the table sped up her heartbeat. Half-past six and nothing to sell yet.

Hurry back, Cade.

                             ~

A church bell rang eight times as Cade drove into Richmond. Ten minutes later, he guided old Sam into his small barn behind the bakery. An unfortunate burning smell wafted over from the outdoor kitchen. He sighed. The morning apparently had presented some challenges for Meg, who had never burned anything before today. He unhitched his horse.

He'd unload later, but Sam needed some care before Cade could get to the baking he was itching to do.

"Well? Are you going to help me?" Hands on hips, Meg stood in the doorway to the barn, her cheeks flushed.

"Almost done brushing down Sam." Sunlight fairly crackled against her auburn hair, turning it to the shade of burning coals. She sure was pretty. A man would have to be blind not to notice. "If you want to help, you can pour some oats from that burlap sack into his feed box."

"There's only a couple dozen egg rolls left in the display case." She made quick work of filling the bin. "Along with two baskets of muffins and a plate of biscuits."

His heart sank. "That's enough oats. Old Sam here is the only horse eating it. Did we have a lot of customers?"

"Four." Her chin dipped toward the bodice of her high-necked blue gingham dress.

Actually fewer than normal. It had been worse than he'd thought. Part of the reason he'd hired her was so that he'd be able to open the bakery doors for business even if one of his frequent overnight excursions kept him away past dawn. She had *opened* the doors at eight. He reckoned that was something.

"I was tempted to put the burned biscuits on display but thought better of it. They're not up to your standards."

"Get some rest, old boy." He patted Sam's neck and put the brush away. "Good decision. Let me take a look at the displays before I start baking."

Meg followed him through the back door and then hurried toward the front room. "I'll check on customers."

After folding up his sleeves, he lathered his hands, face, and arms with lye soap at the indoor kitchen basin. No time to shave. A day's growth of whiskers would have to suffice. He ducked his thick hair under the flow of cold water from the indoor pump, one of his pa's renovations before he passed on.

Cade grimaced at a charred smell that wafted over from a

table. Glancing over his shoulder, he spotted two baking sheets of biscuits far past the over-done stage. No need to examine the bottoms. He knew they were black as soot. He'd see if he could salvage them in a recipe later. Doubtful. Surveying the mess, he scrubbed his wet face and hair with a hand towel.

Long strides took him into the bakery, blessedly empty of customers. Not as fortunately, the display tables were nearly as empty. Meg had not exaggerated the problem.

The worst of it was he had no sponge or yeasted dough ready, which made up the base of many of his baked goods.

"My apologies." Meg crept to his side. "Nothing went as planned."

"I'll start breakfast cakes and Yorkshire puddings." He pushed the dividing door open and held it for her.

"Yorkshire pudding?"

"Popovers, really, since these won't contain beef drippings." He grinned. "You can grease the gem pans for me while keeping an eye out for customers."

She nodded. "Are you going to tell me about last night?"

"Nope." He'd given Isaac the news from Richmond. Isaac, a fellow Unionist in addition to being a conductor on the Underground Railroad, gave him some news about troop movements near his home that Cade planned to pass on to Paul at his earliest opportunity.

Too bad there was not a moment to spare for the task right now. It was difficult to say if such facts would help the Union generals by the time the information reached them. He and his fellow Unionists in Richmond did the best they could to fight this war in their own way.

Meg's shoulders stiffened at the rebuff.

When she asked no more questions, Cade gave his concentration to his baking.

They worked as a team. To his amazement, within an hour generous supplies of breakfast cakes and popovers were displayed in the front room. Sally Lunn and tea cakes were in the ovens, which had finally cooled to an appropriate heat.

Sales picked up as Cade continued to bake, keeping three ovens full.

Meg made another batch of biscuits that turned out golden brown.

"I have sausage in the cellar for our lunch." His mouth watered at the aroma of freshly baked biscuits. "Hold out a half dozen of those and I'll make gravy."

"I'll eat the burned ones."

"Slice off the charred bottoms." He sighed. "I will too."

Her gaze flew to his. A smile, her first of the day, lit her eyes. Green, the color of grass on a summer's day.

He had to stop noticing such things, especially when he didn't know what all she was involved in.

There was a basket of muffins in the window. It meant something, though he didn't know what. He prayed she was careful.

Meg ate between customers. "Popovers are gone, and I just sold the last of the tea cakes. Will you make more?"

"Too late in the day. Just sell what we have."

Supplies weren't nearly as available as they had been a year before. He couldn't afford to waste them. He had schooled Meg on building fires in the oven on the first day to achieve the best baking results and had taken her lack of questions for experience.

He'd teach her again. Monday. Tomorrow was the Lord's Day. He never missed church if he could help it, for he needed the Lord's steady hand on his shoulder to keep his courage up.

Then again, what did he have to lose if he were caught spying? His life? Not such a loss to anyone but himself.

And he was ready to see his sweet Evelyn and little Cade in heaven, whenever God called him home.

CHAPTER 5

*M*eg watched for Cade to enter the church building from her place beside her cousin.

"Who are you looking for?" Bea craned her neck.

Jay, seated beside his betrothed, looked over his shoulder.

Meg flushed to be caught looking for her employer. "Cade Yancey. I thought if he was sitting alone, I might…I mean, he must be lonesome." She'd observed no evidence of him courting in the few months they'd been acquainted. She'd first met him at a party at Elizabeth Van Lew's home. That evening had been her most enjoyable by far since … when?

Since before Thomas died.

"I don't see him." Bea's gaze traveled along the crowded pews. "Jay, will you wait for him by the door and invite him to sit with us? Since Aunt Trudy is sitting with her sister's family, there's room for one more here."

"Of course." Jay half rose.

"No, please." Meg reached across Bea to clutch his arm. She wanted such an invitation to come in a more natural way than waiting for him at the door. "The service is about to begin."

"True." Bea studied her. "We'll invite him to lunch. Uncle

39

Isaac and Aunt Meredith will also be there today, if no battles nearby prevent them."

"Lee's army has pushed the Union army farther away with these daily battles." Jay gave a slow smile. "The rumble of cannons grows fainter with each one."

Smiling radiantly, Bea patted his arm.

This wasn't good news for either Bea or Meg, who both supported the Union. However, Meg understood why Bea was happy for her fiancé. The couple had worked through their differing loyalties with respect and love before deciding to marry.

Meg looked around once more and spotted Cade sitting alone in the back row. He gave her a smiling nod, which she returned.

He had forgiven her for yesterday's fiasco. The more she worked with him, the more she liked him. That was as far as she allowed her thoughts to go.

~

*T*he elegant table where Cade had sat in between Meg and her cousin, Carolina, at lunch made him uncomfortable, for he'd seldom been in such surroundings, and never for a meal. He spoke only when necessary, which thankfully wasn't often. Carolina talked more than any woman he'd ever met, and as a bakery owner who waited on customers all day, that was saying something.

It had been a long time since anyone cooked him a meal. He relished every bite of his lunch, especially the onion soup, roasted chicken, and cucumber salad. Even the plums pickled like olives and the cole slaw garnished with fried oysters, though new to him, left him longing for a larger portion.

He noticed underlying tension between the older siblings,

specifically Isaac and Victoria. Everyone there was family except him and Jay—and Jay soon would be.

Cade wondered why Mrs. Trudy Weston, the hostess, had invited him. Though he attended the same church as the majority of these folks, he only really knew Meg, and she had been a silent observer throughout the meal, same as he.

"I heard shot and shell coming from your general direction while we sang the opening hymns this morning." Looking at Isaac, Jay settled back in his chair, his fingertip circling the rim of his cup of coffee.

"We were already halfway here when it started." Isaac, seated in between his wife and his sister, Trudy, shook his head in a mixture of frustration and resignation. Gray lightened his brown hair liberally, and Cade guessed him to be in his mid-fifties. "No one was on our land this morning."

"Battle sounds stopped by the time we arrived here." Meredith, a pretty brunette her husband's junior by possibly a decade, shuddered. "I've grown accustomed to seeing soldiers in our vicinity, but I will never accept as normal the thunderous roar of shells ripping through homes and trees and men."

"Nor should you." Trudy Weston half reached her hand toward her sister-in-law, who was seated on the other side of her husband. Gray curly hair had been tamed into a bun, leaving the wavy sides to the confines of multiple white combs. An elegant, high-collared blue dress enhanced the blue of her eyes. "You suffered enough ruin at last month's battle to last the war."

Cade appreciated his hostess's calm demeanor and good sense demonstrated throughout the meal. A good judge of character and a fair judge of age, he guessed Trudy to also be in her fifties and younger than her brother.

"One would think so." Isaac's right hand curled into a fist. "Though most of our damage came from soldiers trampling our crops."

"Of course, you are welcome to stay here as long as you like." Trudy gave her sister-in-law a gracious nod.

"Perhaps staying here for the next couple of days is a good idea?" Meredith raised finely-arched eyebrows at her husband.

"Let's see what the day brings, my dear." He patted her hand as he glanced at Victoria.

Soldiers seemed to be on the move throughout the vicinity. Cade figured himself lucky that his overnight excursion had been Friday night instead of last night, for the Swansons' plantation was somewhere near Seven Pines on the Williamsburg Stage Road, the same road he'd traveled before taking side roads. No, not luck, he thought, but Providence.

Two women entered the dining room and began clearing the table. Cade hoped that the ladies, possibly mother and daughter from the resemblance, were among the significant number of black families who lived as free citizens in the city. He hoped Trudy Weston paid her staff.

"When Lee's army is done with the enemy, they'll be nowhere near the capital." Jay gave the woman taking his plate a smile. "Thanks for another wonderful meal, Clara."

"I've missed your cooking." Meg handed her an empty plate. "Thank you."

"You just stop by anytime you've a mind to, Miss Meg." She inclined her head.

These interactions increased Cade's hope that the women were paid workers.

"I second that invitation." Trudy gave her an affectionate smile. "Clara, we're ready whenever you want to serve the cake."

Bea straightened her back with a glance at Meg.

Jay gave a smiling shake of his head at his fiancé and then looked at Meredith. "You'll soon be able to rest easy that you're safe in your home, Mrs. Swanson."

"It's good to know you're confident in our army." She smiled at him. "I share your faith in them."

"Mr. Yancey, how long have you lived in Richmond?"

Cade was surprised at Isaac's question. After his initial brief answers about owning a bakery and hiring Meg, the family had almost ignored him. "Thirty years now. My father and mother moved here from England when I was two."

"I didn't know you were born in England." Meg's fingers touched her parted lips.

"County of Norfolk." He considered how much of his background to reveal to Meg's family and decided little harm could be done. "My father desired to seek his fortune in the former colonies. He sold our bakery and moved us here."

"A big adventure for a little child." Isaac's keen brown gaze studied Cade.

"I still recall the salty smell of the ocean." And his brother, who had been buried in its murky waves. He tamped down the long-ago memory of the infant who'd died on the ship. How different his childhood might have been had he lived. For his parents, too, for he now understood how the loss had been the start of his father's downward spiral. Having survived the death of his wife and son, it was now a tad easier to forgive the way his father had treated him.

"Did you help out in the bakery as a youngster?"

"From the age of four." He grinned. "My pa's specialties were bread and rolls and such. Mama's pies and cakes were popular with customers. My first baking lessons were from Mama until Papa noticed I had a knack for making dough. After that, the family concentrated on my breadmaking skills."

"I can testify that the bread is the most delicious I've eaten." Meg's smile held a hint of pride.

"High praise, indeed." Trudy clasped her hands together. "I will buy bread there whenever necessary. Clara bakes most of what our family consumes."

"She's a fine baker. Those egg rolls were delicious." Cade

didn't want to ruffle any feathers for Clara's sake. "I'd appreciate your business for whatever Miss Clara doesn't provide."

The door opened. "Here's Clara now. She made you an orange cake, Meg, to celebrate your birthday." Trudy's blue eyes twinkled at Meg, who flushed.

Clara brought in a cake with white icing and laid it with a flourish on the sideboard. Her daughter followed with plates and silverware.

Everyone smiled at Meg. It seemed they had all been in on the surprise. Except for the holidays, it had been six years since Cade had participated in a family celebration. He feared he didn't belong at this one.

"Thanks for making the cake, Clara, but it's not my birthday." Meg fingered a cameo broach on the high collar of her green dress.

Clara began slicing the cake.

"Your birthday is Tuesday." Bea grinned at her. "Everyone's here today, so we decided to celebrate now. Are you surprised?"

"Very. Thank you, everyone." Her smile encompassed them all. "It's been awhile since I celebrated the day."

"Understood." Trudy gave a crisp nod. "But this year you are among your loving family and friends. Many happy returns of the day, my dear."

"I'll give you my gift in the parlor." Bea's blue eyes sparkled.

Cade, who had nothing to give, felt even more out of place. Why had he accepted this lunch invitation?

~

Once in the parlor, Meg received a beautiful green satin dress from Bea, Bea's sister Annie, and Jay. Aunt Trudy gave her a dark blue moiré dress, its watered silk soft against her skin. Trudy's own dressmaker had made both.

Meg's last dress purchases had been for mourning, which

she had finally packed away. She appreciated the personal and thoughtful gifts. She'd wear the satin gown to church soon and then save it for special suppers and events. The blue dress was perfect for church and picnics.

In addition, there was a delicately woven white wool shawl from Victoria and Carolina, and white gloves from Isaac and Meredith. All were beautiful items that she wouldn't have been able to afford. She must watch every penny to continue sending coded messages to Washington City.

Everything was extravagantly useful. Her gratitude at the party planned by Trudy and Bea filled the hole of loneliness left by missing family members.

Of course, there was nothing from Cade, who had not known of her birthday.

She thanked everyone as distant rumbles began.

"Another battle." Bea sighed, her face almost resigned.

"Yes." Jay, sitting beside her on the sofa, clasped her hand. "This one seems further away."

"I'm thankful Michael sent word yesterday that our land suffered little more than a few damaged trees on the west side." Victoria stared out the window.

"You were more fortunate than I, Victoria." Isaac stood. "If you young ones will excuse us, my wife and I will visit with my sisters."

"It's a beautiful day," Bea said after they left. "Let's go to the garden."

"The children will love that." Carolina, with Gabby and Daniel, led the way.

Bea and Jay followed.

Cade offered his arm to Meg. When she rested her hand on the sleeve of his gray jacket, she was unprepared for the thrill that ran through her at the warmth of his muscular arm. Why, she hadn't felt such a reaction to a man since Thomas.

Unsettled by her thoughts, she kept her face lowered lest Cade sense her embarrassment.

"I can say my goodbyes by the garden." Cade spoke in a low voice. "My apologies for interrupting a family celebration."

"No, please stay. Bea and her sister Annie are my closest family. Since you're my employer, I know Bea wants to get to know you better." So did Meg, she realized as she looked up at him. She'd never touched him before and hadn't realized he was quite so tall, towering over her by nearly a foot. It surprised Meg to discover she liked his height.

In fact, almost everything about the man intrigued her.

"Are you certain?"

"Completely." It was pleasant to have someone here specifically for her.

The opportunity for private conversation ended when they entered Trudy's well-maintained garden with its stone walk, magnolia trees, and ornately-carved white metal furniture.

The whole day had been like a wonderful oasis in the midst of war.

Even so, a battle in the north occasionally shook the ground.

CHAPTER 6

Cade baked a walnut cake for Meg's birthday on Monday evening. It had been one of the cakes that his mother sold in the bakery, one of the few cake recipes he remembered by heart. He iced it and stored it in the cellar, hoping she liked his surprise.

"Many happy returns of the day," he said the next morning when Meg arrived shortly after dawn.

"You remembered." Her smile lit up the kitchen. "Thank you, kind sir." Pulling her skirts wide, she curtsied.

"My memory's not that poor." Cade laughed. It was actually excellent. He never wrote down secrets he learned, feeling it safer not to have a written record. "We celebrated two days ago."

"True." She set to work on her now daily routine.

They both remained busy all morning. Cade made them sandwiches for lunch and then retrieved the cake, one of his favorites.

After that, he had to wait five minutes for the store to clear. "Meg, I have a little surprise for you."

Her eyes widened.

"It's a trifling thing." It had been years since he'd baked a cake, and he was nervous.

She followed him into the kitchen and then gasped. "Cade. You did that?"

Heat spread up his face.

"It's lovely." She stuck a finger in the white icing. "Delicious. I love the taste of vanilla. What kind is it?"

"Walnut."

"My mother used to make those when I was a child." Her smile broadened. Happiness only enhanced her natural beauty.

"Mine too. She always warned me to each lunch first."

"I guess, as responsible adults, we ought to follow her advice."

He grinned. "It's all right to act like a kid sometimes."

"Let's do that." She laughed.

"Cake first."

"Absolutely." She stepped closer and placed her hand on his.

His hand shook slightly at her soft touch. It had been so long...

"Thank you, Cade." Meg's smile faltered as her green eyes searched his.

A tap on the dividing door brought him back to reality.

"Anyone there?"

Meg dropped her hand as the door was pushed open.

"Pardon me, but can I buy a loaf of white bread?" A mother with two children hanging on her skirt darted a glance between them.

"Of course." Meg scurried after her without a backward glance.

A good thing, too, because Cade had the sudden urge to kiss his employee.

That wouldn't do at all. The widow needed to feel safe around him.

~

*C*ade was able to pass several important messages on to Paul in the next few days. The Confederates had driven Union soldiers back to Harrison's Landing on the James River. In reality, though the Union army had been about five or six miles from Richmond at the battle Meg witnessed, it was still only thirty miles away. It might as well have been one hundred miles, judging from the relief on customers' faces as they spoke of it to Cade.

Those customers had no idea how much information they provided about Confederate soldiers to the Union army via Cade's messages to Paul Lucas.

Wounded soldiers from the battles filled the hospitals. Temporary medical facilities had been opened and quickly filled. Many citizens were involved in nursing the soldiers. Wagons toted the dead to the cemetery, sad sights that nearly robbed Cade of his breath. The worst were the family members frantically searching for their husbands and sons in the various hospitals. Cade wished he could ease their desperation. Their sorrow kept him awake at night until exhaustion claimed him.

War was a terrible thing.

He closed the bakery early for Independence Day. With the hospitals full, there were fewer public celebrations. Cade attended a band concert, something he especially enjoyed. He didn't ask Meg to join him, for he knew she had plans to join her family for a picnic by the river. Also, he didn't want to give her the wrong impression. He was not ready for courtship.

Yet he was lonely. Had been so for six years.

Cade looked forward to church on Sunday and hoped it brought another invitation to the Weston home. He'd learned that Meg spent every Lord's Day with her family. It had been nice to be part of a family, even for a few hours. His own ma and pa had died years ago.

On Saturday, while Meg was out front waiting on customers, there were four taps on the back door. A boy of perhaps thirteen needed passage to the next safe location. Runaways were supposed to come only during the night, but this was the second person in a row to arrive unaccompanied during the day. He'd have to get a message to the families sending the fugitives to him. Anything done during daylight carried greater risk.

He hurried the boy named Jacob upstairs and explained in whispered tones exactly what came next.

The boy listened as if his life depended upon it. He explained he was from North Carolina and intended to reach the safety of Fortress Monroe, for he'd learned the Union army opened its arms to runaway slaves there. Cade agreed the boy's plan was a wise one.

As he descended the stairs from his living quarters, Cade reflected that he wouldn't receive an invitation from Trudy Weston for lunch tomorrow. Because he wouldn't be at church at all.

～

"Where do you suppose Cade is today?" Bea led the way to a private sitting room on the second floor of Trudy's home the following afternoon.

"I've no idea." They had kept their distance from one another since her birthday. She had the distinct impression he had wanted to kiss her when a customer barged in. Perhaps she had been mistaken, yet the interruption had been welcome. Cade also seemed surprised by her touch. Likely that was all it was. "Jay's working?"

Nodding, Bea closed the door behind them. "He'll be here for supper. I'll tell him the news then."

"What is it?" Meg sat on the sofa while Bea opened every

window in the cozy room with chairs and sofas arranged in a semicircle.

"I'm going to Washington City now that the battles have shifted from Richmond." Bea perched beside her and arranged her half-hoop pink dress over her knees.

"Good." Meg didn't own any hoops and was sadly out of fashion. She wondered if Cade liked the hoop dresses.

"Aunt Trudy will go with me. Having an extended visit with her sister has made her miss her brother all the more."

"After learning that her brother Isaac cheated them all of their inheritance last month, no doubt Aunt Trudy needs to see your father." Meg released a pent-up breath. She'd promised Uncle Hiram, Bea's father, that she'd leave Richmond whenever his daughter did. Her presence on the trip wasn't required, though, since family accompanied Bea.

"Aunt Trudy has forgiven Uncle Isaac for altering Grandfather's will. She's even forgiven the lies Uncle Isaac told Grandfather to put his siblings in a bad light." Bea clasped her hands together. "That doesn't mean she'll allow matters to remain as they stand. Since Aunt Victoria's husband owns more than double the land of our family's plantation, she only regrets her brother's dishonesty."

"It sounds as if your father and Trudy want to discuss the matter." Meg recalled the destruction a battle caused to Isaac's plantation. That devastation was small compared to the hurt the man's greed caused his siblings. He'd bared his heart to Trudy when she came to comfort him after the battle ended. Meg would never forget the compassion Trudy demonstrated toward her broken brother.

"They've corresponded by mail and telegram." Bea nodded. "I hope an agreement can be reached that gives them both a small plot of the inheritance. I'd like to see Father receive a significant portion of the five hundred acres the original will apportioned to him."

"Perhaps they will pursue such a course after the war?" Meg saw wisdom in waiting. There was enough to deal with in the meantime.

"I can suggest it." She leaned forward. "Aunt Victoria will return home this week. We'll begin travel preparations after that. Aunt Trudy is enjoying their visit. She may spend a few weeks with her sister after the wedding this fall."

"So you have a date set?"

"Not yet."

Bea looked so forlorn that Meg smothered a chuckle. She remembered those precious weeks with Thomas before the wedding. "Enjoy this time of planning. Much will change after your marriage."

"I know. That's why I want to spend several weeks with Annie." Her expression lightened. "If I can persuade her to travel to Richmond with me, we'll all be together until the wedding. Jay can't take more than a few days away from Tredegar—and that's not guaranteed. We'll go to New York City after the war for our wedding trip."

"Sounds lovely." Happiness for her radiant cousin bubbled up inside Meg. "When will you leave for Washington City?"

"Next week. Perhaps Monday." She clapped her hands. "I can't wait to see Annie and Father."

"I miss Annie too. Give her my love." Bea's sister Annie had stayed in her childhood home after her marriage while her husband John served the Union army somewhere in Virginia. Meg had grown even closer to her cousins when living with them over the fall and winter until she and Bea had traveled to Richmond in February. Those months had been eventful. Martial law had been enacted in March, leading to unwarranted arrests like the one of former Representative John Botts. "Now that I'm working at the bakery, I don't have time to volunteer at the hospitals. Are you still there?"

"I've been at Chimborazo Hospital nearly every day this

week. Wounded from those daily battles filled it. Tents have been erected for new patients." Bea shuddered. "I had to walk past a wagon filled with dead soldiers on their way to Hollywood Cemetery. No caskets. Not even a blanket covered them."

"Tragic." Meg was glad she'd escaped such a sight. "Perhaps I could leave the bakery early one day a week and volunteer at Chimborazo." It was a long walk. She had skills to help, having worked there from February until she'd begun at the bakery. She'd ask Cade.

The parlor door burst open. Gabby and Daniel ran into the room with Carolina on their heels. "My apologies." She brushed back wisps of brown hair that had escaped the twin braids pinned to above her ears. "They want to play with you in the garden. I kept them occupied as long as I could to give you a nice long visit together."

Bea laughed. "Who wants to stay inside a stuffy parlor when the sun's shining on a hot summer day?"

"Not me!" Gabby grabbed Bea's arm. "I'll go with you."

"Me too." At three, Daniel mimicked everything his five-year-old sister did.

Carolina held out her hands, palms up. "Is that all right?"

"It's perfect." Meg held out her hand to Daniel, who put his small palm against hers. "I'm ready for a bit of sunshine as well."

～

*E*lizabeth Van Lew, whose Union support had cemented her friendship with Meg, stopped by the bakery the next afternoon during a lull in customers. Cade, who seemed tired and more quiet than normal, was cleaning the outdoor kitchen.

"Miss Elizabeth, how lovely to see you." Meg didn't dare speak of Unionist secrets with the front door open to invite folks inside. Thankfully, Elizabeth was always just as careful. "What may I get for you?"

"Two loaves of bread." Elizabeth raised her eyebrows and gave a slight nod out the door.

"White bread?" Meg took the unspoken message to mean someone watched her from the street.

"Please."

Before Meg moved away, Elizabeth mouthed, *Come to my home after work.*

Meg inclined her head to show she understood. After that, the bread was paid for and inside the basket on Elizabeth's arm.

"Good day to you." Elizabeth gave a crisp nod.

"And to you. Come again soon." Meg moved to the window display and made a fuss of rearranging the muffins as she glanced out the window in every direction.

A tall, thin man wearing an inexpensive suit lowered his wide-brimmed hat over his eyes and strolled after Elizabeth. He kept about fifty yards between them, pausing to look at window displays twice. When Elizabeth turned a corner, he sped up after her.

Meg moved away from the window. She didn't know the man, but he bore all the traits of an experienced spy.

Elizabeth had complained to Meg several times of being watched. Today Meg had witnessed it for herself. She hoped to learn more from Elizabeth later in the afternoon.

⁓

"I know you are as devastated as I am to see General McClellan's army driven from our very doorstep." With a slight shake of her head, Elizabeth Van Lew sipped her tea in her elegantly furnished parlor.

"It's a blow, for the Union had a chance to end the bloodshed." Meg sank back against the comfortable cushioned chair and surveyed her disappointed hostess seated opposite of her. "Perhaps they will march back to the capital again soon."

"I pray that is so. I had prepared a room for General McClellan to stay here while conquering the city." She held out one hand, palm up. "For naught."

"All is not lost." Meg set her teacup on a side table and leaned forward. "The worst thing we can do is give up."

"I shall never give up." Elizabeth lifted her chin. "We must not lose."

"Agreed." Meg wished she knew the outcome, but God alone knew that. "Folks like us, each doing our part, may help to turn the tide."

"I believe that." Determination filled Elizabeth's eyes. "In light of that, I have a note for you to pass on to your Northern contacts."

She crossed the room to a bookcase where bronze animal statues were displayed. Meg craned her head for a better view when Elizabeth picked up a bronze dog sitting back on its haunches, front paws playfully in the air. This was upended and a circular page extracted from a hollow inside. Elizabeth replaced the statue.

Meg marveled that a common statue had become a hiding place. Even knowing something was there, she couldn't see anything amiss from her spot across the room.

Elizabeth handed her the paper. "Thank you."

Meg placed it in her reticule, wondering how long she could provide this service for free.

"Winning this war will be thanks enough for me." Elizabeth sat and sipped her tea.

"For both of us." Meg figured, when put that way, one and a half dollars was little enough to pay. "You were followed this afternoon, just as you implied."

"You saw him?" Her eyes widened. "He was a Southern gentleman, but that was all I was able to glimpse."

Meg described him. "Oh, and he had a brown mustache."

"Him and half the city." Elizabeth sighed. "I've been followed before, but this one was persistent. No matter which way I turned, he followed."

"This wasn't his first time following someone."

"Then you must be careful also. Do not walk directly to your boarding house." Elizabeth's brow wrinkled. "Why did you move from Trudy's home? Weren't you comfortable there?"

"Oh, very comfortable, indeed." She had moved out to protect the gracious Southerner who supported the Confederacy even if she hated slavery. Not something Elizabeth needed to know. "Once Cade Yancey hired me, I moved to be within a block of the bakery."

"I see." Her brow was still puckered as she studied Meg. "Is there any news for me to pass on?"

"If I learn anything from my customers to pass on, I'll come see you." Elizabeth had her own Union contact. Meg had a sudden idea. "And if you have information for my Northern contact, come by the bakery and buy two loaves of bread."

"What if the bread has all sold?"

"That happens every day." Meg frowned. "Why not buy two of any baked good?"

"Then you'll know to come to my house after work." Elizabeth nodded. "A brilliant plan."

Meg liked it too. It kept her from walking to Elizabeth's home for no reason.

CHAPTER 7

*C*ade locked the bakery's front door at two o'clock on Thursday afternoon.

"Would you mind if I left early tomorrow?" Meg wiped down the empty tables in the front room.

"Why?" Muffins were in the window today. She always hurried on her way the days biscuits were displayed. He sensed a pattern but didn't yet understand its meaning.

"I worked at Chimborazo Hospital every week this spring—and almost daily when battles warranted it." She paused and looked up at him, her green eyes pleading. "It's been over a week since those daily battles stopped, and I didn't help once."

Her desire to serve those hurting was admirable. "What time?"

"Noon?"

"All right. Leave after you've eaten lunch, for you'll be too busy to eat at the hospital." If runaways came to the door today, he'd have to take them on their way tomorrow night. Not ideal. Longer stays here increased the danger for those pursuing the fugitives to find them.

"Thank you, Cade." Her smile warmed her green eyes.

He hurried to the kitchen, eager to be out of her presence. He'd wanted to kiss her on her birthday and couldn't allow loneliness to drive his actions. Or did his admiration for Meg run deeper? His heart had been dead so long that he didn't know.

He was scrubbing the stove when she entered a few minutes later. Now that the baked goods were sold, her lilac perfume was more noticeable. It suited her.

"Why don't you bake pies and cakes to sell? A man came in looking for an apple pie today. That's the third one this week." She hung towels on hooks to dry.

"They must not be from around here." Local folks knew what they'd find on display in his bakery. "Haven't sold those since my mother passed on."

"But you know how to make them."

"Not my specialty." He went back to scrubbing.

"When you sold them, did you sell the pie plates also?"

Cade shook his head. "Mama used to ask customers to return them when they were done. Most didn't. When she started charging them a dime extra to borrow the pie tin, they all returned them to get their dime back."

"Your mother was a wise woman." Meg giggled.

He liked the sound of her laughter. "That she was."

"I'll bake the pies." Her eyes brightened. "We can clear off one of the tables, put benches around it, and sell individual pieces of pie so folks can eat here."

"More dishes." The cost of running the bakery had jumped when he hired Meg. Her idea of selling individual cake slices had paid off. This sounded like too much trouble. It was true profits had been slashed with rising prices of ingredients. Perhaps she'd noticed. Not much escaped the intelligent woman.

"I'll wash them."

He grunted. After her morning baking was completed, she

had freedom to take on an extra chore.

"So I can bake pies?"

"You know how?" He met her eyes.

A guilty blush gave her away. "I can learn."

"I don't have time to teach you." A twinge of disappointment surprised him. Selling individual servings would have increased profits.

"You kept your mother's recipes. I'll ask Clara to teach me."

On the verge of denying her request, he reconsidered. Miss Clara had something in common with his mama—talent. "We'll see."

"I'll go over there tonight to ask her."

"You don't give up easily, do you?"

Curly waves of auburn hair swayed when she tilted her head up at him. "That's something we have in common. And a good thing too, right?"

It was her first indirect reference to the fact they both spied on the Confederacy.

Maybe she was beginning to trust him.

❧

As Meg walked to the hospital Friday afternoon, her thoughts turned to Clara's agreement last evening to teach her to bake pies. Though Meg was excited to learn new skills, her goal was to learn more information from customers. She'd overhear seemingly innocent conversations as guests lingered over slices of pie.

More information flowing to the North—that was always her goal. That it also helped Cade gave her a sense of peace.

Meg spent a grueling afternoon at the hospital and stayed to feed supper to the men in the old ward where she had volunteered many weeks. In the month since she'd been away, new patients had filled most of the beds. It was good to be back, actively doing something to help others.

After the men ate, the surgeon's assistant explained the medicine each soldier required. The harried worker trusted Meg to administer medications to them because he'd worked with her already. It was dusk when she left, exhausted and hungry. A feeling of being watched had her looking over her shoulder, but unless someone watched from the woods on the side of the road, there was no one. Hastening her pace, she soon put the woods behind. Children chasing fireflies in front of homes instilled a sense of safety, but she was thankful to reach her temporary home.

When the door closed behind Meg, she was greeted by Mrs. Ferris, who exited the parlor by the stairs. "Where have you been so late, Mrs. Brooks?" Her landlady's eyes narrowed.

"Please, call me Meg." She brushed wisps of hair back from her face. "I worked at Chimborazo Hospital today."

"You helped our soldiers?" Mrs. Ferris's face broke into a relieved smile. "Then you must be hungry. Come along with me to the kitchen."

"I'll just wash up first, if I may, and meet you there." The modern conveniences of a water closet and a bathing room went a long way to make up for her sparse accommodations, for her room was a quarter of the size her bedroom had been at Aunt Trudy's home.

A few minutes later, a ham sandwich and a glass of milk awaited Meg on a square table in the corner of the spacious kitchen, already cleaned from the earlier meal. "Thank you, Mrs. Ferris. Sorry for missing the six o'clock serving hour." She sat and asked a silent blessing on her meal. "I fed supper to my patients before leaving."

"Chimborazo is a mighty big place, but not large enough to serve all our wounded soldiers, more's the pity. Too many of our young men have died or will be crippled for life." The older woman sat on the corner of the table beside her. "You talk as if you've been there before."

"On many occasions. It hurts to see the devastation to so many men brought on by war. I do what I can to relieve their suffering. I most often work in a Tennessee ward." She sensed her proprietor's distrust waning as she talked. Her empty stomach was grateful for the meal.

"That's mighty fine of you. How do you like your job at the bakery?"

"I like it. The owner is a good and honest man, and I like waiting on customers." The bakery's kitchen was twice the size of this one. "The indoor kitchen has two stoves, just like this one. You rent eight rooms, right?"

"And every one is full." Mrs. Ferris suddenly looked as tired as Meg felt. "I'm careful who I rent to, so you can set your mind at ease about riffraff living down the hall."

"I'm happy to hear it." Her landlady hadn't mentioned that fact before. Perhaps she did trust Meg a little.

"Well, I've got a bit more to do before putting my feet up for the night." Mrs. Ferris stood. "Wash your dishes when you finish, will you? And sleep well, Meg."

This had been the most honest conversation she'd had with the boarding house owner. And this was the first time she'd called her by her given name.

~

*M*eg had stayed up late to compose another letter to Ina, one filled with information given to her by the soldiers. Some of it was old news yet seemed too important to ignore, should it not be already known by Union generals.

Biscuits had gone into the window display that Saturday morning.

When she walked toward the Main Street hotels where Mrs. Jordan usually stayed, it was almost as if she felt eyes boring into her back. Each time she stopped at a window display to take a furtive look around, she saw nothing amiss. There were folks gathered on street corners. Mothers hastened young children down the sidewalk. Men smoked cigars as they talked outside businesses.

Nothing seemed different.

Yet something was wrong. She felt it in her unsettled spirit.

If someone followed her, like that man who had followed Elizabeth, then he or she mustn't witness Meg passing on a letter to Mrs. Jordan.

Oh, no. The woman she sought was two hundred yards distant at the next street corner.

Mrs. Jordan gave a casual look in her direction.

Meg gave a slight shake of her head and then took a right, away from the letter carrier.

The roads Meg chose took a winding turn toward the crowded town square, where she admired the statue of President George Washington riding a horse. She tried to act as if that had been her intended destination.

All of a sudden, Mrs. Jordan stood at her side, also observing the statue.

"I'm being watched," Meg whispered, barely moving her lips.

The letter carrier said nothing. She moved away, her eyes on the first president's statue as if fascinated by it. A moment later, she had vanished into the crowd.

The woman's skill astounded Meg. Very few watching would have even noticed her presence.

Meg lingered another minute to allow Mrs. Jordan time to flee the area. Then, still uneasy, she walked to her boarding house.

If someone had followed her around the city, she prayed all they saw was a lone woman out for a stroll.

~

*C*ade was happy to accept an invitation to Trudy Weston's home the next day after church. Other than Jay, he was the only guest, which was far more to his liking. They dined in the family dining room, a smaller room with a smaller table. Conversation centered around an upcoming trip.

"We leave Tuesday morning." Trudy's eyes sparkled with excitement.

"If not for the recent battles, we'd head north straightaway." Bea sighed as she toyed with her salad. "As it is, I won't see Annie until Saturday."

"Possibly Sunday, if there are delays in Tennessee or Kentucky." Trudy patted her arm.

"I wish you passed through Chattanooga." Jay shook his head sadly. "My sister would welcome you in her home for an overnight stop. Mama misses you both."

"And I miss Mary, my dearest friend in the world." Trudy stared out the open window on softly falling rain. "It's good that your mother went to Tennessee when the Union army neared Richmond this spring, Jay."

"Her nervous state escalated with every battle." Worry darkened Jay's green eyes.

"Miss Mary calmed somewhat once she saw Blanche." Meg glanced at Cade. "I, along with Mabel, Clara's daughter, accompanied her to Tennessee in May."

"That was good of you." Cade was glad to be included in the conversation.

Trudy's brow wrinkled. "I'd reroute our trip if I didn't know she can safely return to Richmond whenever she desires."

Mrs. Weston was a mite optimistic, in Cade's view. The Union army would return...the only question was when. He glanced at Meg, whose cheeks flushed as she bent over her plate. She sure looked pretty in her new green dress, which deepened the color of her eyes and complimented her auburn hair. His brows lowered to recall his head wasn't the only one that turned her direction at church, but his jealousy wasn't warranted. After all, he wasn't courting her…though the thought had crossed his mind.

"True." Jay's shoulders relaxed. "Mama plans to stay with Blanche through August."

"Is Annie happy to see you coming?" Meg smiled broadly, as if certain of the answer.

"Ecstatic." Bea beamed at her. "Aunt Trudy, you'll not be bored. Annie has something planned for nearly every day, in between sorting and sending food and supplies for the soldiers."

"I'm happy to help with that, too." Trudy's face brightened.

"I wish you were coming with us, Meg." The corners of Bea's mouth drooped.

"I'm content here in Richmond for now." Meg's glance darted to Cade before returning to her cousin. "Save something for me to do for the wedding."

"I'll try." Bea laughed. "Annie has such plans. There may not be much for either of us to do."

Meg laughed. "I believe you."

"I'm glad you wore your new green dress today." Bea glanced at the lacy high collar. "I was right about that shade of green, Aunt Trudy."

"Agreed." Trudy smiled at Meg affectionately. "It enhances the color of your hair and eyes, Meg. Simply stunning."

"Th-thank you." Meg's blush reached her hairline. "Perhaps I will wear it to the wedding."

"Please do. Except no one will notice me." Bea grinned at Jay.

"You always have my complete attention." Jay clasped her hand. "And doubly so on our wedding day."

Cade looked away, embarrassed by the affectionate display. Bea was a lovely woman, but, in Cade's opinion, Meg's beauty outshone hers, even in the simple gingham dresses Meg daily wore to the bakery.

~

*H*arold, Aunt Trudy's driver, stopped in front of the bakery on Tuesday morning as Cade unlocked the front door.

"Harold will bring me back once the train pulls out." Meg felt guilty about leaving Cade with both the responsibility of customers and the baking.

"That's fine, then." Cade clasped her hand to help her inside the landau. After she was seated, he rested his hands on the door of the open carriage and spoke to Aunt Trudy and Bea. "I'm praying for your safe travels, ladies."

"Thank you, Cade." Trudy extended her hand to him. "I'm counting on you to watch over our sweet Meg while we're gone. She's very dear to us."

"I will." He released her hand. "Be careful on your way."

Meg fought back tears at his promise as they drove off. "He means it. He will pray for your safe journey."

"I also believe he'll watch out for you." Trudy's sharp eyes missed little.

"I've been on my own for—"

"Two years." Trudy finished her sentence with a sigh. "Yes, we know. Yet we all need family. Friends. Folks we can turn to in times of crisis. I think Cade is that type of man."

Meg's instincts told her he was someone to rely on. "He has a strong faith."

"I like him all the more for it."

Bea studied her cousin's expression. "Shall I tell Annie about Cade?"

"Tell her that my new employer treats me with kindness.

That he's a church-going man." Meg wasn't ready for anything more.

"I'll do that." Bea glanced at the blue sky. "We have perfect weather for traveling, Aunt Trudy."

"Other than being a mite hot, and so early in the morning, too." Trudy's expression turned serious as they approached the train depot. "Meg, should you have any problems at all, go to Clara and Harold. They will help you in whatever way necessary."

"That we will." Harold spoke over his shoulder.

"Ask them for a ride in the landau, even if it's only for pleasure."

"Clara wanted me to tell you to come for meals. Sundays or anytime," Harold added. "Pardon the interruption, Miss Trudy."

"Not at all. It's good for Meg to know you all welcome her." Trudy leaned forward as the landau halted at the depot. "We'll write you often. Send a telegram should there be any trouble."

Tears sprang up in Meg's eyes at Trudy's kindness. She and Bea loved her. "I will. Thank you."

"Jay will be working longer hours while I'm gone. He said to tell you he can come whenever you need him." Bea gathered her basket and reticule from the seat. "All you have to do is send for him, and he'll come to your aid."

The next few minutes passed in a rush. All too soon, it was time for passengers to board.

Meg hugged her adopted aunt. "Thank you for everything. Godspeed, and I'll be praying for your travel. Let me know when you arrive."

"We'll send a telegram." Trudy kissed her cheek. "And we'll see you in a few weeks." She climbed the steep steps with the help of the conductor.

Tears ran down Bea's cheeks as she hugged Meg. "It doesn't seem right to leave you here. Especially since we'll have such fun while you're working."

"Then have double the fun on my account." Meg laughed, choking back her own tears. "I'll miss you. Give Annie a hug from me."

"I will." Bea laughed. "Remember what a cold, rainy day it was when we arrived?"

Meg gave a mock shiver. "I do."

"The warmth of today makes up for it." She smiled. "Who knew I'd return as a betrothed woman?"

"God alone." A whistle blew. Meg covered her ears. "You'd best get on the train. Don't worry for me. I will see you soon."

Bea climbed the steps. "I wish Jay could have seen us off this morning, but he couldn't get away from work. I'll miss him."

"I know. You'll be back soon though." Meg waved her hand. "Godspeed, dear cousin."

Bea disappeared into the car. Meg, fighting tears, searched the windows until she found her loved ones. Then she waved goodbye until gray smoke hid the train from sight.

Despite her brave words, she felt alone again, as she had in Chicago after Thomas died.

Her thoughts flew to Cade. No, she was not alone at all.

CHAPTER 8

he feeling of being watched intensified. Three days after Bea left, Meg burned the letter she'd tried to deliver to Mrs. Jordan nearly a week before in the bakery's indoor oven. All her letters from Ina, her fellow scout in Washington, were burned as soon as Meg read them.

If someone suspected her of spying, there would now be no written records to use as evidence against her.

"What's this?" Cade stood at the open back door.

"Wh-what do you mean?" Meg slammed the oven shut.

He placed two cinnamon cakes on a side table before crossing the room. He opened the oven and peered at the coals. "You just burned a document. I'm not a fool, Meg. What's happening?"

She stared at him, wondering how much to reveal.

"This isn't the first time." A wary look clouded his blue eyes. "Is something wrong?"

"I...I'm not certain."

"You've been worried for a few days. I've waited for you to tell me."

Her heartbeat quickened at the concern in his eyes.

"What's troubling you?" Compassionate blue eyes searched hers. He stepped closer.

If she confessed to being a spy and he went to the authorities, she'd be in jail by sundown. But he wouldn't report her because he was also a Unionist spy.

"Please. Won't you trust me?"

Meg looked up into his compassionate face, and her resolve melted. They were on the same side. "I fear...someone is following me." A man following a lone woman was concern enough to share without revealing spy activities.

"Who?" His shoulders straightened.

That broad chest, mere inches away, invited her to lay her face against it. "I've not seen him. Merely felt his presence."

"Yet you're certain it's a man."

She shivered. "Yes."

"One of Clayton's detectives?"

The force that had arrested so many Unionists since March. "I pray it's not them." A shudder went through her.

"When did it start?" Cade rubbed his clean-shaven chin.

"Last week. When I worked at Chimborazo."

"You plan to go again today?"

"I want to." It was risky with the wooded stretch she'd have to pass in order to get there. "One day a week is all I can manage."

"I can drive you there in my wagon."

"You'd have to close the bakery early." Her heart swelled at the protective suggestion. "I'd rather ask Harold, Aunt Trudy's driver, to take me. He's offered to drive me wherever I need to go in my aunt's absence."

"Excellent idea." Tension eased from his face. "And until we figure who this fellow is, only go to work, church, and the like. Don't go anywhere out of your regular routine."

His advice was to stop spying for now. She understood. "I'll try."

～

*T*wo hours later, Cade watched Meg leave for her aunt's home. He was tempted to close down the bakery and drive her to the hospital himself. Unfortunately, he wasn't above suspicion himself. Should the authorities discover he regularly passed on information to other Unionists, he'd be arrested. Clayton's men were on the lookout for anything out of the norm. Closing the bakery early might invite questions, and he'd rather have nothing to do with the detectives.

Should the local government discover he smuggled runaway slaves further to the north in their quest for freedom, someone might look for a rope to hang him. In the current mistrustful environment, Cade didn't know which was more offensive to Confederates, spying or helping in the underground railroad.

Even so, he had to find the man who had put fear in Meg's eyes. A Confederate spy? One of Clayton's detectives? Or a scoundrel with evil attentions toward a lady?

Every possibility caused his blood to surge. The last had him clenching his fist.

Cade wasn't convinced of Meg's safety around the city. He was always with her at the bakery. She was safe here. And probably safe at her boarding house. He knew Mrs. Ferris, the boarding home's proprietor, was fiercely loyal to the Confederacy. If she suspected Meg of being a spy, she'd turn her over to the authorities without a second thought.

Had Mrs. Ferris found something in Meg's room that gave her away?

Doubtful, for Meg guarded her words even with him. Was she as careful with her possessions? Likely.

Yet it was possible Meg overlooked something.

The smell of something burning spurred him to the outdoor kitchen. He retrieved two loaf pans of Graham bread.

Not ruined. Too brown to sell. Sighing, he wrapped the

bread in a towel. Part of tonight's supper and tomorrow night's supper now.

Leaving the loaves outside to cool, he strode back to the kitchen.

"Pardon me." Someone called out from the front room.

A knock on the dividing door. He rushed to the other room. "My apologies. What may I get for you?"

Two women stood by a dwindling supply of baked goods.

"You only have two slices of cinnamon cake left." One woman in her fifties pointed to a nearly empty plate. "I hoped to buy an entire cake. Do you have any?"

"I do." In the kitchen. He'd forgotten to slice it. A bit of luck. "Let me wrap it for you."

After the women left, Cade's thoughts returned to Meg. She'd be safe with Harold driving her to and from the hospital.

The man following her didn't know she wasn't walking, but he did know she volunteered at Chimborazo Hospital last Friday. He'd probably figure she followed the same schedule every week and lay in wait for her again.

Cade decided to head over himself after drill practice. There was a worrisome stretch of woods.

Someone might be lurking there. If so, Cade would be there to see where the fellow went next.

~

Not knowing when Meg planned to leave the hospital, Cade went home after his last drill practice only long enough to store his musket in his living quarters. Then, in case someone monitored his own movements, he set off at a meandering pace toward the east side of the city.

Once he was comfortable that no one followed him, he quickened his pace toward Broad Street.

Chimborazo was the largest and best organized hospital in

the city. Located about a mile east of Richmond, the former barracks made a fine medical facility. Unfortunately, its one hundred and fifty buildings had proved inadequate for the number of wounded from recent battles. Many tents had been erected to house the overwhelming number, and even these weren't enough. Multiple hospitals throughout the city had staggered under the load.

Cade's thoughts turned to Meg as he strode past a row of homes on Broad Street. He was proud of her for tending the hurting, no matter the color of their uniform. His admiration for her grew daily.

His Evelyn would have done the same, God rest her soul.

The woods were ahead. He waited until a horseback rider rode out of sight before entering the forest. Bushes nestled among tall trees a dozen feet from the road.

With the quiet tread that he'd learned in order to avoid his pa as a child, he searched the forest. No one hid in wait.

That was good, but it didn't mean he wouldn't come later.

Cade hoped he would, for he was itching to find out what the man meant to do next.

Unless it was one of Clayton's detectives. It would be foolhardy to approach one of the detectives to ask his intentions.

He prayed it wasn't, for that meant the authorities suspected Meg of being, at the very least, a Unionist. At worst, a spy.

Cade settled behind the bushes to wait.

His stomach growled. Certainly not the first meal he'd missed in aid of a friend.

❧

"*M*eg's being followed." Cade barely waited for Virginia, Paul Lucas's wife, to leave to whisper his concern. They sat in his small yet comfortable parlor in his two-story brick home. Paul, whose wife had introduced him to

Evelyn eight years before, owned a thriving furniture store on Marshall Street a five-minute walk from the bakery.

"Clayton's men?" The short, balding man in his forties gripped the arms of his cushioned chair.

"Don't know." Cade raked a hand through his thick hair. "Meg hasn't seen him. I spent two hours in the woods waiting for him. Nothing." Meg had passed by in a landau at dusk, her body tensed as if poised for flight. "Her carriage dropped her off at her boarding house, so she's safe for the night." He'd checked for a light in her window before walking to Paul's home.

"She didn't see him. You didn't either." Paul raised his eyebrows.

"True."

"Perhaps she imagined it."

"Doubtful. She's a level-headed woman."

"Elizabeth Van Lew recommended her as someone who can help us."

"Meg's got her own contacts. She may not be interested." Cade rubbed the stubble on his jaw, as rough as sandpaper, as he considered what little he knew of her. "She's a spy. That much is certain." He explained about the baked goods in the window display.

"Who is she working with?" Paul's brow furrowed.

"Don't know."

"She doesn't trust you?"

"Not with her life." He didn't yet have that level of trust for her either. He must believe she would not betray him even if she were under great pressure.

"Keep an eye out for this man following her."

Cade nodded. He didn't need help with the situation. Not yet, anyway. It was good that Paul knew of a potential problem in case something happened.

"Since there's a possibility that Clayton's detectives suspect

Meg," Paul said, "don't tell her any secrets. If there's any sign of trouble, let me know."

Cade walked to the bakery on deserted streets. It was nearing the ten o'clock curfew.

He hastened his pace. No need to give the detectives, who roamed the city day and night, cause to stop him.

CHAPTER 9

"Hello, Meg."

In the act of combining baked goods onto one plate for the display case in the front room, Meg stiffened. She'd know that voice anywhere. How had Thomas's good-for-nothing brother found her?

She whirled around to face him. "Good morning, Lance. Here to purchase baked goods?" She knew that wasn't his reason for tracking her down. He had a scruffy brown beard the same color as his hair, covered by a slouch hat that he hadn't removed upon entering the bakery.

"Oh, I'm here for a lot more than baked goods." The thirty-year-old took a few menacing steps toward her.

"That's all we sell." Meg stood her ground, not about to let her only brother-in-law know her stomach lurched at the sight of him.

"I know." He circled the display table she leaned against. "I know a lot about you. I've been here better than a week."

"Oh? What brings you to Richmond?" Meg prayed Lance didn't notice the blood draining from her face. He'd been the one following her. She'd sensed the danger. The man had tormented her husband—his own brother. She'd witnessed his ruthlessness.

"You weren't in Chicago."

So, he had traveled to Illinois looking for her. Why? He had promised Thomas he'd stay away. A shiver started at the pit of her stomach.

Slow, heavy tread on the floorboards circled her behind the table. Cade baked in the outdoor kitchen this morning. Lance probably knew this. She closed her eyes, steeling herself. The last she heard, he had moved from Colorado to the silver mines in the Nevada Territory, which he apparently left to look for her. That didn't bode well for her safety.

What did he want from her? Thomas had given him every-thing the last time he'd visited.

～

Cade entered the kitchen with three loaves of white bread in his arms. His senses were immediately alerted. Something was wrong. Nothing was amiss in the kitchen. Then he heard a stranger's menacing tone from the front room.

"You weren't in Washington City."

No need for light footsteps. Cade's booted feet struck the floorboards as he slammed into the dividing door.

With one glance, he took in the threatening stance of the bearded stranger and Meg's tense posture. Cade's eyes fell to the man's chest, wide for a man half a foot shorter than he.

No shield-shaped badge. Not one of Clayton's men.

"Got more bread here. Mrs. Hanson will be back for it any time now." Cade spoke as if nothing were amiss. "Mrs. Brooks, will you get the muffins from the oven?"

There were none and Meg knew it.

"Of course." She left the room without a glance at the stranger.

Cade watched the sweep of blue gingham dress disappear behind the door. Then his friendly manner slipped away. "What do you want?"

"A loaf of bread."

"No."

The man's grin died as Cade advanced toward him. He stepped back. In his haste, his hat fell off his greasy hair.

"I saw the look you gave Mrs. Brooks, my employee." A threatening look, intended to frighten. Cade didn't scare so easily. "You're not welcome on my property."

The man ducked to retrieve his hat. Made a play of dusting it off.

As if any of its dirt came from the bakery's spotless floors. The man's bluster didn't fool Cade.

He strode toward the door.

"Don't come back."

He turned, a menacing light in his eyes. "Oh, I'll be back. You aren't here all the time, are you?"

Did the man know he'd been gone overnight on Sunday? This was Saturday. How long had he been watching Meg—and him—to know this?

"I don't advise it." Folding his arms, he widened his stance. If there was to be a fight, he'd be ready for it.

The stranger shoved on his hat and was gone.

That fellow was trouble. How did he know Meg?

❧

*M*eg cringed as she listened at the door. Cade had thrown him out, almost literally, but Lance would come back. He always did.

Light footsteps warned her to step away before the door opened.

She met his concerned blue eyes.

He put a finger to his lips. "We'll talk later," he whispered.

When there were no customers to interrupt them. Meg nodded. Truthfully, she was too shaken to speak. She longed to lay her cheek against Cade's broad chest, feel the comfort of his strong arms around her.

Disarmed by her thoughts, she turned away.

Lance robbed, swindled, connived, and hurt everyone in his path. She hated that she had brought trouble to Cade, though gratitude filled her that Aunt Trudy and Bea weren't in Richmond.

"Work in the kitchen the rest of the day."

"But—"

"I'll tend to customers." His face turned grim. "And don't go outside. I don't trust that scoundrel not to return."

"He'll return," Meg whispered. Lance was like the proverbial bad penny. He always came back.

Cade placed his warm, gentle hand on her face. "I know."

Startled, she looked up into his compassionate eyes. She covered that strong hand with hers.

His eyes searched hers. "You can trust me."

Meg stared at the closed door long after he'd returned to the front room.

Had she been alone when Lance confronted her…

A shudder pierced through her.

Cade was a good man. *Thank you, God, for sending me Cade. Protect both of us.*

~

*C*ade locked the door promptly at two o'clock and strode to the kitchen. His mind had played through many scenarios since he'd taken over waiting on customers. He was ready for the truth.

"Who was that man?"

Meg had scrubbed the kitchen in his absence. Something seemed to crumple inside, if the empty look in her eyes was any indication. "I'll tell you. Can we sit?"

After closing the windows and curtains, he joined her at the table, straddling a spindle-backed chair on the corner adjacent to her. "Speak softly. I'd not put it past that scoundrel to listen at the window."

"I wouldn't either." Meg looked at each of the three windows as if searching for a silhouette. "I'll speak quickly, since you must leave for drill practice."

"The War Office rescinded the order requiring businesses to close at two o'clock. Since daily drills are no longer required, I told them yesterday was my last practice. I'm not serving Home Guard. Next week, we'll resume closing at five o'clock." He folded his hands. "Tell me about that man. Take all the time you need."

"His name is Lance Brooks."

Cade gave his head a little shake. "Brooks?"

"He's my husband's brother."

He drew back. "I thought you were a widow."

"I am. Thomas drowned in a boat accident two years ago." Her eyes darted to the closest window.

"My apologies. Tell the story your own way." He forced his shoulders to relax.

"Thomas and Lance were the only siblings who survived to adulthood. Thomas felt guilty about surviving a fever that took the lives of his two sisters and his parents lavished him with love and gifts. He became the favored child until he completely recovered. Lance was jealous. It was only a few months, but Lance felt neglected. Both sons were loved and treated well, but Thomas said Lance treated him differently afterward. Thomas adored his brother, even when he mocked him." Meg raised troubled green eyes to his. "I see now that's where the trouble began."

"What trouble?"

"Before I married Thomas, Lance went West. Looking first for gold. And then silver. Success favored him, but he spent or gambled away everything he found. The man idolizes money. Every few months Thomas would learn that his parents had sent Lance more money. I've no doubt he wasted every penny." Her face hardened. "Thomas's parents died and left the house to both sons. Thomas wanted to rent it and keep it in the family for sentimental reasons. Lance insisted it be sold. He wanted his half."

Remembering Lance's menacing manner to his sister-in-law, Cade had little doubt the man knew how to obtain what he wanted.

"Lance came back the following year. He demanded Thomas's share of the inheritance." She tugged at her sleeve. "That was shortly after my mother died, so I imagine Lance figured we had inherited sufficient money from her. Anyway, Thomas refused. Lance said it wasn't a request." Meg's jaw set. "He threatened my husband. His own brother."

What a scalawag. Cade's hand formed into a fist.

"I pleaded with him not to give in to his brother's bullying. Against my advice, Thomas spoke with him alone." She wrung her hands. "I've no idea how Lance convinced him to give him our share. However, Thomas asked a lawyer to draw up papers that said he owed Lance nothing more. Any debt Lance claimed we owed was paid in full after that, even though both sons had received an equal share of the inheritance, as stated in the will.

Lance wanted everything for himself. He signed the document as a condition of receiving the payment."

Robbed by his own family. Cade could only imagine the humiliation and hurt Thomas suffered. Then he recalled how his own father had treated him. He'd even said he'd wished his younger son had survived instead of Cade. Perhaps he did understand Thomas's pain. And Lance's, if it came to that. Yet that's where the comparison ended, for Cade had chosen a far different path.

"What happened?"

"Lance left Chicago. We prayed he was out of our lives for good." Tears filled her eyes. "Thomas drowned a week later. He had borrowed a friend's boat to go fishing. He wanted solitude, I guess, to work through the wrong dealt him. I never saw him alive again."

The sadness in her eyes slashed through his defenses. Taking her hand, Cade raised her to her feet and enfolded her in his arms.

~

*M*eg rested her wet cheek against Cade's broad chest as he cradled her in a gentle embrace. The comfort of being held in the compassionate man's arms was the deepest she'd experienced since Thomas died. She felt protected and unwilling to leave its safety.

Yet they were alone in the bakery. She shifted, and he released her. She missed his warmth immediately.

"My apologies for losing control like that." Meg accepted the plain white handkerchief he offered. "It rarely happens."

"I believe you." His thumb wiped away a tear in a caress.

Her eyes flew to his.

"About everything."

What was it about this man that made everything he did

seem the right thing to do? She didn't know. "I trust you with Thomas's secret. Not even my family knows."

"I understand why you kept it hidden." He nodded. "And I understand why you had to speak."

"I have nothing to give Lance, I wonder what he wants." She sat and drummed her fingers against the table.

"He'll not steal another dime from you."

Meg looked at his set jaw. "We know he's able to follow me without being seen. What can we do?"

"The most important thing"—he pushed up his sleeves—"is that you engage in no more secret activities until we're certain Lance is gone."

Meg gasped at the intensity of his whispered words. They'd never spoken of spying. A friend and fellow Pinkerton scout, Hattie Lawton, was still in a Richmond prison for spying. She had pretended to be the wife of Pinkerton scout, Timothy Webster. He had been hanged in Richmond. When Meg had finally found her, Hattie had warned her to stay away from her, telling her not to place herself in danger by being seen with her. Meg had heeded that advice to protect herself and keep important information flowing from Richmond to Washington City.

Dare she acknowledge her secret letters? No. Cade knew enough already. "Were I involved with that, I'd agree."

"Of course." Cade studied her face. "A fellow like Lance would use such knowledge to squeeze every last penny from you."

True. A chunk of ice formed in her stomach and spread throughout her body. Lance was not above blackmail.

CHAPTER 10

$\mathcal{C}$ade walked Meg home, where she planned to remain until he came to escort her to church in the morning.

On his way back to the bakery, he kept a sharp eye out for the rascal. Though Cade felt Lance's presence on the street, he never set eyes on him.

Slippery as a weasel.

After learning Lance's background, Cade knew he couldn't protect Meg when he was out of town. Overnight trips—indeed all his secretive missions—must stop until Lance left the city. If what Meg said were true, it seemed the man would stop at nothing to get what he wanted.

What *did* he want? Meg worked at a bakery and lived in a modest boarding home. What did she have that Lance traveled to Richmond to obtain? It was a puzzle.

A frightening one.

Cade set to cleaning the outdoor kitchen and considered whether to bring Jay, Bea's betrothed, in on Meg's problem. The man seemed steady enough. He was Meg's family—or would be once he married Bea.

But Cade didn't know the man well. He decided against it as he finished scrubbing.

A bird landed on a table. He looked beyond the bird's wings to a scruffy face. Lance stood just beyond his property. How long had he been there?

Dropping his rag, Cade crossed the space and was face to face with him in a split second. "I warned you."

"I ain't on your land." Lance held his arms wide. Whistling, he sauntered away.

Brazen wretch.

Cade had a good mind to chase him down.

~

*M*eg hadn't just been frightened by Lance when he'd shown up at the bakery. He'd jeopardized all her careful plans to support the Union. What could he possibly find to use against her? Meg prayed for protection and then considered every detail connected with her spying.

There was nothing for Lance to find at the bakery. What if he sneaked into her boarding house? She kept her room locked, yet Mrs. Ferris had a key. Meg paid extra to have her bedding and clothes washed weekly, so a maid also had access to her room. It seemed likely that the maid kept the door unlocked while doing the laundry, and then locked it after putting clean linens on the bed.

If that was the case, anyone could have been in her bedroom. Meg searched it, twice, for any evidence that could be used against her.

Good. Not one letter from Ina.

She read all of Annie's correspondence that had arrived while she was in Richmond. Other than writing of her husband being a lieutenant in the Union army, Annie gave no details the Confederates would care about. Still, one never knew how someone might twist words or phrases for nefarious purposes.

What might Lance do with the information? Who knew how his twisted mind worked?

Too risky to keep personal correspondence. It was best to burn the letters in the bakery stove. Not here, where other boarders might witness and wonder.

Aware that Lance had followed her for more than a week, she thought back over what he'd witnessed. She must assume he knew everywhere she went.

The bakery, where he'd made himself known to her.

He certainly knew where she lived, knowledge that sped her heart rate.

She'd been to St. John's Church. Her senses were always attentive to nearby conversations on church grounds. She would have noticed his scruffy presence.

Wait. Bea. Aunt Trudy.

Was that Lance's interest in her? Their wealth?

How could he know? Meg wasn't a blood relative to Aunt Trudy. Or Trudy's siblings, Isaac Swanson and Victoria Jones, wealthy plantation owners.

No, Lance likely didn't know about Isaac or Victoria. They'd already been gone from Richmond when he began stalking Meg.

At least, that was her fervent prayer.

Meg paced in her small room, trying to reason what drove her brother-in-law. Ten steps to the door. Ten steps back to the window. Over and over.

It was a good thing Bea and Aunt Trudy were on their way to Washington City.

Her steps halted. If Lance saw them pick her up from the bakery Tuesday morning, he knew they'd left.

Why stay if their wealth was his aim? He couldn't know how long they'd be gone.

What then was his purpose?

Meg had gone through a portion of the money from the sale of her house. She hadn't smuggled any coded messages to the North after knowing she was being watched. Cade was right that curtailing all spying-related activities was a top priority.

How frustrating that one man could halt her important work. Often, she sent portions of Richmond newspapers—those reporters provided more valuable information to the Union than they realized—with comments about some minor bit of news. The important intelligence for Ina would be found elsewhere on the page.

If someone confiscated Meg's carefully-worded letters, they wouldn't mean anything to them. She and Ina had designed a scheme where common items had double meanings. 'Aunt Cora' was a regiment, followed by a number and any word beginning with the same letter as a Southern state and an actual city identified where troops camped. No one but Ina understood its meaning. Anyone reading them would wonder what was special about Aunt Cora's two vases, when Meg actually referenced two Virginia regiments camped in the town mentioned.

Troop locations were valuable information for Union generals.

Even if that snake, Lance, got his hands on one of the notes —which he hadn't—he would not understand.

None of Ina's notes survived past the day she received them. She'd just searched every hiding spot in her room. There were no documents to link her to spying.

It was best to display muffins in the bakery window to keep Mrs. Jordan away.

How were they to convince Lance to leave her alone? Thomas had planned for the future and thought he had protected himself and Meg.

Unfortunately, he'd been blind to the worst of his brother's flaws.

∾

*C*ade whistled on his way to Meg's boarding house the next morning. He'd spent an hour on his knees last evening. Then he pondered the situation most of the night. If neither of them passed on any information against the Confederacy in the next week or so, Lance would have no ammunition to use against them with General Clayton.

Besides, Cade had a hunch that Meg's spying wasn't the reason Lance hunted for her. The ne'er-do-well had stumbled onto something he thought to use to get his way.

From the background provided by Meg, Cade figured the gambler wanted money. Were a man determined to play games of chance, he'd find them in the city.

Of course, something else might drive him. Cade sighed as he spotted Meg, eye-catching in her new blue dress, waiting on the porch. She would be the best one to discover Lance's motives.

"Good morning." He grinned at her, determined not to let Lance believe that he got under their skin. "What a fine day for a stroll to church."

"Good morning to you." Meg's expression lightened as she joined him on the sidewalk. "Those clouds look like they hold rain to me."

"So they do." He glanced at the overcast sky.

"You're in a good mood." She laughed.

"So I am." Laughing with her released the tension from his shoulders. He crooked his arm. "Shall we?"

She rested her fingers on his sleeve. "We shall."

Cade liked the feel of her small hand on his muscled arm.

Perhaps she did, too, for a smile lit her eyes as they set off at a leisurely pace.

"Anyone watching might think we have not a care." He winked at her.

"Agreed." She giggled.

"Don't let a certain person know he's getting to you." He should escort her to church every Sunday. This was fun.

"You're a wise man."

"I have a wise Father." He covered her hand with his. "A wise Heavenly Father, that is."

"Indeed, you do. I do as well."

"Seems like we have some things in common, Mrs. Brooks." He quirked an eyebrow at her.

"I believe so, Mr. Yancey."

~

*M*eg loved Cade in this carefree mood. She'd never seen him like this. They reached St. John's Church all too soon and found Jay Nickson awaited them.

Perhaps he'd hoped Cade would escort her.

The three sat together near the back, with Meg in the middle. This church was a safe place. Surely Lance had no power over her in the Lord's house. She almost wished Lance Brooks would cross their path on the church grounds. In her present mood, she feared she'd laugh uproariously at his threats.

Then she sobered, for Lance did hold power over her if he knew her secrets.

When the pastor bowed to pray, Meg's prayer was for protection—and that Lance never discovered secrets to use against her. Or against Cade.

For Lance would destroy them to get whatever he was after. In a heartbeat.

~

*M*eg followed the men outside after the service, darting furtive looks in every direction. If Lance was in the crowd, he concealed himself well.

"Do you have plans for lunch?" Jay glanced from Meg to Cade. "I didn't receive a telegram from Bea yet so they were delayed at least a day."

Meg gave a start, suddenly ridden with guilt that she'd forgotten about her family's travel in the midst of her anxiety over Lance. "Bea will send a telegram to you straightaway upon arrival. Aunt Trudy promised to send me one as well."

"I feel rather out of sorts." Jay grinned sheepishly. "I've been with Bea nearly every Sunday since she arrived."

Meg had been with them most of those days, too, though she understood his thoughts were focused on his fiancé. "Harold and Clara invited me to dine with their family. After that, Clara will give me another lesson on baking pies."

"Which kind?" Cade asked.

"Peach."

"An excellent choice." He looked at Jay. "Meg wants to set up a dining area at the bakery and start selling slices of pie."

"Inspired." Jay nodded. "Let me know when it starts. I'll be a customer."

"Good." Meg tilted her head at Cade. "See? I told you customers will enjoy it." And she looked forward to overhearing sensitive information to send North.

"Well, Cade, old boy, want to dine with me? My cook is nearly as talented as Clara's."

"I believe I'll accept your offer." He turned to Meg. "I'll stop by afterward and escort you home."

"That's kind of you, but Harold offered to drive me." Her disappointment at the need to turn down his offer surprised her.

"Perhaps he won't mind if I ride along." His mischievous smile lent a twinkle to his blue eyes.

She laughed. "I very much doubt it. Very well. Come to my aunt's home around four o'clock."

"I'll be there."

"Look there. Harold is waiting by the street."

Meg followed Jay's glance. Her smile died.

So was Lance.

CHAPTER 11

*C*ade helped Meg into the closed carriage. Bless Harold's thoughtfulness for choosing that over the landau due to the ominous gray clouds overhead.

There were a few gray clouds in his own mood, if truth be told. Lance had been brazen indeed, for he'd followed Meg to church.

"I will come for you at four o'clock." Cade kept his voice low. Lance had disappeared into the crowd, but Cade didn't want to be overheard.

"Did you hear from Miss Trudy?" Harold, Trudy's driver, stood next to Jay. "She figured on being in Washington City yesterday."

With a war going on, lots could happen on the meandering route the ladies had been forced to take. Cade would feel better himself once they arrived safely.

"Or today at the latest." Jay clapped him on the back. "I'll be a little on edge until we hear. Bea promised to send a telegram, so I want to stay near to home. If I hear first, I'll come here. I'd be obliged if you let me know when you get word."

"Sure will." He climbed into the driver's seat. "We'd best get going. Clara's looking forward to having Miss Meg with us all afternoon."

Cade lifted his hand in goodbye as Meg gave him a confident smile from her window. It warmed his heart that her independent spirit reasserted itself today.

He scanned the crowd. Lance was here somewhere. Question was, did he intend to follow Cade or Meg?

~

*C*ade lingered in Jay's parlor after lunch. The betrothed man didn't want to budge from home until hearing from Bea. Cade understood his growing anxiety, for he'd probably wait at the telegraph office himself for news.

"I appreciate you accepting my invitation to lunch, Cade." Jay stared at a mantle clock, as if willing the minute hand to move faster. "Been waiting for news since I got off work yesterday and praying nearly every moment for Bea and Aunt Trudy's safety. Thanks for giving me something else to think about."

"It's only half-past two." Cade studied the younger man's wrinkled brow, growing a bit uneasy himself. Richmond citizens had learned to cope with the battles—some far too close for safety—not to know how quickly fighting started. He prayed the women hadn't encountered delays for those reasons. "I expect you'll hear soon."

Jay rubbed his hands over the cushioned chair arms. "I pray so."

Cade did too. If Jay really needed a distraction... He rubbed his jaw. He'd spent enough time with him today to take the man's measure. Jay was honest. He worked at Tredegar, which supplied munitions to the Confederate army. The ironworks had its secrets, yet Jay never hinted at them. Much as Cade wanted to pass such information along, he appreciated Jay's loyalty. He was a man who wouldn't betray a secret.

"I apologize for my preoccupation." Jay forced a smile. "Is Meg doing well? At the bakery and in her new home?"

It was the opening he needed. "Well, she does have a unique problem. She's in some danger. This may not be the best time to give you such news—"

"It's a very good time." Jay's eyebrows lowered. "Bea charged me with looking after her cousin in her absence. What's the trouble?"

Cade summarized what Meg had revealed about her brother-in-law's past behavior and his present menacing actions without revealing Meg's fear that Lance might discover her spying. He explained that the wretch had even made threatening moves toward himself.

"You're kidding." Jay glanced at his bulging muscles. "The man can't be bigger than you."

He gave a brief description as thunder rumbled outside. Not a battle brewing, an actual storm, Cade was happy to note.

"Wait a minute." Jay straightened. "I saw that fellow wandering about the graveyard while I waited for Meg to arrive." He shook his head. "That one's a bad character. I hate to think he's threatening her. Does he want money?"

"He didn't have an opportunity to tell her what he wanted. I caught him trying to frighten her and threw him out of the bakery."

"Good man."

"I wish he had balked at it, given me reason to pick him up and toss him out by the seat of his pants." Cade clenched his fist. "I'd have done it none too gently, mind you."

"I'd like to have seen that." Jay chuckled and then quickly sobered. "The fact that he didn't resist shows he's either scared of your size and strength or at least respects it."

Cade hadn't considered that. "He was there this morning beyond the carriage where Harold waited."

"You don't say." Jay's eyes darkened. "The scoundrel."

"Quite brazen to stalk her on church grounds. And while she's in the company of two strong men who can fell him in one punch. Imagine his actions if she were alone."

"I don't like the sound of this." Jay's fingers formed a steeple. He tapped them against his chin. "Would she be safer staying at Trudy's house?"

"Doubtful. Her boarding house is full. I can't see the man attacking her there."

"You say he's a gambler."

"For years, apparently."

"There are plenty of disreputable gaming halls in Richmond." Jay's eyes narrowed. "If he plays and loses more than he has, he'll be in worse trouble. The streets can be mighty dangerous for a gambler with unpaid gambling debts."

"Maybe that already happened. The fellow is very good at hiding." Cade was, too, and grudgingly accepted that the wretch had some skills at melting into a crowd. "I can vouch for that myself. I looked for him this morning and didn't spot him before church."

"Long practice at avoiding detection, perhaps?"

Made sense. Not from spying but from hiding from gamblers to whom Lance owed money. "I think you may be onto something, Jay."

Someone applied the door knocker. Jay bolted from his chair. "One moment, please."

The telegram? Cade stood, tensing for the news.

Jay returned, waving a sheet of paper. "They arrived safely. Praise the Lord."

"Praise the Lord, indeed."

Jay tapped a loose fist on his chest. "A great relief."

"For me as well." Cade, grateful for Jay's insights, reflected that Paul wasn't his only friend in Richmond. "Shall we walk over to Trudy's and tell Meg and the rest of the household the news?"

"Let's leave now." Jay grabbed his beaver hat. "That steady rain pelting the roof won't even bother me with such good news to share."

～

"I'm glad they're safely in Washington City." Meg expelled a long breath. Harold had invited Jay and Cade back to the kitchen, where delicious aromas emanated from both ovens. "Though it's unfortunate they were held for questions by Union forces in Nashville."

"Nashville fell under Union control this summer. Questioning delayed them so long they missed their train's departure and had to wait until the following day." Jay sighed. "Bea didn't elaborate on the problem. I'm certain they'll tell us more in their letters."

"They are safe now." Cade clapped Jay's back.

"Praise God." Jay's voice vibrated with emotion. "If Bea's father doesn't return with her, I may fetch her myself."

"A fine idea." Meg wondered if Jay might be better served taking his own carriage directly to Washington City. Choosing a careful route through Virginia was an option now that fighting had moved away from Richmond.

"We got our own telegram." Harold strode into the room and showed it to Clara first. "Miss Trudy says they're both fine."

Clara read it, a smile growing as she gave it to Meg. "It's just like her to bring a ray of sunshine with her words."

"*Dearest Harold and Clara, we arrived safely.*" Meg held it aloft for Jay, who peered over her shoulder as she read aloud. "*Most went just as planned, but we had an unplanned overnight stay in Nashville. The Union army, who has taken control of that city, took an uncommon interest in a Richmond citizen and her northern niece. I'm happy to say gracious manners prevailed in the end and we were given passes to prevent a recurrence in Tennessee. I was happy to arrive at our destination to hug Annie and my dear brother Hiram. Please share the news with Meg, Jay, and the rest of my loyal staff. A letter will follow. Sincerely, Gertrude Swanson."*

"A military man would have to be a scoundrel to treat Aunt Trudy with anything other than kindness. And Bea." Jay's brow cleared. "Sounds like Trudy's unfailing Southern courtesy won the day."

"I reckon you have the right of it." Harold nodded. "Ain't never met a more gracious and kind woman than Miss Trudy."

"Bea's mother, my aunt, was the same." Meg smiled as she returned the paper.

"I will send Bea a telegram." Jay folded his own message and placed it in his coat pocket. "May I reply for all that we've received them?"

"That would be a kindness." Meg, who had little money to spare for the expense, nodded.

The rest agreed.

"How did the cooking lesson go?" Cade raised his eyebrows at Meg, who laughed.

"I have a long way to go before I'll feel comfortable charging hard-working citizens for my baking." She grinned. "However, Clara had a suggestion."

Cade's glance darted to the cook, who clasped her hands together.

"Now, Miss Meg's baking is coming along. In the meantime, we wondered…that is, we know you need pies…" She glanced at her husband.

"Clara and I wondered if she can bake pies for the bakery." Meg put an arm around her friend, feeling her nervousness in the trembling of her shoulders. "We'd buy the pies from her daily to sell by the slice."

"I got some peach pies we made today. Should be ready by now." Clara wrapped towels around her hands and opened the oven.

Within seconds, two golden brown pies rested on a board. The heavenly aroma of baked peaches made Meg's mouth water.

"Meg says folks keep asking for pies." Cade grinned. "I may have to try a slice before deciding."

"These are too hot. Give them a few minutes." Clara straightened. "I can also make other flavors. Like blackberry, blueberry, apple, cherry—"

"Don't forget crabapple and pumpkin." Harold seemed as eager as his wife.

"Two different types a day, two of each, is enough for a beginning." Cade's brow wrinkled. "What will Mrs. Weston say?"

"Oh, this is only 'til she gets back." Trudy wiped her hands on her apron. "I have time only while she's gone. Now, I'd buy my own ingredients and not take anything from the pantry, mind you."

It seemed important to the cook that everyone understood that detail. "Of course." Meg was encouraged by Cade's smiling enthusiasm.

"While the pies cool, do you mind if we borrow the parlor for a few minutes?" Jay looked at Harold. "I want to send that telegram, but I need to speak to Cade and Meg a few moments."

"Sure thing." Harold opened the door for them. "If Miss Trudy were here, she'd say 'you're always welcome.'"

"Thank you." Meg knew it was true. How they all loved the hospitable woman.

She followed the men down the hall, wondering what Jay wanted to discuss.

CHAPTER 12

*A*s soon as Jay closed the parlor door behind them, he turned to Meg. "Cade told me of your trouble with your brother-in-law. I know everything."

Everything? Meg's startled glance flew to Cade. Surely he hadn't told a staunch Confederate supporter about her spying.

Cade gave a slight shake of his head.

No one made a move to sit on the comfortable couches as they stared uneasily at each other. Steady rain pelted the window panes.

"What do you want me to do for you? I can hire someone to have the fellow followed."

"He's sneaky." Meg studied Cade's expression. His impassive face gave nothing away. Had the men discussed solutions?

"I spotted him today," Cade said.

Meg's throat tightened. How had the man become so adept at hiding?

"Jay's idea has merit." Cade's quiet voice cut through her confused thoughts. "To learn what Lance wants, you'll have to talk to him. A crowded city street during daylight hours is my preference."

"Mine too." She shivered. "I don't trust him."

"I went to school with a detective in the city," Jay said. "He's built a good reputation. A limp kept him from mustering into the army, but it doesn't prevent him from doing his job."

"I...I haven't enough money in Richmond to hire a detective." Meg's face flamed. "Part of the money from selling my Chicago home is in Uncle Hiram's bank."

"Don't worry about the expense. This is my gift." Jay glanced from Cade to Meg. "Bea would say the same, were she here."

"Cade," Meg asked, "what do you think?"

"It's a sound plan. I'd feel better to have a detective following behind you to watch for Lance." His eyes held hers. "Let's set a day and time when we'll all follow as you set out to take a stroll. You must seem to be alone or Lance won't approach you, as we learned today. Encourage him to talk. Ask him bluntly what he wants."

"Let's do it after the bakery closes for the day." Meg straightened her shoulders. Lance would follow her, especially if she didn't walk to her boarding house.

"Exactly."

Cade's eyes were steady, assured. Just like the man. "I want to put this behind me. Does Tuesday give you enough time to make the arrangements, Jay?"

"I'll ride to see my friend, Michael McCane, directly from the telegraph office. Let's work out the time you will leave, your destination, and your route before I go."

Before they left the parlor, each one knew the plan.

The detective added an extra layer of protection.

Meg prayed Michael McCane was not only available but also trustworthy.

~

*H*arold brought two peach pies and two blackberry pies promptly as the bakery opened at eight o'clock the following morning.

"Those are beautiful." Meg stared in awe at the golden brown crusts with cutouts of peaches on two and a cluster of three blackberries on the other.

"Clara will be right glad to hear you said so." He looked up as Cade entered the front room. "She baked bits of peach and berry-shaped dough on the top so you can tell what kind it is before you slice it."

"Clever." Cade sniffed. "Blackberries. I don't see how folks will be able to resist the aromas in here."

"*I* can't resist." Nothing Meg baked had ever looked this delicious. She was glad the talented baker who created the masterpieces was teaching her these skills.

"Come on back and I'll pay you."

Meg placed the pies in the display case with the plates and utensils behind them. The newly arranged table and chairs accommodated six guests. Meg doubted six people would enjoy the pie at the same time, yet it was nice to dream. She marveled that her idea had borne fruit in a most unexpected way.

The men returned while she placed a basket of muffins in the window.

"Miss Meg, I'd like the honor of buying a slice of peach pie. It's my favorite." A proud smile lit Harold's dark eyes.

"You must be my guest. It's my treat." Cade indicated with a nod for Meg to do the honors.

"No, begging your pardon." Harold straightened his shoulders. "I want the privilege of buying the first slice of my wife's pie. I saved room for it from breakfast." He patted his stomach. "I'd eat it, even if I didn't."

Laughing, Meg put a slice on a plate. "Have a seat, Harold."

"I'll join you. There's ten minutes until the next loaves come out of the oven." Cade held out his hand for a loaded plate. "Meg?"

"Oh, I can't wait either."

Sitting beside Cade, Meg savored every bite.

But not as much as Harold, who beamed at them across the table.

~

"Good morning, Meg." Elizabeth Van Lew came to the bakery two hours later.

"Good morning, Miss Elizabeth." It was the first time the woman had returned to the bakery since they'd agreed on a code. They were alone in the front room, as Cade was still in the thick of baking. He needed additional items because they were to resume closing at five o'clock today. "I trust you are well."

"Very well, now the rain has stopped. Though it's as hot as ever." Elizabeth glanced out at a sun-drenched street. "We didn't have an opportunity to talk at church yesterday."

Meg reflected that Elizabeth didn't know what a fortunate thing it was, since Lance had been watching. "No, I was distracted yesterday."

"Oh?"

Best steer the conversation to a safer topic. "Yes, Aunt Trudy's cook gave me a baking lesson." She pointed to the serving area. Halves of two pies had been sold, but it was early yet. Meg expected to sell more in the noon hour. "I can serve you a piece of pie here if you like."

"It looks delicious. If I weren't in a hurry…"

"Of course. What may I get for you?"

"Wrap up two pieces of cinnamon cake, please." Elizabeth gave her a steady look.

Two of anything meant Elizabeth had a message for her to

forward, meaning Meg must come to her home for it. Impossible with Lance watching. "How about three cakes? Two isn't convenient at the moment."

Elizabeth's eyebrows shot up. "You're right. Three is better."

Meg made a move as if brushing back her hair. "Being watched," she said, while her hand covered her mouth.

Her eyes widened. "Understood," she whispered.

Elizabeth scurried away as soon as her package was ready.

Meg was glad her fellow spy readily accepted her dilemma.

As she greeted the next customers, a young couple with an infant, she reflected that a confrontation with Lance tomorrow couldn't come soon enough.

*C*ade glimpsed Lance after escorting Meg safely home that evening. Since she promised she'd stay home all evening, Cade strolled over by the gambling halls to lead the unwelcome troublemaker on a merry chase. He maintained a steady pace, easily followed, and finally spotted the scruffy beard one hundred yards behind him.

Lance maintained enough distance between him and his prey to run for shelter.

Good to know.

Cade stopped by Jay's home about seven.

"I just got home, old boy." Jay led him to the parlor. "Are you hungry? I'll ask Esther to make another sandwich for you."

"Obliged to you." Preparing a sandwich didn't add undue burden for Jay's cook, and the pair needed to talk.

"Let me go tell her and wash a bit of the day's grime away."

"First, tell me if Mr. McCane agreed to our plan."

"He did."

A wave of relief washed over Cade as Jay strode from the

room, for he wasn't alone in watching over Meg. With a villain as slippery as Lance, another pair of eyes was welcome.

While he waited, Cade crossed over to stare out the window onto the residential side street in the city's wealthier Church Hill neighborhood. Jay lived in a modest home away from the richest families.

Movement behind a spreading magnolia tree across the cobblestone street caught his attention. He rubbed his eyes and looked again. Sure enough, someone knelt behind the low branches.

It had to be Lance.

Cade stepped back several paces from the window to move out of sight. He watched the figure and waited.

Five minutes.

Ten minutes.

Finally, his patience was rewarded. Lance stepped away from the magnolia leaves that had concealed him.

Proof that Lance had followed him. Now Meg's brother-in-law knew for certain where Jay Nickson lived. Another friend of Meg's to trail.

Cade didn't take too kindly to being stalked, even if he had led the man on a merry chase. A slow burning anger began to simmer.

Tomorrow, if all goes well, you'll get your comeuppance.

~

*I*t was still sweltering at nearly dusk that evening when Cade reached his home. He figured Lance had found something better to do, for he hadn't felt eyes on his back the whole way.

Perhaps he'd found a card game somewhere. Lance had probably determined by now that Cade was early to bed and early to rise.

Not much fun to watch as the sun went down, for in summer, that was when he made his sponge for the morning's bread.

His hands were a watered floury mess when someone tapped four times on the back door.

Not a moment to spare to clean his hands. He wrapped a towel around the right one and opened the door. Two small black boys stared up at him with dark, frightened eyes. Probably eight and ten years of age.

"Hurry inside," he whispered. He should have sent word to have the other stations send the fugitives on to the next station until Lance was gone. His heart sank. It was too late now.

The boys skedaddled into the kitchen. Cade locked the door after them, praying Lance was on the other side of Richmond.

He placed two fingers on his lips and then pointed to the table and chairs. They sat and ate the rolls he set before them and drank two glasses of milk each while Cade finished his sponge and covered it in a two-gallon stone jar.

"Well, boys," he whispered, "where are you headed?" Cade always allowed fugitives to tell him what they wanted first, because one time a neighborhood boy had come simply to ask for a meal.

"Fortress Monroe. That's where our pa went." The older one spoke between bites. "You know where that is, Mister?"

Cade nodded. These boys were so young to run away, yet it was a good thing too. Unless they were caught, slavery would one day be only a distant memory for them.

As he prayed it was going to be for everyone once the war ended.

"I'm Cade. I need you to whisper all the time you're in my home. All right?"

They nodded.

"What are your names?"

"I'm George, like my pa," the older one answered. "This here's my brother, Max."

"A pleasure to meet you." Cade washed his hands at the basin. "Come over here. Wash your face, arms, and hands before we go upstairs. No talking now."

The boys seemed happy for the lye soap. They had one sack between them. Cade had clean children's clothes for them in the hidden closet. They'd also leave with another sack, one filled with food.

Not tonight though. He'd have to keep these boys at least two days, maybe longer, until the threat imposed by Meg's brother-in-law was gone.

The curtains were drawn, as they had stayed since Lance surprised them on Friday.

He ushered the boys upstairs and showed them to their windowless room. "You can sleep on the bed in here tonight, but if someone comes, hide in here and close the door tightly." He opened the hidden closet. "I'll refresh the water and bring more food in the morning. You'll be with me a couple of days at least."

"That's good." George said. "Max is tired from all the walking."

"Understood. You both will have a good rest." Max had yet to utter a word on his own behalf. Too frightened to speak? Could the boy talk? "You'll need to be quiet all day. Only whisper to each other. Nothing else. There's a bakery beneath our feet. Folks come in and out all day. We can't allow them to hear you walking about."

George's eyes widened. "We'll be careful."

Cade showed them everything they'd need through the morning. "I'll bring you plenty of water to wash yourselves." He lit the lantern on a chest beside a large bowl and pitcher. "Soap too. Once you're clean, pick out some clean clothes to wear." He'd wash theirs sometime in the morning. He'd be busy tomorrow after work figuring out Lance's motive. At least Cade prayed all went well and he had an opportunity to confront Meg's former brother-in-law himself.

He wished the boys had come two days later. Everything would have been so much easier without this additional burden.

CHAPTER 13

eg tried to calm her jittery nerves the following afternoon. She had seen Lance sitting on a bench across from her boarding home last night until darkness fell. The man must have known about curfew, for he was gone by half-past nine.

He meant to shred her peace. He'd done it, for she'd tossed about in bed all night and awakened resenting him all the more for disrupting her life. She hadn't ventured out alone since his visit to the bakery though he hadn't returned to confront her again. No doubt Cade's physical stature gave Lance second thoughts about bothering her there.

Yet he'd threaten a woman alone. Coward.

The knowledge brought her a semblance of calm.

All that changed today. Why had he followed her to Richmond? He'd taken a lot of time and considerable trouble to get here, given the uncertain travel problems caused by the war. Did it have something to do with Thomas? Her curiosity spiked, because she didn't know what happened between the brothers.

Thomas had never told her what Lance had said to make him agree to give over his inheritance from their parents. To her many questions, he'd only answered that the signed papers protected their future.

He'd drowned a week later.

Lance had hounded his parents for money. After their death, he'd turned on his brother.

Now that menacing behavior was directed to her.

Lance had stolen from her all he was going to get.

~

*C*ade cleaned both kitchens and then joined Meg in the bakery. "Clara's pies sold well."

"All gone by one o'clock. Word is spreading about eating here. Two people ate their cinnamon cake slices here. We may want to offer other individual baked goods."

He couldn't think about that right now. Nervous energy made it difficult to focus on anything beyond the task ahead. "Not much left to sell." The boys upstairs needed supper before he left. Best take it now. He put a generous supply of biscuits and muffins on a plate.

He looked up from his task to see that her eyes had a haunted look.

"Has this ugly business with Lance caused you to think more about your husband?"

A nod.

She didn't know he understood that loss. He never talked about Evelyn. To anyone. Not even long-standing customers mentioned his late wife.

"Sorry this has brought that pain back for you."

Green eyes slanted his direction. "Thank you, Cade. For everything."

Loose floorboards creaked by the door. Two customers.

"Do you have any more peach pie?" A woman in calico scanned the displays.

"I'm sorry, it's all gone." Meg tucked clenched hands in her apron pocket. "We'll have more tomorrow."

Noting her flushed cheeks, Cade left with a loaded plate as the woman gushed about the pie she'd enjoyed the day before.

He prayed they caught the scoundrel disrupting Meg's peace tonight.

~

Cade emerged from the bakery exactly five minutes after Meg and set off in the same direction. It took only moments to recognize Michael McCane from Jay's description. Brown curly hair. Muscular frame. Brown coat and trousers. Patterned vest. Beaver hat. He carried a cane as he nonchalantly trailed Meg down Marshall Street. The cane made the detective's limp barely discernable.

He'd never met Michael, but Cade noticed how well he blended in with Richmond bystanders and pedestrians, gentlemen dressed in a similar fashion. He was neither dressed in the finest of suit nor the cheapest.

Meg walked at a leisurely pace up ahead. She carried a reticule and a basket, as was her normal custom.

So far, so good.

Cade surveyed the crowded streets on the sunny afternoon. Families drove past in wagons. Couples strolled arm in arm. Men smoked cigars outside of stores. A man held a newspaper aloft and pointed at a column to another man. Gentlemen talked on street corners. Children pushing large hoops along the opposite sidewalk with a stick gave pedestrians an unexpected hazard.

Lance must be there somewhere.

Recalling the hundred yards the man seemed to prefer, Cade slowed his pace. Shortly afterward, Lance emerged from a side street and followed Meg on the same side of the street.

Good. Very good. On this occasion, *Cade* was the follower.

Jay, dressed in the clothes of a working man, waited at George Washington's statue on Capital Square, Meg's destination, with Troy, a friend from Tredegar Ironworks. They would stay near enough to intervene should trouble arise.

Cade didn't plan on being far behind.

The detective's job was to keep Lance in his sights, no matter what happened. He would trail Lance to his living quarters or wherever else he went while in town, which had been impossible while he remained hidden.

From his position behind everyone, Cade enjoyed a first-hand look at the ways Lance avoided Meg's detection. Every time she glanced around, he either dodged into a doorway, stood with his back turned to a group of men as if peering into a store window, or held a wide-brimmed hat aloft to shield his hair and face from being seen as he stooped to pick something up from the sidewalk.

Not bad, really. The man had been practicing the art of concealment for some time.

Interesting, though not surprising. He and Jay had suspected as much.

The streets grew more crowded as they neared the center of town.

Lance increased his pace, actually passing Michael, who, like a professional, didn't appear to notice him. Afterward, the detective turned around and looked directly at Cade before resuming his stroll.

So the detective had known both Lance and Cade were back there all the time.

That one look comforted Cade.

Wait. Where was Meg?

~

*M*eg turned down Tenth Street. A sudden chill on her neck warned her that Lance was near.

She gripped her basket. No less than four men watched out for her. Even the crowded streets would protect her. If not... She touched her reticule and the hard surface of her pistol. She knew how to use it should Lance try to harm her.

Capital Square was up ahead. She scanned the crowds for Lance, Jay, Cade. No, Cade was behind her.

There were no familiar faces.

Bracing herself, she stepped onto the grass in the uncrowded square. Children laughed. A family ate a picnic supper on a blanket some thirty feet from the first president's statue. A couple of men stood with their backs turned to her. Not as many people as she'd hoped.

"Hello, Meg."

Lance was behind her, close enough that she felt his breath on her neck. She closed her eyes. Opened them. No weakness in front of this coward. "Lance. What are you doing here?"

"I might ask you the same thing." He fell into step beside her. "You knew I'd be back, didn't you? A signature on a piece of paper from Thomas's lawyer means nothing to me."

"You signed a legal document promising that you'd never approach us again. You said you were through with us." How Meg wished he had meant it.

"I lied." He grinned. "I'll never be through with you. You're family."

"No. Not family. All that died with Thomas." They halted at the statue. No one else was close enough to hear their conversation. Where were Jay and Troy?

"About that." His voice turned into a low growl. "Why didn't you inform me of my brother's death? I had a right to know."

"No, you did not." Meg spun to face him. "We washed our hands of you the day you stole Thomas's inheritance."

"Tsk. Tsk. Stole...such an ugly word." His brown eyes, the same color as Thomas's, held a hardness that had never been in her husband's. "Thomas wanted me to have it."

"You're lying." The man was a cad. "He refused to give it to you. Initially, at least."

"Oh, believe me. He agreed willingly." He leaned closer. "After I told him what I wanted to do with you."

Her stomach lurched as bile rose up in her throat. Lance's leer revolted her. Meg raised her arm to slap him, but he caught it, clamping his fingers over her wrist in a vicelike grip.

She gasped, biting back her scream. She didn't want the authorities to come and investigate Lance, for then they'd investigate her own Unionist activities. There was too much to find. Lance might be in jail, but so would she, for entirely different reasons.

No, she must handle this alone if Cade didn't come.

"Not wise, Meg." He lowered her arm to give an appearance that he held her hand. "Now, you're going to walk with me. Don't give me any trouble, or it's going to be very painful for you later."

Her mind refused to consider what he threatened to do.

"Let me go." He pinned her right arm between them. Her weapon was in her reticule hanging from her left arm. If she struck him with the gun, it was doubtful the blow would be hard enough to force him to release her. Instead, she tried to wrench herself free without attracting attention. *Cade, please come for me.*

"I suggest you release the lady." Cade bore down on them. He smashed one booted heel on Lance's toes.

Lance yelped and released her. He started to run.

Cade's hand closed around his arm. "Not so fast, fella. You're going to answer for what you've done to this lady."

Michael McCane strode up. "Miss, do you require some assistance?"

Meg looked up. This must be the detective, based on the relieved look Cade gave him. "Yes, please. This bearded man threatened harm to me."

Michael looked up at Cade. "Do you need help?"

"Want to hold onto him? He has a habit of disappearing."

"A pleasure." Michael's hand clamped down on his shoulder.

Cade released him and turned to Meg. "He tell you what he wants?" Cade stood near enough that his strong arm brushed against hers.

She couldn't look at him. Her face flamed in humiliation. The man wanted something far worse than money. "Me," she whispered, hoping Michael didn't hear.

Poor Thomas. How this threat must have weighed on him.

"That's not going to happen." Cade leaned over and spoke in Lance's ear, and the cad's eyes widened in fear.

"Fancy meeting you all here. Need anything?" Jay strode up with Troy.

"This fellow's leaving the city." Cade jerked his head toward Lance. "Tonight. He requires assistance finding the railroad station."

"He's in luck. I know just where it is." Jay surveyed him. "Let's accompany him. Make certain he doesn't lose his way."

"That's a mighty fine idea." Cade widened his stance. "We'll even accompany him to his living quarters so he doesn't get lost between here and there. Will you be all right, Meg?"

"Of course." Meg's emotions battled among relief that Lance was leaving, anger for what he'd done to his brother—and to her—and humiliation that all these men knew what he wanted from her. "I don't *ever* want to see you again, Lance."

"What do you say, Lance?" Cade's face hardened.

"Fine by me." He nearly spat the words.

"That didn't sound too friendly." Cade turned to Jay. "Gentlemen, don't you think an apology is in order?"

"Most assuredly." Michael, without decreasing his grip on his shoulder, gave Lance a steady look.

Jay clenched his fist.

"No. I don't want to hear his empty words." Meg held up her hand. "No apology will suffice. Change your ways, Lance. You were raised differently. Turn back to what your family taught you and save yourself."

"You've been given grace when you didn't deserve it." Cade reached for her hand. Her fingers closed around his in a convulsive grip. "I reckon I can match it. We'll escort you as a man, not a villain. But I warn you—don't try my patience."

"I'll go like a man." Lance's gaze dropped to the grassy earth. "And you'll never see me again, Meg."

The promise, though seemingly sincere, brought her no comfort. Now the danger had passed, it suddenly seemed as if she viewed everything from a distance, as in a dream.

"We can handle this one, Cade." Jay looked at her with concern. "Meg needs you. She looks about ready to fall."

Cade's head jerked toward Meg. He put a comforting arm around her.

A sudden sense of safety washed over her. She leaned against his chest.

"I'll take care of her. I'll be obliged if you make certain that he's on a westbound train tonight."

"You have my word." Jay shook Cade's hand.

Meg buried her face against the comforting warmth of Cade's chest. Strong. Dependable. Trustworthy. Everything Lance wasn't.

She felt Lance's gaze but didn't turn his direction. She looked instead at the bulge in her reticule. Her weapon. Had Lance been successful in dragging her away... Shuddering, she closed the door forever on those dark reflections.

"Thank...I shall never be able to..." Her voice faltered.

"Our pleasure, ma'am." Michael tipped his hat at her.

Meg watched them walk away, her heart aching for all the man had done to the family that loved him. Thomas had adored him when they were boys.

"Take me to Aunt Trudy's, Cade." Her shoulders drooped. "I want to be near family tonight, even if they aren't home."

CHAPTER 14

$\mathcal{C}$ade, alarmed at Meg's pale face and dazed look, guided her to nearby Broad Street, where he paid for their passage on a half-filled omnibus.

Children gripped the back of the roofed vehicle with open sides, their faces toward the street behind them. A mother sat with closed eyes, as if snatching well-deserved rest. Two bearded gentlemen in coats and vests read newspapers.

Cade sat beside Meg on the wooden bench, his leg against hers in case his presence brought her any solace.

That scoundrel had tried to kidnap Meg, threatened to rape her. Her dead husband's brother had catapulted the strong, independent woman into a nightmare.

"It's over." He leaned to whisper for her ears alone.

"Is it?" She looked at him with dull, green eyes.

"Yes. He'll never hurt you again."

"Maybe not." Her gaze dropped to her wringing hands. "What he did in the past was plenty enough."

What had Lance said to her in those three minutes while Cade held back to give Meg an opportunity to learn what the villain wanted?

Cade hoped she trusted him enough to tell him someday. He prayed for her the rest of their journey.

Minutes later, the omnibus halted in front of St. John's Church. They were near Trudy's home.

"Meg, we'll have to walk now." Cade helped her to her feet. Then, carrying her basket, he held her hand while she exited the vehicle. "Much obliged." He nodded to the driver when they both stood on the sidewalk.

The driver drove on to the next stop.

"Just a little further now." He placed her trembling hand on his crooked arm and covered it with his. "Meg, you can do this." She must walk. The alternative was that he carry her—which he could easily do, since she was of trim stature—but that would bring unwanted attention. Folks would rush to help them. In her present emotional state, she'd shrink from strangers.

Vague green eyes met his.

"You're in shock. Let's walk to Trudy's. We're almost there."

"Trudy's." She blinked.

"Yes. One step. Now another."

They started down the hill.

It was a good thing the other men had escorted Lance from town. After seeing Meg in such a bewildered state, Cade would have preferred to send him off nursing a bloody nose, or worse. His vehemence surprised him, for he usually shunned violence.

As they neared the home, Harold ran to the street with Clara at his heels. "What happened to Miss Meg?"

"I'll explain everything inside."

Clara wrapped an arm around Meg's waist. Harold opened the door, and she and Cade got her inside the parlor before anyone else spoke.

"Meg, what's happened to you, child?" Clara guided her gently to the couch.

"Oh, Clara." Tears spilled down Meg's cheeks. "Poor Thomas."

Clara raised her eyes to Cade. "Her dead husband?"

He nodded. "Lance, his brother, has been following Meg. He's a scoundrel. What he had in mind to do…"

Clara, a fierce look in her eyes, drew her shoulders back.

Meg covered her face with her hands. "How could he?"

"Hard to say what turns some men into animals, as if they turned their backs on the sense the Good Lord gave them. They all will get their comeuppance when they stand before Him on Judgement Day." Clara patted Meg's shoulder. "Important thing is that it's over. And no one here is gonna let him anywhere close to you."

"Promise?" Meg looked from her to Cade.

"Promise." Cade answered for all of them. "Meg asked to stay here with you. Is that all right? For a few days?"

"She can stay here as long as she wants." Clara lifted her chin. "That's what Miss Trudy said all along anyway. I'll take her upstairs."

"Need my help?"

"I got her." Clara shook her head. "Harold, send Mabel to me."

Her husband left the room.

Cade watched the pair ascend the stairs, marveling at how a good woman made all the difference. Clara knew just what to do, and Meg instinctively responded to her compassionate care.

"We'll get you a nice bath, and then I'll bring you a bite of supper. How does that sound?"

"Good. But my clothes—"

"Did you forget Miss Bea convinced you to leave a few things here?" Their voices trailed away as they disappeared down the second-floor hall.

Cade's chin dropped to his chest. How he wished he could have protected her from this. They all imagined the gambler wanted money. It was the means Lance had planned to use to steal it from Meg that they'd focused on. His error in judgement was a costly one he'd regret to his dying day.

"Mr. Cade?"

He opened his eyes and focused on Harold's concerned face.

"Can you tell me what happened? Clara needs to know so she can help Miss Meg."

"Of course." He braced himself. "It's not a pretty story."

"You look like you was wrung through a wringer yourself, if you don't mind me saying so. A good strong cup of coffee won't do you no harm." He indicated the back hall with a nod. "Let's talk in the kitchen."

Cade followed, reflecting that Trudy Weston was blessed with a caring staff.

~

Several nights of restless nightmares caught up with Meg, and she fell asleep that evening soon after consuming a bowl of vegetable soup for supper.

Awakening before dawn, she found that the shield her mind had erected over her heart after Lance left had melted away.

Meg was in the bedroom, decorated in shades of yellow, where she had spent the spring. She felt safer somehow. While it was a comfort to be here, Bea wasn't asleep on the other side of the wall. Aunt Trudy wasn't down the hall. How she longed to tell them what happened.

She crept to the window, open to allow night air to cool the room, without lighting a lantern. Her thoughts were darker than the night.

Though Lance had hurt her—she had bruises on her wrist to prove his rough treatment—that wasn't what caused her deepest pain.

No, it was what that monster had said and done to her husband—his brother—that sliced through her soul.

Thomas hadn't been the same after giving Lance the inheritance money. She and Thomas had planned to build a new home in a small town that needed his skills as a doctor. He had worked with another doctor for years and dreamed of being on his own. He felt he was finally ready. All he'd wanted to be was a country doctor, even knowing patients sometimes paid for services with a jar of blackberry jam or pickled beets.

Thomas had been both a gentleman *and* a gentle man. Strong on the inside. Faithful. A churchgoing man. Meg had fallen in love with him for those qualities.

Lance had never been like his brother. She had given him a wide berth, especially after seeing the havoc the older son wrought on his loving parents. Had he threatened them to get money? When her in-laws died in a bridge collapse, Thomas had been surprised that none of the money mentioned in the will was in the bank. Only the home remained.

She and Thomas heard from Lance more often after their parents' deaths. Each letter contained requests for money.

"He's had a run of back luck at the gambling hall," Thomas would say. "Let's send him something to tide him over." Or, "A gambler is after Lance. He's paid the man all he's due. Unfortunately, the gambler disagrees. My brother only asks for enough to live in a boarding house for a month while he gets back on his feet. I'm going to send it."

Meg stared up at the starry sky. They never should have helped him, for it started a pattern.

It was that last visit that destroyed Thomas. Now she understood why. Lance threatened to rape her.

Her husband kissed her goodbye at dawn the next Saturday. He had been a strong swimmer yet had drowned a dozen feet from the riverbank.

For the first time she wondered... Had his drowning been her husband's last intentional act?

No! It couldn't be suicide.

Yet her heart whispered that it was possible. Had she always feared this possibility in the deepest place in her soul? An area of her heart that went too deep for words?

For Thomas's sake, for truth's sake, she must consider it. There'd been plenty of tough days. They had planned for a family. After one miscarriage, Meg was never pregnant again.

She turned her mind from that grief, shifting her focus to Thomas's struggles with an effort.

Once brickmaking became too difficult for his aging father and her in-laws made a home with them, she and Thomas planned for them to all live together in that dream home in the country.

That didn't come to fruition either.

Still, would that have been enough to cause Thomas to want to die? What had Lance said to him?

Wait. Had the rogue implied Meg wanted him too?

Bile surged to her throat, gagging her. She'd die before she let that scoundrel touch her.

But what if Thomas believed it?

No, he knew her so well. He couldn't believe such a lie.

She didn't know what Lance had said to Thomas, but she despised him for saying it. He had tormented Thomas, one way or another, for years.

Thomas, you didn't kill yourself that day, did you? The answer her heart sought didn't come. A good man died that terrible day while his brother lived to play another hand of cards.

Unshed tears threatened to choke her. *Oh, Thomas, why didn't you ask me for the truth? Far from desiring your brother, I could barely force myself to speak civilly to him after his unreasonable demands. I loved you. Your brother planted those seeds of doubt. For how long?*

Heart breaking afresh for Thomas's pain, Meg fell to her knees.

~

*C*ade caught an omnibus ride over to Trudy's home on Wednesday evening to save time. Had only one day passed since they confronted Lance? He planned to leave with George and Max when the sun went down, assuming Meg didn't need him.

Within a few minutes, he knocked.

"Mr. Cade." Harold opened the door wide. "We expected you."

"Good evening." Cade gave him clean pie pans from the day's pies. "Customers gobbled up every slice again today."

"Clara will be pleased." Harold stared at the metal pans. "I 'spect you want to see Miss Meg."

"Yes, please." Cade removed his bowler hat.

"Wait in the parlor, if you will." A wary look crossed his face. "I'll ask Clara about visitors."

Didn't sound promising. Cade paced the length of the room until he returned.

"Miss Meg's having a bad day." Harold shook his head, a concerned look in his eyes. "Clara said something's taken Miss Meg to a real dark place."

Cade's heart ached for her pain. He'd seen the shock on her beautiful face himself.

"You're certain that man didn't hurt her?" Harold eyed him.

"Positive." They'd been in his sight for the entire interchange. The brim of his hat crumpled in his hands.

"Then something that scoundrel said liked to destroy her spirit. That's what Clara says."

"Can I talk with her?"

"She ain't up to talking. Can I tell her you're praying for her?"

"I am." He nodded. "Without ceasing. Will you tell her for me that I stopped at her boarding house last night so Mrs. Ferris

122

wouldn't worry about her?" The woman had expressed concern and then informed him the room was paid for through Saturday. She demanded next week's rent to hold the room past that date. He'd paid it, making certain the proprietor knew it was coming from Meg's salary to protect her reputation.

"Sure will."

"I'll come again tomorrow. Thank you all for taking care of her."

He forced his feet to take him out the door and away from her.

Tonight as he traveled to the next station on the Underground Railroad, he'd pray for the boys' safety and Meg's shattered heart. First, he had another stop. He lengthened his stride and headed to Jay's house. After learning of Meg's precarious emotions, it was imperative he ensure that Lance had taken that westbound train.

~

*T*he first pickets outside Richmond were behind them. Cade had explained that he sang songs to let the boys hidden in the wagon know how the trip was progressing. George said their pa used to sing to them. They knew some church songs. It warmed Cade's heart that such a simple practice on his part meant so much to them.

He'd miss the boys. It had been nice to have children in the home. It increased his longing for—

Don't think about Little Cade. Best concentrate on getting these boys to safety. That was how he'd gotten through the months following the tragedies. Focus on the task at hand. He whispered a silent prayer they'd find their pa at Fort Monroe.

Forests up ahead, thickets where Confederate guards had waited in the past, prompted another song to remind George and Max to trust God whenever they were afraid.

"O God, our help in ages past, our hope for years to come,

"Our shelter from the stormy blast, and our eternal home."

No one halted him in the forest. Not surprising. The armies had shifted locations. Glancing from left to right, he whistled another verse of the tune he'd just sung. Crickets sang. An owl hooted. His grip on the reins gradually relaxed.

If all went well, they'd be at Isaac's house in another hour. The compassionate man was accustomed to Cade waking him up in the middle of the night, and his wife often gave them all a bit of cheese with bread—a welcome snack, not only for the nourishment but for the hospitality it provided.

He prayed for Meg, not knowing the darkness she faced, and that she'd soon trust him with the burden.

They rambled away from the woods. The words to one of his favorite hymns, "From Every Stormy Wind," seeped into his soul.

"From every stormy wind that blows, From ev'ry swelling tide of woes,

"There is a calm, a sure retreat: Tis found beneath the mercy seat."

"That one's also for you, Meg," he whispered. *Lord, please help her.*

CHAPTER 15

*M*eg regretted missing Cade's visit the day before. She hadn't been able to talk or even dress herself. Only cry. And pray. She'd done a lot of both, reminding her of those terrible grief-filled days following Thomas's death. Bea's whole family had been there. Uncle Hiram had taken care of planning the burial and all the legal details. Her cousins had stayed with her a month, caring for her when she couldn't lift a finger to care for herself. After they left, the reality of her new situation struck her. She had to find a job to replenish food in the empty cupboard. That gave her a reason to get out of bed in the morning and dress for the new day.

A shudder went through her. She had no desire to relive those difficult days.

Yesterday had been spent on her knees in prayer. This morning, she awoke to birds singing outside her window, as if to remind her of God's compassionate love. Nourishing meals strengthened her. She'd brushed her hair and pinned it back with combs in preparation for Cade's visit.

Life didn't sit still while one grieved the past. There were things she must do. A visit to Elizabeth to obtain notes she must forward. Tomorrow was Friday, her usual day to work at Chimborazo. She'd volunteer at the hospital and move back to her boarding house. On Saturday, she planned to work at the bakery again, which she missed.

And she missed Cade.

According to Clara, Cade had visited Mrs. Ferris on her behalf. So thoughtful. So like him. Unlike her, who hadn't spared a thought for her landlady's worry.

Meg waited for him in the upstairs parlor, calmer now that he was coming. The men who had come to her aid this week—Cade, Jay, Troy, and even the detective, Michael—showed her she didn't face her enemies alone.

In some ways, her loneliness had deepened since coming to the Confederate capital. Traipsing on the city's streets alone to deliver her messages left her vulnerable, especially after the hanging of Timothy Webster. Even though she hadn't worked directly with Timothy, his execution both saddened and frightened her.

Danger also accompanied her on her missions. It was vital the flow of information continue. One never knew the bit of information that might tip the scale in the North's favor.

Lance had interrupted her important work. Cost her nearly two weeks of delivering messages. Who knew what that information, added to others, might have accomplished?

Another wrong to lay at Lance's feet.

Half-past five. Cade was likely finished cleaning up the bakery. He'd come soon.

It surprised her how much she longed to see him.

~

"*H*ow is Meg?" Cade stepped inside the Weston home and took off his hat. It was Thursday, and he hadn't seen her in two long, exhausting days.

"Some better." Harold accepted his hat and placed it on a side table. "She's waiting for you. I'll take you to the family sitting room upstairs."

Nervous yet encouraged that she wanted to see him, he followed close behind. His eyes drank in her forlorn face above a purple dress.

"It's lovely to see you, Cade." The corners of her mouth lifted slightly as she indicated a chair to her right.

He bent on one knee to clasp her hand to his heart. "It's good to see you, Meg. I stopped in yesterday."

"Clara told me." She studied his hand dwarfing hers. "My apologies for missing so much work. I'd like to take one more day off to work at Chimborazo tomorrow."

"That will be good for you." Cade gave her a smile, hoping to convey his whole-hearted approval. "The proprietor of your boarding home wanted next week's payment in advance. I paid it and told her it came from your salary."

"Thank you. I'll make certain she hears it from me too." She looked down at their clasped hands. "I'm sorry I wasn't able to talk with you yesterday. I'm ready now."

"Good." He released a long breath and then sat on the edge of the adjacent chair, still retaining a gentle clasp of her small hand. "I've prayed for you."

"Yes." Her fingers curled around his. "It seems strange to say so, but I felt those prayers."

"You've donned half-mourning?"

Her fingers fell away from his, leaving him with a longing to comfort her.

"I left clothing here, mostly from my mourning for Thomas that I'd worn long past society's conventions anyway." She folded her hands without looking at him. "Though mourning clothes fit my mood."

So her pallor did have something to do with Thomas. He waited for her to continue.

"Memories of what Lance did to Thomas have haunted me this week." She took a deep breath and told him what happened leading up to her husband's death.

Cade listened with compassion for the young couple who had learned too late that Lance would stop at nothing to obtain all his parents' money. Even, it seemed, tormenting his brother with his feelings for his wife.

Blood surged through Cade's veins at the humiliation on Meg's face—as if any of this were her fault.

"I don't know details. Thomas closed up like a clam about it." She raised troubled green eyes to his. "What has tormented me this week is that Thomas may have believed I cared for that wretch, returned his feelings."

"Impossible that anyone who knew you would believe you'd step out on your marital vows."

"Do you...is it possible Thomas believed I wanted to? That he took his own life out of anguish?"

Cade nearly fell off his chair. No wonder she had suffered these past days if that was what troubled her. He wished Lance was still in town. He'd like to have another talk with him.

"I can't countenance the thought of Thomas not believing I loved him."

"You and I have trained ourselves to look at situations rationally."

"True." Her green eyes darkened. "You feel I'm being irrational."

"Not at all." He covered her hand with his own as he looked into her eyes. "I think Lance excels at befuddling your thoughts."

"He did that to his whole family." She nodded. "He's not in Richmond?"

"Left Tuesday evening." Cade couldn't keep the satisfaction from his tone. "Jay and Troy escorted him on the train themselves and watched the window where he sat until it left the station."

"Good news." Relief lightened her expression.

"About the other thing." Cade straightened his shoulders. "You say Thomas was a good swimmer."

"And only a dozen or so feet from the shore when the boat capsized. The river had a depth of some ten feet." She stared at her hands.

"He was fishing. He likely bent over too far to fetch a fish from his line."

"That was the sheriff's thought." Her brow wrinkled. "He had a knot on the back of his head that surely rendered him unconscious."

"From the capsized boat, right? He fished alone, you said?"

"Yes. The sheriff had seen such accidents happen before." She raised her eyes to his. "The lawman believed it an accident."

"It certainly wasn't a self-inflicted wound." If Lance had been in town when Thomas drowned, Cade would suspect him. Without any evidence to the contrary, he had to accept the lawman's explanation.

"You're right. There's no evidence that it wasn't an accident." She reached for his hand. "Lance was the one who planted seeds of doubt."

"Don't let him win." Cade spoke in fervent tones. "You know Thomas best. I'm certain he loved you."

"He did." A tear slid down her cheek. "And I loved him."

"I know." Her sorrow broke his heart. She'd endured so much. Cade stood and opened his arms.

❧

*M*eg rested her cheek against Cade's steady heartbeat as his arms went around her. As he cradled her against his chest, comfort seeped into her very soul.

Slowly. Amazingly strong. Stitching her heart back together, with the pieces in all the right places. How did one man's touch heal so much in so little time?

Gratitude welled up in her for all he'd done for her. Gratitude and something else. Something she wasn't ready to probe.

Meg only wanted to rest in the arms that held her gently. Compassionately. Lovingly.

She stepped away, embarrassed to have allowed him to hold her so long. "How can you, a man of few words, know just what to say?" She smiled to lighten the moment.

Mournful blue eyes met hers. "Because I lived it."

CHAPTER 16

*M*eg gasped. "You mean, you're a…"

"Widower." He turned away. "Six years now."

"I'm sorry." He really did understand her anguish. It bonded them together beyond the spying. Beyond the job they shared at the bakery. "Want to tell me about it?"

"I will." He walked to the open window, shadowed now with the sunshine moved to the western horizon. "I don't talk about it much."

"I understand." Meg stared as his broad shoulders, drooped under the weight of remembered sorrow. Oh, yes. She understood.

"Evelyn and I had been married about a year when she told me I'd be a father the following summer."

Meg closed her eyes against waves of sorrow in him, in her. The big man with a big heart had also lost a child.

"I was happier than I had a right to be."

Cade certainly deserved his share of happiness. Why did he have such a low opinion of his worth? He had hinted at his father's ill-treatment of him.

Silence stretched between them, only broken by clopping hooves on the cobblestones outside.

"It was April. April fourteenth, 1856. I was working in the bakery when Evelyn called for me from our living quarters. Told me to fetch the doctor. I saw the blood so I sent a customer for Dr. Ebbing. I didn't know what to do. Just held her hand until the doctor got there. I knew it was too early for our son to live. I'd never prayed harder." He looked over his shoulder at Meg. "Until this week."

Tears trickled down her cheeks. She remembered the blood, too, from her miscarriage.

"Dr. Ebbing's face confirmed my fears. Our son was too tiny to live. Not much bigger than my hand." He stared at his palm. "That wasn't the worst of it. Evelyn lost too much blood."

Meg's heart broke for him.

"She told me his name was to be Cade, after me." He gripped the window sill. "She was too weak to hold our son, so I did it for her. I cradled little Cade and positioned her arms around him. We stayed that way until…she passed."

Meg stood still, waiting for the man of few words to finish his story.

"I held little Cade for hours. Dr. Ebbing said to let my neighbor nurse him. That was the only time I let him go. Except for those few minutes, his whole life was lived in his father's arms."

A sob broke from him. Meg rushed to his side. Sliding her arms around him, she held him while he grieved. She prayed for him.

Just as he had done for her.

~

*L*ong strides took Cade back to the bakery. Raw emotions had been too much for him. The comfort of Meg's arms had begun to heal him. Her compassion also stirred his heart with emotions he thought long dead.

He had wanted to kiss her.

Love for her had grown without his permission. After all Meg had endured this week, no doubt his feelings were unwelcome.

He didn't want to be like Lance.

No, he wasn't like Lance. The man was worse than a ne'er-do-well.

That didn't mean Cade's attentions were any more welcome. He, a common baker, had nothing to offer such an extraordinary woman.

He unlocked the back door and sat on a chair. The kitchen was spotless. Sponge didn't need to be started for another two hours. Eating held no appeal.

A breeze lifted the curtains. He looked out toward the west. His little family was buried side by side in Hollywood Cemetery, a few feet from Cade's parents.

No one in the world had known the whole story of that terrible day. Now Meg knew.

Why had he told her?

He was tired. That was it. His sleepless night was to blame for his emotions getting the better of him. Once he rested, he'd be himself again.

Calm. Steady.

Yes, a good night's rest would restore him. Meg would understand why he'd accepted her comfort in his grief.

A beautiful woman like her wouldn't be attracted to a big oaf like himself. He'd best concentrate on keeping his ears open for bits of information to pass on to Paul and sneaking fugitives to the next safe station on the Underground Railroad.

Worthy causes, both.

So why did his heart suddenly feel so empty?

~

*H*aving arranged for Harold to pick her up from the Van Lew mansion in an hour, Meg walked to Elizabeth's home the next morning.

Birds serenaded her walk. Their song had a sweeter sound than she'd noticed for a while. She looked around and finally spotted a robin on a branch above her, head tilted as if it knew a secret. Smiling, she continued her stroll. She stopped to smell roses lining a hedge. What a beautiful day, even with those clouds overhead. Not the puffy kind so welcome on a July day. Still, a little rain might cool the oppressive Virginia heat, which she'd learned to tolerate.

Discovering Cade was a widower had shocked her, and the loss of his infant son had brought back her own loss. He had left suddenly after baring his soul. She assumed he rarely gave into his emotions. The only sob he allowed to escape had pierced her heart.

His suffering and the faith that brought him through it had made him a compassionate man. She thanked God that their paths had crossed.

Meg gave a start to see a thin, sedately-dressed woman on the sidewalk ahead of her in the direction of the city.

"Miss Elizabeth." Meg waved as her friend headed toward the busy thoroughfare, Broad Street. She quickened her pace. "I was just coming to see you."

"Meg, why aren't you at the bakery?"

"I had a little problem to take care of." She tilted her head. She had warned Elizabeth that someone watched her earlier that week.

"Is the problem resolved?" Sharp eyes studied her.

"It is." Meg didn't wish to elaborate. She'd given too much of her emotions to Lance. He'd receive no more. "Would you like to return to your house?"

"Yes, perhaps a pleasant visit is just what we both need." Elizabeth fell into step beside her. She nodded to two women talking with a fence between them. They looked away, chins tilted in the air. "It's good to see a friendly face."

"Always." Meg had noticed chilly behavior from a handful of neighbors toward Elizabeth in the past and wondered at its cause. Perhaps they suspected her Unionist support though, from what Meg had observed, Elizabeth was always careful.

Inside, they went to Elizabeth's parlor. She shut the door behind them.

"Now, I must ask. Are you certain the people watching you are gone?"

"I am." Meg looked around the elegant parlor at the little statues, expensive furniture, and opulent furnishings.

"Your confidence has convinced me." Elizabeth placed her basket on a table. "I've sent some messages northward by other messengers. You understand you're not my only contact." She extracted a note from the same hidden compartment in the statuette as previously. "Here are two more."

"I can't get them sent until tomorrow. Is that soon enough?"

Elizabeth nodded. "It's the knowledge itself rather than swift delivery."

"Thank you." Meg, without reading them, tucked them into the shoulder of her plain blue calico dress. "I hesitate to broach a rather delicate topic."

"A forthright manner is best." Elizabeth studied her.

Perhaps it was acceptable to ask for help funding the expense of sending Elizabeth's messages to the Union. "You don't know how I get the information out of Richmond. There is some expense involved." A hefty sum. Meg's savings in the city bank had dwindled.

"And I've never given a penny toward it." She covered her mouth. "My dear, I had assumed your wealth was in the same class as your aunt's until you accepted a job at the bakery. Say no more." She extracted some bills from her reticule. "This should help."

"It will." Twenty dollars. This would fund several weeks of messages. A blessing indeed. "Thank you." The bills were tucked next to the messages.

"Since you aren't working today, would you care to join me on my walk to town?"

"I'm going to Chimborazo from here, or I'd be pleased to stroll with you."

"Perhaps another time." Elizabeth led the way out.

Meg touched her shoulder. Paper crinkled.

This money would help, especially since she'd missed three days of work this week.

~

*C*ade delivered another message to Paul Friday evening. A customer had shared information about prisoners while enjoying a piece of Clara's pie.

"So there was an exchange of prisoners outside of Richmond on July twenty-second."

"Three days ago." Cade nodded. "At Aiken's Landing on the James River." It was a small place some twenty miles south of the city.

"The generals already know this, of course, but I'll pass it along so our fellow Unionist stay informed. Is that all she said?" Paul indicated a plate of cookies on the table between them in Paul's sitting room.

"Only that there are plans for more exchanges." Cade ate a molasses cookie in two bites. Tasty.

"Good to know. I expected to hear from you sooner about

the person following Meg."

"Turned out to be a personal problem unrelated to her Unionist activities." Though if Lance had discovered Meg's spying arrangements, they'd have had bigger problems.

"Are you certain?"

"Depend on it." The rest was private. Paul's strong curiosity about everything happening in the city made him a good spy. To protect Meg, Cade had no intention of satisfying it. "Anything I need to know?"

"See this?" Paul pointed to his watch chain.

Cade frowned at the peach seed hanging from the chain. "Does that mean anything?"

"Sure does." Grinning, Paul rocked in his seat. "See that three-leaf clover inside the seed?"

He hadn't noticed the clover, apparently on some type of hinge. "I do now that you've pointed it out."

"Even better. Watch." Paul turned the hinged clover inside the peach seed upside down. "That means it's safe for Unionists to talk." He turned it right-side up. "This setting means it's not safe. Maintain silence when you see it."

"Clever." Especially since he hadn't noticed the decoration on Paul's watch chain until it was pointed out.

"I've got one for you." He extracted two seeds with hinged clovers from inside a plain wooden box on the mantle and laid them on the table in front of Cade.

He fingered the rough seed. Practiced flipping the clover up and down. "I'm supposed to attach this to my watch fob?"

"Exactly." Paul, studying his reaction, rested an elbow on the table. "It's an extra layer of protection while we're in public."

"But few folks know of my Unionist support." It was less dangerous that way. He was more careful than most spies.

"There are more of us than you think. This gives another opportunity to quickly pass on information, as we had to do in the last few months when both armies camped so close to Richmond."

Those weeks had been busy and tense trying to separate truth from rumors. "Why did you give me two? In case I lose the first?"

"Don't lose it. Can't risk supporters of the Confederacy wearing them. You can see the danger caused by the loss of even one seed."

Cade gulped. A spy, believing he spoke to a trusted Unionist, could pass secrets to Confederate supporters. Dangerous, indeed.

"The other one is for Meg. Tell her to make it into a pendant. That's what the other women are doing."

Cade's body tensed. "She isn't working with me on Unionist activities. She has her own ways of forwarding messages."

"What are they?" Paul drummed his fingers on the table.

"We don't talk about it. I've learned to trust her."

"That is what I wanted to hear. You're the best judge of character in our lot." Paul eyed him. "Perhaps that's because you are the most trustworthy."

"Yet I spy on my customers, my neighbors." It was a dilemma he'd struggled against since the war started.

"You never lie."

"No." Cade shook his head. He'd heard too many broken promises from his father to bear falsehoods. Even when questioned about fugitives, he'd always figured out a truthful way to answer queries. "Can't lie. Makes it difficult to live this spying life." His tormented soul reconciled the spying and smuggling of fugitives by weighing the good that awaited them in the North.

"Keep reminding yourself it's for a worthy cause." He pointed to the peach seed still lying on the table. "Consider giving that to Meg. She's courageous—has to be to work on her own as much as she does."

Cade thought of her facing Lance. Yes, courageous was an apt description.

"Of course, she does communicate with someone in the Union somehow. I'd like to have her work alongside us."

"I'll think on it." Cade pocketed both seeds. Did wearing it increase her danger? Or lessen it?

He'd pray about it, long and hard, before deciding.

CHAPTER 17

*I*t felt as if a butterfly took flight in Meg's stomach Saturday morning as she walked to the bakery. The sun was a soft yellow dome on the horizon when she let herself into the back door.

"Good morning." Cade kneaded dough with floured hands without looking up. "Good to have you back."

"Good to be back." Meg put on a bib apron. "Am I baking the usual?"

"I'm out of baking powder. Can you make that first?"

"I've never made it." Meg raised her eyebrows. "Do you have a recipe?"

"In my head." He didn't look at her as he gave her the list.

They'd shared the most tragic moments of their lives two days before. He hadn't met her eyes or given her that lopsided grin when greeting her. Was he embarrassed? She quickly prepared baking powder per his instructions with a troubled spirit.

Ah, he must be self-conscious because she wrapped her arms around his neck to comfort him. Heat flooded her face. She hadn't considered any awkwardness he might feel. She'd been too grateful for all he'd done for her.

"Do all your usual baking." Cade continued to knead, the dough becoming soft and pliant in his skillful hands. "I've a taste for apple fritters, so I'll make those later."

"One of my favorites. Hope there's enough for me to eat one as my breakfast." She smiled at his profile.

"I'll make certain of it."

This was ridiculous. "Cade, please don't be embarrassed about Thursday."

He stiffened, then resumed kneading.

"I'm glad I told you about my past because what you said and did"—heat rushed up her cheeks again—"comforted me."

Cade stopped. His blue eyes met hers in a long, steady look. "I'm glad."

"And I'm happy you trusted me with yours." She touched his muscular arm, which tensed beneath her hand. "Now I know."

"Now you know." He stared down at her hand.

"Let's have no awkwardness between us." She gave a firm nod. "We're friends."

"Friends."

She wondered at his resigned tone. Hadn't she just bared her heart to him again? "I'll get started on the biscuits." Some needed to be displayed in the window today. The letter she'd composed last night also contained Elizabeth's messages for Mrs. Jordan to carry northward.

Time to resume her not-so-normal, dangerous life.

And she had Cade to thank for it.

She liked him more every day.

~

*F*riends. A gift, true enough, and all he had any right to expect. He was thirty-two, way too old for dreams of a wife and family.

The bakery had just opened, and Harold was dropping off the daily pies. He and Meg talked in the front room.

A footstep sounded overhead.

Cade waited for Meg to dash through the door and call his attention to an intruder in his apartment.

It didn't happen. Good. She hadn't noticed.

A mother and daughter of about six had tapped four times on his door at midnight. Ursula, the mother, knew the code, so he invited them in, despite his misgivings. He had made it clear to the three station masters who sent fugitives to him that he preferred to shelter only families or males of any age because there was no woman to attend them. It hadn't been a problem before the war started, because all the station masters brought the runaways directly to his home. Then each had decided it was too dangerous to smuggle the folks into the Confederate capital. Cade had learned his home was often bypassed, as it was deemed safer to stay away from Richmond.

Everything about smuggling folks to the next safe house was fraught with danger.

Women alone were an added concern for Cade. Not only did he not have a wife, mother, daughter, or sister to care for the needs of a female, he also didn't want any woman in his care worried for her virtue.

When Evelyn was alive, that hadn't been a problem. Not that he ever treated any woman less than honorably. They were in no danger from him. He just didn't want anyone to be afraid.

Ursula was a feisty one. She said her daughter Deborah would never cotton to hiding in the hidden room, which was an enlarged closet. She informed Cade they'd stay in the bedroom all night and all day. He warned them to keep quiet so customers wouldn't hear. That sobered Ursula, and she'd promised to speak only in whispers.

Cade resolved to take them to Isaac's tonight. This family hadn't come far—a two-day walk from Richmond—and were ready for the freedom in the north, even if they had to walk every step of the way.

Though it was good to know they were willing, Cade was happy to inform them they'd ride a good bit of the way. He didn't know much beyond that and couldn't answer most of Ursula's rapid-fire questions. Station masters tended to be a secretive lot. They had to be, or they'd end up in prison.

Cade glanced at the ceiling again, praying the noise was an isolated incident. He sighed, for he wasn't certain which one, mother or daughter, was more likely to forget the rules and call attention to their presence. Most of his customers knew he lived alone. Meg certainly was aware of it.

Tonight's trip meant he'd miss church—and sitting with Jay and Meg. It had been pleasant to belong again.

As a friend, of course.

He toted a tray with four loaves to the outdoor kitchen. The morning was getting away from him, and he had eight more loaves to bake after these were done.

$\approx$

A mother and her son, too young for school, enjoyed slices of pie in their one-table café corner.

The number of baked goods on display had dwindled. Meg combined what was left on plates for the remaining four hours. Cade's policy to make everything fresh daily was likely the reason he often sold everything.

It thrilled her that the apple fritters had all sold by ten o'clock. She'd convince Cade to prepare them at least weekly.

Better yet, she'd learn to make them and free Cade up for the breads and rolls that were his favorites.

"Thank you for the cherry pie."

Meg looked up with a smile. "It's our pleasure. Come again."

The little boy waved as he stepped out the open door.

Something crashed above Meg's head. Cade must have fallen.

She rushed into the kitchen to find he was coming through the back door. "Cade, something fell in your living quarters."

"Probably some books." He glanced at the ceiling. "I'll go check."

"There's an intruder." She pointed to his musket hanging on a rack. "You'd best take a weapon."

He shook his head. "The neighbor has a curious cat. Animals sometimes find their way into open windows. It's nothing."

"Be careful." She folded her hands at her chest. That crash had been far too heavy for a cat, though a small animal could have knocked over a stack of books.

Meg listened for Cade's light tread on the uncarpeted wood stairs. Heard the door creak open and close behind him.

Her gaze fastened onto a rolling pin. Perfect. She picked it up and crept toward the stairs on the far side of the kitchen. If Cade needed help, she'd be up those steps in a flash.

"Yoo-hoo." A woman's voice. "Is anyone here?"

Drat. A customer.

"Yes, ma'am. Be right there." The creaking of floorboards overhead was the only sound. Likely it had been a cat, just as he'd said. She rushed to the front room where a young woman in yellow gingham stood expectantly. "What can I get for you?"

"I see there's half an apple pie left. That'll be just perfect for dessert for me and my three little ones. I don't want to eat it here. Can I take the whole thing?"

No one else had requested to take a metal pie pan home. Meg pondered. Then she remembered how Cade's mother had handled the dilemma. "Of course. We'll need the pan back tomorrow. Umm, that is, Monday. We're not open on Sunday."

"Fine by me. I live on the next street over."

"Good. That'll be fifty cents. Ten cents each for four slices and ten cents for the pie pan."

"Ten cents for the pie pan? I said I was bringing it back Monday."

Meg widened her smile. "And when you do, I'll return the dime."

"I don't want it that badly." Lifting her chin, she glared at Meg. "Good day to you."

"Good day." Meg was sorry to lose the sale but glad she'd stood her ground.

Mrs. Yancey's plan had been a sound one.

Then she remembered the intruder.

~

"Everything's fine." Cade held out both hands, palms down, at the sight of Meg's worried face at the bottom of the stairs. "There was no cat in my living quarters by the time I got up there."

"Was it a mess?"

"You could say that." Deborah, the little girl, had been playing and knocked over a pile of books. Not in the window-less bedroom where no one could see them. No, she had been in his sitting room, where open windows allowed breezes to blow his curtain apart. Neighbors might already have spotted her. Sweat broke out on his forehead. "I'll clean it up later."

"I'm glad it wasn't an intruder." She returned to the front room, and he heard her greet a customer.

It was sweet of her to worry for him. He basked in her concern. It had been a long time since someone wanted to take care of him.

At least she hadn't questioned a cat causing the ruckus in his living quarters.

He swiped at his wet forehead. He hoped Ursula and Deborah cooperated tonight. If they talked while hidden in his wagon, all of them were in danger.

CHAPTER 18

$\mathcal{C}$ade remained in the bakery until sundown. More uneasy about this trip than he had been in years, he prayed fervently for this night's travel. Then he closed every window in his apartment before knocking on the bedroom door.

"We're sorry for making a ruckus today." Ursula put her arm around her daughter. "We hope it didn't bring you any trouble."

"I hinted that a cat might have found its way inside."

"That was right smart of you." Ursula patted her daughter's shoulder. "We each got new clothes from the closet, just like you said. Our old ones are here." She held up a burlap sack.

"I have a bag of food for you to take with you as well." Cade rubbed the back of his neck. This mission felt riskier than most. "Once we leave this room, we won't talk until I get you safely to our destination. Agreed?"

They nodded.

"No whispers. No movements. Nothing."

Deborah's eyes widened. She pressed against her mother.

"I don't want to scare you, but if anyone hears you, it puts us all in danger." Cade studied their contrite faces.

"What do we do?"

Cade explained everything they needed to know. Ursula repeated it for Deborah. The girl's eyes widened to learn of the confined space where they'd hide for hours, something that seemed to terrify her.

When Ursula finished her explanation, he prayed for them.

Afterward, a fresh resolve lit Ursula's eyes. "We won't talk."

"If we're caught, you'll be returned to the plantation. I'll go to prison."

She hugged her daughter. "Sing to us often. It'll help."

"I like *Silent Night*." Deborah tugged on his hand. "Do you know that?"

"I'll sing that song and others too. Often. Now I'll extinguish the lantern light before I open the door. It's dark. Once I open the door, not a word."

Lord, help us.

~

"*H*alt." Pickets stopped the wagon in a clearing about six miles from Richmond.

"Whoa." Cade pulled back on the reins. Old Sam was such an obedient, well-trained horse that he responded to the slightest touch. "Evening, gentlemen." He counted ten, no, twelve guards. He hoped this wasn't trouble, for he hadn't seen them until they entered the road. The toe of his boot nudged against the musket wrapped in a blanket at his feet. It would do no good against twelve guards.

"Your pass." One soldier extended his hand.

"Of course. It's right here." Cade retrieved it from his pocket and gave it to the one in charge. "Nice evening. Those stars sure are pretty."

The soldier held the page up to the wagon's lantern. "Cade Yancey. Mr. Yancey, what's your destination?"

"I run a bakery. I need to replenish my supplies."

"Mite late for such an errand. What's inside the wagon?"

Cade's heartbeat quickened. "Empty sacks for supplies." Most pickets let him go after reading his pass.

"Don't mind if we look, do you?"

"Not at all." *Please, don't move.* Cade feared for the little girl. *Please, God, help them be still.*

"Joe, take a look."

Cade shifted to one side so the soldier could climb up and peer inside the enclosed wagon, open only in the front.

"He's right, corporal. Nothing but sacks." He leaped to the dirt road.

"All right. A local sheriff asked us to keep a lookout for runaway slaves. A mother and daughter." The corporal returned Cade's pass. "If you see them, let us know."

They were looking for this family this far from the city? "Ain't seen no one on the road." Cade's heart hammered in his chest. They were all in more danger than he'd realized. He slackened the reins, and Old Sam began plodding again. "Much obliged."

Moonlight shone down on the open road five minutes later. No place to hide here. Cade looked back. No one followed.

His heartbeat returned to its normal rhythm.

Ursula and Deborah must be terrified. Maybe a song would help.

"Silent night, holy night, all is calm, all is bright

"Round yon virgin mother and Child. Holy infant so tender and mild,

"Sleep in heavenly peace, sleep in heavenly peace."

He hummed the second verse and then the third.

Peace entered his heart. He prayed the song and the wagon's rocking motion would lull little Deborah to sleep in heavenly peace.

~

"Will you give to our bazaar?" A fashionably dressed woman about Meg's age stopped her at the corner of Ninth and Broad Streets.

"Pardon me?" Meg looked around the sidewalk at the statuettes, paintings, expensive fans, and decorative items arranged on tables and shelves around the four women in hoop skirts.

"We have plenty of finery to choose from if you want to buy." The pretty brunette swept a white-gloved hand toward the display. "We're raising money to support the Confederacy. Our dear wounded have suffered much from these unfortunate battles."

"Agreed." Meg had seen the suffering first hand. She hated it. However, supporting the Confederacy financially was another matter.

"Of course, you do. Women like us must help by doing our part." Bright blue eyes stared at her as if to hold her captive until she bought something. "It's a very warm day. Of course, it always is on the first Saturday in August, but that's beside the point. You need a fan. I see you don't have one in your basket."

"No, I don't." Meg shifted her basket, empty except for a linen cloth covering the letter intended for Mrs. Jordan, away from the woman's hand. "But I'm unable to purchase a fan this evening."

"Perhaps you're right." The woman glanced at Meg's blue gingham dress, of far inferior quality than her own pink delaine gown. "We do accept donations. Your country needs every dollar you can give."

The fashionable woman wanted a whole dollar? That was steep. "Will you be here for a while?"

"Oh, yes, we patriotic women must perform our duty, and I know you'll do all you can for our soldiers. We'll be here another hour today. You'll also find us here many afternoons."

Good to know. She'd avoid this corner in the future. "I appreciate all you do for patriotism's sake." Not a lie. It was admirable. It was simply that the charity was intended for the wrong recipient. "Thank you."

The woman nodded graciously.

Meg hurried away, sorry that she'd ventured this far down Broad Street before turning toward Main. As she headed down Ninth Street, her distracted thoughts led back to Cade.

She'd been back to the bakery a full week. She'd thought the personal conversations she'd had with Cade would bring them closer. Instead, though he always treated her courteously, he avoided her.

It was a puzzle.

Like that cat in his apartment the week before. She hadn't seen any cats climb up the side of a house and enter through a second story window. That didn't mean it *couldn't* happen, but *did* it happen quite that way?

And what about those overnight trips? Why didn't he leave to purchase supplies immediately after closing the bakery? She understood the mills offering the greatest savings were some distance from Richmond. Was the ten o'clock to dawn curfew the reason?

She had the impression the only reason he mentioned his supply trips was because he often arrived back home after dawn, when her shift began.

Unless she missed her guess, Cade was involved in dangerous activities beyond his spying.

Or it was possible that his spy activities demanded more of his time than hers did.

She prayed they would soon trust each other. It would be thrilling to work with him on dangerous missions. They'd watch out for one another much the same as her fellow Pinkerton scouts had watched out for her in Chicago after Thomas died.

Maybe she'd ask Cade again about his overnight supply trips. He offered to walk with her to church. He'd missed services the week before and never explained why. She understood the man well enough to know he didn't miss church services without a good reason.

The more Meg knew of him, the more he intrigued her.

CHAPTER 19

"Good morning." Cade's heart jolted at the sight of Meg on Sunday morning. She sure was pretty in that gingham dress the color of ripe limes, but it was the happy glow in her eyes that stole his breath.

"Good morning to you too." She tucked her hand in his arm. "Isn't it a lovely day?"

He looked around. Dew had already dried on the grass, a healthy green lingering from Friday's rain. Sunflowers in a nearby yard were open toward the sun that beat down on them relentlessly even as early as half-past eight. Yet puffy white clouds dotted the blue sky. "It is indeed."

"I'm having lunch with Clara's family again today. Then she'll give me another lesson in pie baking. Want to come?"

His spirits lifted at the invitation. Then he thought better of it. "Clara won't want another baker in the kitchen when she's teaching you."

"Why not?" She tilted her head up at him, her wide-brimmed straw hat shading her eyes. "You said yourself that pies aren't your strong suit."

"True." Plans that kept him with Meg most of the day

certainly appealed to him. "I can come over after you dine together." A diner near church was open for sandwiches and soup. He wouldn't have to walk home and back.

"Clara said to invite you to join us for our meal."

"Is that so?"

"You've impressed her." Meg looked toward the church as the bell began to toll. "Selling her pies. Praising her baking. Helping me when I needed a friend."

A friend. A timely reminder, for his heart had begun to sing at spending the day in her company. "My privilege."

"So please say you'll come." Her fingers tightened on his arm as she looked up at him.

"I will. And thank you."

His friend's radiant smile warmed every part of his lonely heart.

And she was completely unaware of it.

～

"I asked Clara if we could use this downstairs parlor for a few minutes before we leave." Meg opened the door to the large, elegant yet cozy room. They'd laughed often during the baking lesson. Not surprisingly, Cade's skill with pie crust matched Clara's. It was the various fillings that he'd never taken the time to master.

Cade raised his eyebrows as he sat beside Meg on the mauve couch. "You want a private conversation we can't have at the bakery?"

"Exactly. We're often interrupted by customers or the need to watch out for our baking and such." It was time they addressed a major mission they had in common.

"What's on your mind?" He folded his hands.

"Let's whisper for this conversation."

His glance darted from the closed door to the open windows. "Shall I close them?"

Good idea. "Let's do." His attention to details must make him an excellent spy.

When they had returned to the couch, Meg took a deep breath. "We both support the Union while living in the Confederate capital."

He gave a wary nod. Speaking of Union sympathies while a guest in the home of a Confederate supporter didn't sit well with him.

"I also know you're involved with spying for the North. As I am."

He eyed her, wondering at her intentions.

"I imagine we both receive a fair amount of information from our customers."

"I'm continually amazed at what they tell us." He gazed steadily at her. "As well as what can be gleaned in newspapers."

"Editors must realize not everyone in this city supports the Confederacy, yet they write as if everyone does."

"I read them, but there's nothing there to pass on to fellow Unionists in Richmond. They all read the same papers. Those with direct contacts outside the city pass on the reported facts."

"I do as well." It comforted her to know others watched the papers to send vital information north.

"How?" He scooted to the edge of his seat.

"By letter carriers. A husband and wife team. She's my contact." Without sharing the name, she explained their methods.

Risky. "Aren't you afraid a letter will be confiscated and used against you?" His knuckles showed white as he rested a fist on the couch between them.

"That's a danger but a mitigated one." She explained a bit about her codes for Ina without divulging her fellow former

Pinkerton spy's name and how she knew her. She needed him to share his own details first.

"Very wise of you." He rubbed his hands together. "I've been praying about asking you to work with the Unionists here in Richmond."

"Yes." Other than Elizabeth sometimes supplying information, she had worked alone while in Virginia. She wanted the support of at least working with Cade. She didn't need to think about it further. "How can I help?"

"First, let's keep one another informed of what we learn."

"Agreed." She leaned forward. "I will continue to send my letters."

"Do that, unless you sense you're being followed."

"Am I?" Her heart rate quickened. She had always sensed Lance's presence when he was around. That feeling hadn't returned.

"I'm watching out for you." Cade covered her folded hands with his own. "So far, no signs of it."

"Good." She released a deep breath. "I have a strong intuition I've learned to trust."

"As do I. Sharpening our skills of observation only increases our effectiveness." He stood. "Notice anything?"

Other than how handsome he looked in a brown coat, matching trousers, and patterned vest in shades of green and beige? She looked closer. "The decoration on your watch fob is unique." And not especially attractive. He needed a wife to help him select such things. Heat traveled up her cheeks at the thought.

"Exactly. I've been wearing it for over a week." He held up the chain. "Did you notice it?"

"No." Her cheeks flushed. So much for her powers of observation. "Does it mean anything?"

"It identifies Unionists to one another." He explained about the clover inside the seed.

"Clever." She was awed that an everyday object could be used to tell others whether it was safe to speak openly. "I'll watch for these."

"I have one for you. Women wear them as necklaces." He extracted a peach seed from his pocket. "If you display it, other Unionists you don't know may casually speak a phrase on the street and then stroll away as if nothing was said. That's happened to me twice since I began wearing it."

"More information for my Washington City contact." She clasped her hands together.

"Shh. Remember to whisper."

"Sorry. I'm excited to work with you. With all of you." It was almost like being back on staff at the detective agency, where others watched out for her and she watched out for them.

"Me too." He smiled at her. "Paul will want to talk with us."

"Paul Lucas?" Elizabeth had mentioned Paul was a Unionist. Nothing more.

He nodded. "I go to him with everything. He has contacts outside the city."

Meg tested the hinged clover, flipping it right-side up. "Unsafe." Upside down. "Safe."

"Exactly. I'll take you to Paul's tomorrow evening. We may find out something during the day to share with him."

"Excellent plan." She smiled up at him. "Now let's try a piece of our raspberry pie."

"Might spoil our supper." He grinned.

"Worth the risk."

It would all be worth the danger if the Union won.

157

CHAPTER 20

Cade escorted Meg to Paul's home the following evening. A day of steady rain had kept away many customers but also cooled the temperature. August fourth already. How his life had changed since Meg had begun working for him seven weeks before. She'd brought a breath of spring air with her. Their relationship was about to change. He prayed it didn't increase her danger, for he realized she'd shoulder it to help the Union win the war.

When they arrived, Paul introduced his wife to Meg and then ushered their guests alone into his sitting room.

"Mrs. Brooks, Cade gave me the good news last evening. Allow me to say that your connection with Miss Van Lew makes working with you as a fellow Unionist all the more appealing."

"Thank you, Mr. Lucas." Meg inclined her head.

"I see you're wearing the peach seed pendant turned upside down." He smiled. "You're a quick learner."

"I've been doing this for some time." She glanced at Cade.

"Now we need to learn more about one another to give the greatest benefit to the Union." Paul retrieved a journal and pen from a shelf behind him. "How often do you send messages to your Washington City contact through a letter carrier?"

"It depends on when I discover something the Union should know. At least weekly."

Paul's pen scratched across a blank page. "Where do you get your information?"

"Most often, it's through our customers." She glanced at Cade, seated beside her.

"As I do." It thrilled him to hear her refer to them as "our customers."

"Knowing when to remain silent is a skill I've learned." She watched Paul write again.

"Anywhere else?" Paul asked

"Through my work at Chimborazo." Her glance flew to a stack of newspapers on a bookshelf. "Newspapers, of course. Conversations on the streets."

"Very good. Anything else?"

She stiffened. "You've asked a lot of questions without giving me any information."

"My apologies." Paul laid aside his pen. "Cade explained much of what we do already. I also meet with fellow Unionists when situations demand our planning together."

"You don't need to go to those meetings, Meg." Cade spoke quietly. "I don't attend them, preferring to keep some anonymity."

"That's my preference too." Uneasiness cleared from Meg's face. "For now."

"Wearing that necklace opens doors to more secrets, as Cade no doubt explained." He glanced at Cade, who nodded. "You'll meet new contacts, people who won't know the particulars of your own methods."

"That's important to me." Meg shifted in her seat. "I'd prefer what I've told you to remain a secret between the three of us."

"We can agree to that." Cade lifted an eyebrow at Paul and

only continued after he confirmed his agreement with a firm nod. "I feel the same. Not telling anyone our secrets is safer, but that won't help the Union. We have to pass on what we know in the safest manner possible and only to folks we trust."

"Who is your letter carrier, Mrs. Brooks?" As Paul asked the question, his glance dropped to his journal.

Meg lifted her chin. "Do you have a trustworthy associate in Washington City?"

Paul hesitated. "Yes, but I don't communicate directly with him. I fear my correspondence sent under a flag of truce will be opened."

She nodded. "You must assume that. Under those circumstances, I can offer a better solution. That's one contact I can reveal."

Paul leaned forward, and Cade held his breath as they waited for her information.

"Mr. and Mrs. Jordan are my letter carriers. I deliver the correspondence to Mrs. Jordan and pay her one dollar and fifty cents for each letter."

Cade frowned. That was a significant percentage of her pay, depending on how often she used the service.

"Mr. Jordan is often gone." She fingered the pendant around her neck. "Delivering letters to the Union capital, I presume. I don't know if they deliver to other cities. That is a question for them."

"Where can I find them?"

She explained, watching him write in his journal.

"Who is your Washington City contact?"

"That I won't reveal. I'm sworn to secrecy."

"Is there anything else you want to tell us?"

She shook her head.

Cade noticed Meg neglected to mention that she wrote in a code using everyday language, not a cypher. She also didn't elaborate on her work that involved Elizabeth Van Lew, whom they all knew. Cade had met Meg at a party in the Van Lew mansion in the spring.

However, Elizabeth had never patronized his bakery before Meg worked there. She'd been there at least twice to his knowledge. Cade figured Elizabeth gave Meg messages she wanted relayed to the Union.

Paul also worked with Elizabeth. He didn't mention it either.

None of them knew Cade worked for the Underground Railroad.

Looked like they all retained a few secrets.

~

*M*eg was pleased that she'd joined the group of Unionists Cade worked with. She kept him informed of her discoveries, which he passed on to Paul. Neighbors knew Paul and Cade were friends, so it made sense for him to pass along information for both himself and Meg. It was a comfortable plan, for she felt her efforts were multiplied by the system already in place.

She used the money provided by Elizabeth to send messages north, combining her own messages with Elizabeth's to save money whenever possible. This allowed her to begin buying newspapers again. Pages from these sometimes went with the letters.

Bea, Annie, and Aunt Trudy sent newsy weekly letters. Her cousins' plans for Bea's wedding included shopping expeditions. Since some items either weren't readily available in Richmond —or only at exorbitant prices—the sisters decided to make purchases in Washington City and send packages to Trudy's home in advance of the wedding. Dressmakers were already stitching their wedding attire that included a new dress for Meg. She smiled that her cousins treated her like a sister. Bea didn't expect to return to Richmond until September. The wedding would most likely occur in October, though the actual date depended on when the most family members could attend.

While Meg missed her cousins and wanted to see them sooner rather than later, her days filled quickly. Elizabeth kept her busy. Confederate General Stonewall Jackson's troops had been in the Gordonsville area in mid-July. A Virginia battle at Cedar Mountain on August ninth was a Confederate win. There wasn't any information that came to Meg after the battle that the Union army didn't already know, so there was no need to communicate with Ina.

Still, she listened sympathetically to her customers and scoured the newspapers throughout the hot August days that followed.

Cade escorted her to church twice and then told her he wasn't going to be there on August twenty-fourth.

She walked to church by herself that hot morning, wondering what other secrets Cade kept from her. She had thought joining the Unionists in Richmond meant the pair would work together on everything.

True, they compared information every evening after the bakery closed. Often that led to newsy letters for Ina. And, if the pair talked too long, Meg ate supper with Cade. Not in his living quarters, but in the bakery kitchen where they were both comfortable. After those occasions, he escorted her home.

Her appreciation for him grew. He was always kind. A fine Christian. A gentleman. Yet his overnight trips troubled her. Why didn't he trust her with the details? What was he involved in?

~

"Word is that fighting took place at Manassas yesterday," Cade said as he locked the bakery door on Friday, August twenty-ninth. "The information about

Stonewall Jackson's forces you sent to Washington City on Wednesday isn't going to reach Union generals in time to impact the outcome."

"Learning of Jackson's march toward General Pope's supply line might have helped had the knowledge come earlier." Meg sighed. "Though our Union troops can win without it."

"Certainly." Cade began scrubbing soot from the stove, a daily job. "Last July, that was the location of the Confederacy's victory."

"Praying for a different outcome this time." Meg washed a baking pan in sudsy water.

"If Confederate reinforcements from the Army of Northern Virginia join the fight, things may get hot for Pope." The last thing Cade wanted was for the Confederates to keep winning and then attack the Union capital or cross the Mason-Dixon to threaten other Union cities.

Meg rinsed the pan under the cold flow from the basin's pump handle. "I like talking about such things with you."

Cade met her gaze across the room. "Feels good to me too." It didn't do any harm to admit it. They were friends, after all, and even closer since she'd started wearing the Unionist pendant. "Did you learn anything worth reporting to Paul?"

"Just the likely location of Pope's army. The Union army knows its own position."

"True." Cade chuckled.

"Can I ask you something?"

"I told you what I heard." Her voice had an ominous tone. He bent over the stove to hide his face. "I may not be able to answer."

"Where do you go on your overnight trips?"

His hands stopped moving. Sweat beaded on his forehead at the abrupt question. "I thought you knew about me getting supplies."

"Then why not leave in the afternoon so you get back before curfew?" She crept to his side and stood there. Waiting.

"I have a bakery to run."

"You don't have to go without a night's sleep. I'll wait on customers and clean up after they leave."

Bless her sweet heart. Her questions were borne of concern, not suspicion. "It's a wonderful offer, but I'm accustomed to going without rest. Thank you for thinking of me."

Someone was concerned for his welfare. It was a pleasant feeling. Meg cared that he often went without a night of sleep.

Just like any friend would do.

CHAPTER 21

*M*eg's worry over the Confederate victory at the second battle of Manassas increased. After it ended, reports were that both Lee's Army of Northern Virginia and Stonewall Jackson's troops were in Frederick, Maryland. She and Cade spent lots of time walking the streets to learn what citizens knew. That combined with what Elizabeth told her went into a letter to Ina the second week of September.

Neither army appeared to threaten the Union capital at the moment, yet Meg prayed for her Northern relatives almost hourly. Other Union cities were in a state of panic, as her Southern customers gleefully informed her.

A letter from Annie awaited Meg at her boarding house on Friday, September twelfth. The opening lines confirmed the panic in towns around the Mason-Dixon line.

As you no doubt have heard, Lee's army is in Maryland. Not too close to the capital, yet closer than anyone likes. Soldiers often march many miles in a single day, or so John says, so they can go in any direction on that march. Everyone knows it, and the cities near the Confederate army quake with fright while planning for the worst. Just last year we all feared a Confederate attack on our city after the first battle at Manassas Junction. We were grateful nothing came of that fear. This time I feel General Lee means to attack us. Where, of course, remains a mystery. Worse still, I haven't heard from John in a week. He tells me what he can, which is usually very little.

Bea is beside herself with disappointment because Father has post-poned our trip to Richmond. Until the Southern army retreats back to the South, we'll stay here. It's difficult to say if this will delay next month's wedding ceremony.

I begin to think it best we invite only our family and closest friends to the ceremony. Bea is distraught for she has dreamed of a big wedding since girlhood. I understand, for you recall my own wedding was a hurried affair in Boston after John's father died. Things often don't go as planned. You know this as well as anyone, dearest Meg.

Meg sat down on her bed. She once had planned to live out her days in Chicago as a country doctor's wife. Yes, she understood change.

Of course, few of our acquaintances will feel comfortable traveling south while a war rages between our countries. There are, almost certainly, a few among our friends who disapprove of Beatrice's beau simply because he lives in the South. I find that a ridiculous attitude, though my loyalty is firmly for the North. (Perhaps I should not write of that since this letter is sent to the Confederate capital.) Anyway, Father says we will host a party for Bea and Jay after everything is resolved. I pray that is soon, for I miss my dear husband more than simple words can communicate.

Bea will write when her heart feels less broken, but I'm certain this is merely a short delay. I miss you, cousin, as does the rest of the family. Everyone sends their love and prayers for your safety and humbly request your prayers for our safety as well.

It was unfortunate their trip was delayed, though Meg applauded the wisdom of Uncle Hiram in his decision, for she agreed with Annie's assessment that Lee planned to attack somewhere in the North. A feeling of foreboding warned that it wasn't going to be a small battle.

Even if her premonition proved false, it was frightful for Northern cities that Confederate soldiers camped tonight in Maryland.

She got on her knees. After praying for her family's protection, she prayed for folks she'd never know in a location she wasn't certain of. Where was the battle expected to be fought? Such intelligence was what they needed to learn.

Maybe Paul or Cade knew more than she did.

~

Speculation abounded among Cade, Meg, Paul, and other Union supporters in the next few days. Cade met with Paul to tell what little he learned. He and Meg often strolled the streets together after the bakery closed to listen to conversations outside businesses and on street corners. They wore their peach seeds with the clover upside down and spotted others wearing them. Some information learned from Unionists on the streets they already knew. It was like digging for clues and finding one he'd already uncovered. Still, they learned enough to make the strolls worthwhile.

Meg's fingertips resting on his crooked arm made those walks in the September sun even more enjoyable.

After escorting Meg home, Cade often met several Unionists while walking about town. If no one was around, they quickly swapped information and then went on their way. He learned that Pennsylvania cities like Philadelphia and Harrisburg were said to be fearful of an attack.

Everyone scrambled to figure out where the Confederates camped, where they intended to attack, and where their troops moved—details the Union army needed.

In the midst of this search for facts, three fugitives had rapped four times on Cade's door on Tuesday night, September sixteenth. Nine o'clock was late to take the fellows, two of them brothers, to the next station, but he was too jittery to sleep anyway.

They'd go tonight.

~

*M*eg awoke before dawn the next morning, filled with foreboding. The bad feeling increased when she arrived at the bakery to find the back door unlocked but no Cade. The stoves in the outdoor kitchen were cold. Unusual, for they were always lit before her arrival.

Worried he was ill, she climbed the stairs to his living quarters. The door was ajar.

She knocked. No answer.

"Cade?" She raised her voice and called out again.

"Cade, are you ill?" She stepped inside a stark sitting room that included a dining table, heat stove, sofa, two cushioned chairs, and an end table with a lantern and clock. The place would benefit from a woman's touch.

Three doors likely led to three bedrooms. Cade had lived here with his parents and then his wife. One was ajar. Probably Cade's bedroom. If he was sick, he needed help.

"Cade, it's Meg." She crept toward the middle bedroom, listening for sounds of coughing, breathing, or cries for help.

"Meg, are you upstairs?"

Running footsteps on the stairs filled her with relief. He wasn't sick in bed.

"What are you doing up here?"

"I couldn't find you." She raised her hands, palms up. "The back door was open. Sorry about intruding in your private quarters."

"No harm done." His eyes darted around the room.

"You didn't leave it a mess." Her tension released with her laughter. "Though you certainly didn't expect company."

"Yes, well, we'd best get to our baking. Customers will be here before we know it."

Puzzled by his abrupt manner, she preceded him down the stairs.

⁓

That was close. Cade knew the windowless room where Meg had been headed had been left in shambles. The boys had taken quick sponge baths using the bowl and pitcher in the room. They changed into clean clothing and left tattered ones in the floor. Dirty water remained where they left it because Cade hadn't had time to empty it the night before.

He didn't even know if the hidden closet had been closed properly.

He turned back and locked the door.

That room needed a good cleaning before anyone saw it.

A huge yawn escaped as he ran down the steps. After he'd brushed down Sam and gave him water and oats, he'd stopped in the outdoor kitchen to light the ovens.

Had the familiar task taken a minute longer...

Sweat ran down his face. Good thing he hadn't stopped at the mill for supplies. Instead, after dropping off the boys at Isaac's, he drove most of the way back and then slept in a wooded area.

He and Meg started on their morning baking, now a comfortable routine, without talking. She seemed to understand that he liked to concentrate on the task at hand until he had several different baked goods in various stages of preparation. He was behind this morning and hoped she guessed he'd overslept. Another yawn was smothered behind his fist.

His decision to take the boys on to safety last night had been a sound one. They'd been excited to be miles closer to freedom. They seemed to trust him and viewed hiding under the wagon's bed as an adventure, a far cry from how Ursula and little Deborah had seen it.

He glanced at Meg's nimble fingers giving the biscuit dough a gentle knead. Her skills had greatly improved in three months.

He'd grown to respect her judgement. Should he tell her about operating a station on the Underground Railroad?

Meg hated slavery. She had said as much in one of their many conversations. However, that wasn't the same as risking your freedom to aid runaway slaves. Hiding them. Giving them food and a change of clothes. Transporting them to the next safe location.

No, silence was key. One thing his mother had ingrained in him was to keep his mouth shut.

That sometimes saved him when his father came home drunk.

Cade worked the dough as his mind traveled down roads he seldom ventured.

Whiskey had turned his quiet father into a violent man. To Cade's knowledge, his father never struck his mother in anger. His son was another matter. Claimed he was too loud, too disobedient, too clumsy. Cade had worked to improve his failings. It never changed anything, for his father always found another reason to raise his fist.

That treatment of her son broke his mother's heart, as it mostly happened when she was away from home. She'd return from her errands to find Cade trying to hide a black eye or a busted lip. She tended to her son's wounds and then confronted his pa, who was immediately remorseful. He promised never to strike his son in anger again.

And broke the promise the next time he came home drunk. The reprieve might last a week or two months.

"Cade?" A soft hand touched his forearm. "Are you all right?"

"What?" His hands stopped kneading as he looked down into concerned green eyes.

"That dough is ready to set for its rise, is it not?"

He followed her pointing finger to the overworked dough. This wasn't going to be his best batch, but he must use it anyway. Had to have something to sell. "It is."

Meg's hand fell from his arm as he set the dough in a bowl and covered it with a linen towel. She pinched a bit from her batch and rolled. "Did something happen?"

"Nothing worth mentioning." He'd put all that behind him at the age of twelve when he and his mother buried his father. "Heard anything about General Lee's battle plans?"

"Nothing yet. Perhaps our customers will know something."

CHAPTER 22

The terrible battle at Antietam Creek near Sharpsburg, Maryland, on September seventeenth, broke Meg's heart. It wasn't clear to her who won but, by all accounts, fighting had been brutal.

On Friday, two days after the battle, Meg tended wounded from Antietam at Chimborazo and discovered that horror for the soldiers hadn't receded. She asked Cade for permission to also leave her job on Saturday to volunteer at the hospital. He readily gave it, and she spent another exhausting day working in her ward almost unaided. One soldier not old enough to shave died before she learned from the surgeon what medicine to give him. Another asked her to write his wife, pregnant with their first child. She had not a moment to spare for the task before he breathed his last breath. That heartbreaking letter was written late Saturday night before she fell into bed, aching for the young lives snuffed out far too soon.

"Word is that General Lee has crossed the Potomac River." Cade strolled to church beside her the following morning.

"That's the best news I've heard in days." Meg whispered, for that type of information was unlikely to please Richmond's citizens, many of whom had been ecstatic that Lee took the battles North. "The fighting has ended?"

"In Maryland, it seems. The armies still skirmish at various places. No particulars on that yet."

"You've been busy." She met his troubled gaze. He wasn't one to gloat over so many deaths, no matter who won.

"We all have. I visited Paul before his family left for church." His sigh came from his soul. "I didn't want victory to come in this way."

Meg didn't either. The cost was far too high.

Her broken heart had no words of comfort. She tucked her hand into his arm. He covered it with his other hand as they walked on together.

~

A regular customer stalked into the bakery two days later. "Mrs. Brooks, did you hear the latest?"

Meg, who carried a plate of sliced cinnamon cake through the dividing door, looked up warily. Her answer was always negative to such questions. She learned more by pretending ignorance. "I don't believe so, Mrs. Finch. What happened?"

"Oh, Lincoln's done it now." Spots of red appeared on each wrinkled cheek. "Do you know what that Yankee president has gone and done?"

"Pray tell me quickly." Meg, her eyes focused on her distraught customer, set her plate on a table.

"You're not going to like it."

"I'm certain you're right." Meg's curiosity reached a fever pitch.

"Lincoln says he's going to free all our slaves come January." The gray-haired woman shook her head so violently that a pink silk flower fell off her hat.

"What?" Meg retrieved the flower, careful to hide her elation. "How can he do that?"

"That's what I say. That Yank has no power to do nothing in the Confederacy." Her eyes flashed. "And now he thinks he can free our slaves?"

"Surprising." That word didn't come close to expressing Meg's astonishment. Did President Lincoln really intend it? Amazing and wonderful were the words she wanted to say, neither of which Mrs. Finch would appreciate.

"The gall of the man. Who does he think he is?"

The election in 1860 had made him the country's president. Meg caught the words just in time. "Are you certain of this?"

"My neighbor's cousin lives in Baltimore. He sent a telegram." Color receded from her face, leaving her as pale as she had been scarlet. "I can scarce take it in."

"You've had bad news." Meg led her to the café table. "May I get you a slice of peach pie? Or a cinnamon cake? I'll buy it for you." Ten cents was a small price to pay for such news.

"That's right kind of you. I'll take the cake. I smell the spices from here. Must be fresh from the oven."

~

"Cade, the most wonderful news." Meg rushed into the kitchen and closed the door behind her.

Cade took in her flushed cheeks, her sparkling eyes. "Tell me."

"President Lincoln has declared the slaves will be freed in January." She clasped her hands together.

Adrenaline shot through his veins. He had worked for so long to see this day that the power of speech left him. He laughed with sheer joy.

Meg ran to him and threw her arms around his shoulders in shared elation.

Cade, clasping her close to his chest, picked her up off her feet, and swung her around. Her blue gingham dress flared like a bell in a tower.

She laughed again.

He looked into her lovely, smiling face. His lips were on hers before he had time to talk himself out of it. Her kiss was every bit as sweet as he'd dreamed it would be.

Her arms tightened around his neck, and she returned his kiss with a hunger that matched his own.

Then she pushed on his shoulders. Immediately he put her down and stepped back.

"Cade, I..." Hands covered her scarlet cheeks.

"My apologies for forgetting myself." He'd embarrassed her. Perhaps frightened her as well, big oaf that he was. She'd told him again and again that they were friends. "I can only say that my joy at the news..."

She nodded. "I'll see to our customers."

He watched her go with a sorrow that matched his earlier happiness.

Loneliness hadn't driven him to kiss her. No, it was something much stronger. He loved her.

She didn't love him. Of course not.

The atmosphere between them, once full of camaraderie, must now be awkward. Stilted.

Meg might even decide to quit her job at the bakery, stop working with the Unionists.

He rubbed his hands over his face. He mustn't allow her to fear him giving her another unwanted embrace. He'd apologize again.

No time like the present.

Cade went into a front room to find a dozen folks milling around. All six chairs around the café table were filled customers enjoying their single serving baked goods. Cheerful conversation filled the atmosphere where he'd expected gloom.

Meg shot him a harried look.

With a nod to her, Cade bent toward the nearest woman. "What can I get for you, Mrs. Thomlinson?"

"I'll take a slice of your sympathy pie."

"Sympathy pie?" He frowned. "I'm not certain—"

"Alberta Birch told me you all were giving away baked goods in your café because of what the Yank president went and did." The woman with gray streaks in her blond hair peered around him. "I'll take apple. That's what my mama used to bake most often."

Free food? "Pardon me one moment." Stepping to a corner, he crooked a finger at Meg. "You're giving away pie?"

"And cake." She bit her lip. "I only meant to give a slice to Mrs. Birch. But then she told her neighbors we were as sad as they are about President Lincoln's decision and that we're giving away food to comfort them."

The bakery funded all his other activities. "I can't afford such generosity."

"We can say it's just for today," she whispered. "It builds rapport, a feeling that we are in this thing with them."

How she managed to look contrite and resolute at the same time… "All right. Just for today."

Her face cleared. "Thank you. Take it out of my salary." She hurried away.

Her weekly salary didn't cover this loss—not that he intended to charge her. He stepped toward the café corner. "Apple pie, I believe you said, Mrs. Thomlinson?"

CHAPTER 23

"This is a portion of the proclamation?" Paul glanced at Meg over the top of the page.

"President Lincoln's preliminary Emancipation Proclamation." Meg glanced at Cade. Things might have been awkward between them after their unexpected kiss, but there had been too much happening all week to dwell on the embrace that shook her from her complacency with their friendship. "The announcement was made on September twenty-second."

"'All persons held as slaves' in the Confederacy will be free. It's effective January first. Very good. You say your Washington City contact sent this to you?"

"On Monday. The very day it was announced." A fulfilling brand of exhaustion made her happy she'd joined the Unionist group. "Mr. Jordan left the same day, in a hurry to deliver the big announcement to his allies."

"That's how I have the particulars in my hand on Friday." He sat back in his chair. "No need for me to tell you all that this is important news."

"We've prayed for this day." Cade leaned forward.

Meg had done the same. She didn't know the motivation that drove Paul's Union support.

"This proclamation will be kept from many slaves. Richmonders will know, of course, but those living in rural areas may not. We'll spread the news."

"Agreed. Perhaps the end of the war approaches." Cade shifted in his wooden chair. "President Lincoln knows much we don't."

"True." Paul held up the page. "May I keep this?"

Meg nodded. "I copied it for you."

"Thank you. I want to pass it on to our fellow Unionists." Paul folded the document and pocketed it. "You're both welcome to come with me."

"It's getting dark. I'll go home." As much as Meg wanted to share in the happiness with other Unionists brought by the proclamation, something held her back from exposing her support to a group of like-minded people. She rose to her feet.

"I'll see Meg safely home." Cade stood. "Thanks to her quick thinking and compassion early this week, even more of our customers believe we're Confederate supporters."

Meg flushed with pleasure at Cade's praise.

"Oh? What did you do?" Paul picked up his stovepipe hat from a wall hook and gave Cade his slouch hat.

She explained the misunderstanding about free food.

"It appears your offer, though costly, may pay off in the end." Paul smiled at her. "Let's hope so. Remember to listen well. Take advantage of all conversations. That's one of the ways we'll help win this war."

❧

*O*ut in the waning light, Cade matched his wide stride to Meg's smaller one on the sidewalk. There were fewer folks out on the moonlit night than when they'd arrived at

Paul's home. They'd dined with his family, an impromptu invitation that Cade rarely received. It must be thanks to Meg's soothing presence. He glanced at her, who peered all around them, silently thanking God once again that there'd been no time for awkwardness between them this week. He understood why she didn't rest her hand on his arm as she used to do. She likely didn't want to encourage him to kiss her again. She had naught to worry about. He'd learned his lesson well.

"Penny for your thoughts?" He grinned at her.

"Thinking about how this week's news will change our country." Her face relaxed into a smile. "For all future generations."

"That it will." Eventually, his Underground Railroad activities wouldn't be necessary. "Too many folks will hide the announcement from those most affected." The ones who'd be freed by it.

"I fear that too. Unfortunate that it took a war for so many to know what freedom feels like."

"That's a fact."

"Cade, about the other day..."

Even in the darkness, the light from a street lamp touched her flushed face. He had thought them free of the awkwardness. Love for her had welled up...and he'd acted upon it. "No need to talk about it. I regret causing you even a moment of worry. It won't happen again."

Startled green eyes flew to his, then dropped.

"My apologies." He'd tuck his love for her deep into his heart. She'd not suffer for his feelings again.

"Well, as to that..."

She paused so long that he thought she'd forgotten what she wanted to say. Perhaps it was better that way. His heart applied the words of rejection to his soul anyway.

"I told my cousin in the spring that the time was coming when I'll enjoy the companionship of a fine man again." She paused at the gate in front of her boarding home. "That day is still approaching."

"Understood." It was a nice way of saying she wasn't ready for courtship and didn't want such attentions from him. What did he have to offer such an amazing woman, anyway? No, she'd pick someone younger than he. Someone not as beat up by life as he had been. "I'm certain that man is out there somewhere."

"Yes." She entered the gate and closed it behind her. She turned and looked into his eyes. "I'm more certain of it every day."

Cade stood as if his feet had sprouted roots in that spot long after she entered the home.

It almost seemed as if she'd offered him hope.

He couldn't afford to grasp it.

◦

*T*hree letters awaited Meg when she arrived home from work on Tuesday evening, September thirtieth. After she dined with her fellow boarders, she hurried to her room to enjoy them. Since the days had grown shorter, she lit her lantern and curled up on her bed to read. First was Bea's letter.

Dearest Meg,

I have the most wonderful news! Since General Lee is out of Maryland and back in the South, Father feels it's safe for us to return to Richmond. I can scarcely believe that it's been two and a half months since I last saw Jay. They say absence makes the heart grow fonder. I can now attest to that truth. And of course I have missed my dear cousin as well. All those months when I saw you daily have given you a special place in my heart, that of a sister. I am thrilled that we will all be together soon.

Watch for us to return on October third or fourth. Jay and I have set our wedding date for October twenty-sixth. It's a Sunday, and he

*has assured me his boss will give him the day off. We will take a
wedding trip later, after the hostilities are behind us.*

*Another advantage of scheduling the wedding on Sunday is that
you will also be free to attend. Please tell Cade he will be invited. You
speak so highly of him in your letters that Annie and I are intrigued.
Indeed, Aunt Trudy also senses something. You can tell me later if
we're wrong.*

Meg tapped the page against her chin. The memory of the
kiss she shared with Cade brought heat to her face even now.
She'd returned his kiss and hadn't wanted to leave his arms. He
was a good man, worthy of her love. But was she ready to
love him?

She shied away from probing into her feelings.

*Father cannot afford to leave the bank for a month, so he will come
later. He assures me that he will be there in plenty of time to give away
the bride. That's me! I must pinch myself when I think of becoming
Mrs. Jay Nickson next month. I will marry the man of my dreams. I
will then be the happiest woman in Virginia. Oh, Meg, I do pray such
happiness comes to you again.*

Bea's joy was infectious. Meg almost envied her cousin.

Annie's note was more practical. It provided the train route
the three of them would take and other details that her sister, in
her excitement, had left out. She warned that the weeks leading
up to the wedding would be busy. Annie begged Meg to take
part in any and all plans.

They could arrive as early as Friday, three days away.

Longing for her cousins and aunt welled up inside Meg,
making her realize how lonely she had been for their company.
She reached for Aunt Trudy's letter.

My dear Meg,

*I can't believe I've been away from Richmond for most of the
summer. Why, it will be fall when I see my dear home again. I am glad
that I will not miss the changing colors of the trees in my own garden.*

Except for my wedding trip—my dear Parker took me to Europe—I have not been away from Virginia for this long.

Clara has written me faithfully. She told me to pray for you most fervently back in July but has reported that you seemed to have turned a corner in your grief. I am comforted to learn of it, if true, for you and I both know the pain of burying a husband. You are so young with much to give. It's my prayer that you come to know your own heart and mind, and that you'll watch for God's leading. Our Heavenly Father often does not guide us with pointing fingers, accompanied by a marching band, to a sign that reads "This way to happiness. This is the way to My will for your life." No, His ways are often more subtle.

Remember when Elijah felt all alone in that cave after fleeing from Jezebel's threats? He was certain that he was the only one left who loved God. Then God told him to go stand on the mountain for He was about to pass by. Then there was a powerful wind, an earthquake, and a fire. God wasn't in any of these. Then came a gentle whisper. God was in that whisper.

What is God whispering to your heart and mind, dear Meg?

I have waited for you to write me of whatever occurred this summer to put you in such doldrums. I can only guess it is a matter too personal for a letter or you have resolved the problem.

If I speak out of turn, I hope you will forgive me for touching on such a personal matter. Clara didn't tell me what happened. If you wish to talk about it, I do hope you know I will listen. Please believe you are as dear to me as Annie and Bea.

A tear rolled down Meg's cheek. The whole tone of Aunt Trudy's letter reminded her of her sweet mother, who might have given similar guidance.

As for the matter with Lance, it was behind her. She would mention the barest of facts to her family, enough to warn them to steer clear of the dangerous man should he come around again, but not of his attempts to kidnap her. Jay was part of that story, and he could choose to tell his fiancée what he wanted to reveal.

For herself, she only wanted it to be over. If she saw Lance twenty years from now, it would be too soon. The man had been poison to his family and to her. She'd pray for his soul, pray that God would send someone into his life to return him to the faith he was raised in.

It fascinated her that Aunt Trudy referenced one of her favorite stories in the Bible. Elijah had triumphed over the prophets of the idol Baal. That success had led to Jezebel's threats of murder. His greatest victory plunged him to his lowest depression, which he suffered alone.

God met him there.

Her Bible was on the chest of drawers. She flipped to First Kings and began reading at the eighteenth chapter.

CHAPTER 24

"*M*iss Trudy sent a telegram last evening." Harold barely greeted Meg Friday morning before he shared the news. "They expect to arrive tonight on the six o'clock train."

"That's wonderful." Meg clasped her hands together, especially excited to see her cousin Annie, whom she hadn't seen since February. "We've missed them, haven't we?"

"Sure enough." Harold's face beamed as Cade brought a basket of rolls into the front room. "Mr. Cade, Clara says to remind you these are the last of the pies, since she'll be too busy from now on."

"She warned it was temporary." Cade grinned and extended his hand. "I appreciate all the delicious pies. They've brought new customers to my bakery."

"She'll be glad to hear it." Harold shook Cade's hand. "She says to thank you. It was nice to earn extra money."

"The pleasure is mine." Cade paid him from the cash box. "When will Mrs. Weston arrive?"

"Tonight, though I 'spect the train will be late." He grinned. "Miss Bea is bringing most of her possessions with her this time. Miss Trudy asked that Mr. Jay bring his wagon for the trunks and boxes. He might have to make a second trip to the depot."

"I'll bring my wagon." Cade looked at Meg. "You want to meet their train, right?"

"Even if I have to walk." Meg barely resisted dancing a gig.

"That's not necessary." Cade chuckled. "I'll take you."

"I would have picked you up from the bakery if Mr. Cade didn't bring you, Miss Meg." Harold grinned. "Miss Trudy will want you both to stay for supper."

Meg knew it was true. "I accept because I know I won't be ready to leave them immediately. Cade?"

"If invited, I'll stay." His eyes lingered on her face.

"Make no mistake, unless Miss Trudy arrives feeling poorly, she'll invite you." Harold picked his hat off the table where he'd set it upon entering. "Clara has given me a list of tasks for the day, so I'd best get to it."

As it wasn't time to open yet, Cade closed the door behind him before turning to Meg. "You're happy."

"Ecstatic." She smiled at him. "Thanks for loaning your wagon. If I know my cousin, Bea will have enough to fill it."

~

*M*eg's prediction and Harold's warning proved correct. Cade oversaw the train attendants loading trunks and boxes onto Jay's wagon. When that was full, his bakery wagon was quickly filled to the brim.

"Is that it?" Cade peered past the attendant's shoulder.

"That's it." Sweat ran down the man's bearded face, despite the evening's chill.

"Thank you." Cade tipped him and his buddy for their time and trouble. "Hope the load's not too much for my horse on these hills."

185

"Shouldn't be. Must be a lot of clothes. Most boxes are light."

That was a relief. "Much obliged." He, Jay, and Mrs. Weston's staff had to unload it all too. Catching Jay's eye, he waved.

Jay spoke to Bea, who clung to his arm as if she'd never release him. In the end, Bea rode beside Jay on the dark streets. Harold followed in a carriage with the other ladies. Cade, alone, took up the rear.

He didn't mind, for the joy on Meg's face was worth any amount of trouble.

The train had been an hour and a half late, a wait that had been difficult for all three of his companions. Jay's face, especially, showed strain and anxiety as he watched to the west for the train carrying his fiancée to him.

The joy of the reunion for all the loved ones had warmed Cade's heart. He was used to being on the outside and didn't mind it. But when Meg took his arm and brought him forward to introduce him to Annie, his heart swelled with gratitude to be part of a family again, even for a little while.

Supper was a more boisterous occasion than he was accustomed to, for conversation between the cousins flowed from one topic to another, never finishing one before the next started and then returning to a previous one.

No one seemed confused by the rapid-fire changes except Cade, who sat between Annie and Meg and across from Bea. The betrothed couple frequently smiled at one another.

Cade almost envied their joyful reunion. Meg had told him she wasn't ready for courtship. There was no assurance she'd give him a second glance even then.

He decided to simply enjoy the evening and future family gatherings he'd be invited to because of his connection to her.

"Meg, will you spend the night here?" Bea asked as they strolled to the parlor after their delicious meal. "Harold can drive you to the bakery in the morning."

"Well, I…" Meg met Cade's eyes. "I told Mrs. Ferris that I was dining out this evening, but she expects me home."

"If you want to accept Bea's invitation," Cade said, "I will stop by your boarding house and inform her where you are." A small errand, indeed, to allow her to give in to the longing in her eyes to stay up late and catch up on the news with her cousins.

"Oh, please do." Annie added her own coaxing.

"If you're certain you don't mind." Meg's green eyes searched Cade's.

"Not at all." It amazed Cade she didn't know he'd go to the ends of the earth for her.

"I can't fathom how you girls have enough energy to talk all night." Trudy's eyes twinkled at them. "I will seek my bed early and greatly fear I won't be up to see you off in the morning, dearest Meg."

Cade glanced at the mantle clock. Ten minutes past nine. Too late to linger, for his hostess was weary from her travels. Besides, he had to make sponge tonight for the morning's bread.

"Please don't." Meg touched Trudy's lacy sleeve. "I will be gone by dawn."

"And I must take my leave." Cade inclined his head toward Mrs. Weston. "Thank you for a delicious meal and warm hospitality."

"My pleasure." She offered him her hand, which he held briefly. "I hope you will accompany Meg often to our festivities this month."

"Most kind of you. I look forward to it." He turned to Annie. The lovely, sedate brunette was calmer than her sister. "It was a pleasure to meet you, Mrs. Finn."

"And you, Mr. Yancey." Annie inclined her head. "Thank you for helping with the luggage. Would you believe my sister left some of her possessions at home?"

He chuckled. "Don't see how that could be the case, begging your pardon, Miss Bea."

She giggled. "Father's bringing more."

"Looks like our wagons will be needed at the train depot again." Cade grinned at Jay.

"That they will." He gave a mock sigh.

"Oh, you will insist on teasing me." Bea swatted at his arm playfully.

"Always." Jay grinned.

"Good night, everyone. Meg, I will see you in the morning." Cade gave her a smiling nod.

Meg took his arm and walked him to the door. "Don't forget to stop by my boarding house. Mrs. Ferris will worry."

"I won't forget." Cade accepted his hat from Harold, who opened the door. "Morning comes early. Don't stay up too late."

"I won't. Drive safely."

As Cade strode to the stable behind the home, he hummed to himself. Meg was happy. He was thankful for her family, who'd brought that happiness.

～

"So, tell us about Cade." Annie curled her legs underneath her on the chaise in the yellow bedroom that had been Meg's while she lived there.

Meg, sitting on the chair near the desk, pretended to need to retie the string at the neckline of her nightgown. "He is as he seems. Strong. Loyal. Quiet. A Christian." And Unionist spy. That was something she'd keep to herself for now. Even though both Annie and Bea supported the Union, spying was another matter.

"I noticed those qualities." Bea glanced at Annie beside her. Bea had learned about Meg's activities in the spring. She knew Meg had been a Pinkerton spy and that she used a letter carrier to send information to the North. "You've become closer friends while I've been away."

Meg, recalling Cade's kiss, lowered her face to hide her blush. "He's a good man and good to me. I-I had some trouble over the summer. It could have gone badly for me."

"What happened?" Annie's brown eyes widened.

Attention swerved from Meg's relationship with Cade, just as she intended. She explained that Lance had followed her before making his presence known. He was still gambling and not above threats to get what he wanted. "Cade met him when he came to the bakery. Lance continued to follow me so Cade told Jay about it."

"I'm glad." Bea leaned forward. "I charged Jay with watching over you while I was gone."

"Thank you for that." Meg smiled at her. "They were able to convince Lance to leave Richmond."

"Did he want money?"

"What do gamblers always want?" Meg walked to the window. Answering Annie's question with a question was deliberate—and evasive. There were some details best left hidden. "Should you see Lance, please avoid him. His treatment of his own family was deplorable."

Annie joined her at the window. "And now he's doing the same to you." She placed her arm around her. "We will keep an eye out for him."

Bea stood on her other side. "I'll tell Father."

"Do that." Meg couldn't suppress a shudder that Lance might try to extort money from her uncle. "Now, let's speak of something more pleasant. What are your plans for the wedding, Bea?"

As her cousin's focus shifted to her upcoming wedding, Meg felt as if she'd crossed a hurdle. She was glad her cousins knew about Lance's character, for she didn't put it above him to ask them for money in the future.

CHAPTER 25

ade escorted Meg to church two days later. It was pleasant to sit with her family, Meg between himself and Annie, the same seating arrangement as at Miss Trudy's family dining room later. Conversation was easier for Cade to follow, as it didn't contain the same fever pitch as the day the ladies had arrived.

"Jay, I've missed your mother terribly these past months. The trouble around Richmond has shifted away from us. Surely that eased the fears that chased her away." Trudy set aside her untouched molasses cake and looked at him expectantly. "When may I expect see my dearest friend Mary again?"

"I had a telegram from my sister just last evening. I was waiting to surprise you." Jay smiled at her affectionately. "Mama is leaving Chattanooga this week. Blanche and the boys will accompany her."

"Splendid." Trudy's eyes brightened.

"I can't wait to meet Blanche, Little Joe, and Donald." Bea turned to Jay at her side and placed both hands on his arm. "And will I also meet my future brother-in-law?"

"Joe can't leave his congregation so long but has agreed to marry us. He'll be here for a week or so." Jay's face lightened. "My whole family will be there." A shadow crossed his face.

Cade imagined that memories of Jay's deceased father brought on gloomy thoughts. Cade fought back envy, for he had never missed his own father.

"Is Will coming to the wedding?" Meg's compassionate gaze shifted from Jay to Bea.

"No word yet." Bea gnawed at her lip. "I miss him so. He's in North Carolina, probably in the Wilmington area. His commander is rather strict."

"He wrote to Father that he was called up to Virginia to help fight in that intensive week of battles at the beginning of July." Annie sighed. "The fighting ended before they arrived. Will and his comrades were ordered back to North Carolina."

"He was in the same state as me"—Bea's fingers curled around Jay's—"yet unable to come to us here."

"A disappointment, to be sure." Trudy's bracing tone seemed to snap her guests from their doldrums. "Let's remind ourselves there is much to celebrate."

"True." Annie smiled at Bea.

"When does Mary expect to leave Chattanooga?" Toying with crumbs around her cake, Trudy looked at Jay.

"On Tuesday or Wednesday." Jay ate his last bite of dessert and pushed it aside. "They will sleep on the train one night and likely spend two nights in hotels along the way. Mama doesn't do well on long trips."

"I can understand that. It's tiring. I enjoyed a lazy day yesterday, leaving my room only to dine with my nieces." Trudy, her gaze resting on Bea, folded her hands in her lap. "Does this mean we can expect them on October tenth?"

"Friday is the earliest possible arrival. You're anxious, I know." Jay grinned at her. "My guess is Saturday. I'll receive a telegram when they leave my sister's home and then again when they stop the night before."

"I'll send Mary a telegram to let her know I'm in Richmond." Trudy rose. "Shall we sit in the garden and enjoy the fresh air? Ladies, perhaps you should bring your shawls against the nip of fall."

~

*I*n the week that followed, Meg's cousins insisted she go to Trudy's home every night after work. It was a pleasure to do so and take part in the planning. They worked on the guest list two evenings and began writing invitations the next. Jay planned to consult his mother about her guests in the days after her return.

The whirlwind of activity left Meg little time to compose letters for her letter carrier. Fortunately, nothing she learned from customers seemed worthy of the letter fee. Instead she told Cade everything and asked him to pass on the information to Paul.

"Do you mind taking this task for me?" Meg asked Cade as he locked the bakery on Friday evening.

"Not at all." He grinned as he led the way to the kitchen. "Annie won't be here much past the wedding, and Bea will be busy with her new married life. Enjoy the next two weeks without worrying about anything beyond your duties at the bakery."

"What about Paul?" Meg began to wash the few remaining dishes on the counter. "Will he assume that I'm shirking my duties?"

"Let me handle Paul." He frowned at the corn muffins he stored in a sack. "He can be a mite bossy, but his heart is in the right place."

"Thanks, Cade." The last of her anxiety slipped away. "You're the best."

There was a knock on the back door. Two knocks. Meg had heard four raps on the door often enough to know it was some kind of code for Cade. What did it mean? They'd grown closer, but still he didn't trust her with his secret.

"It's Bea and Annie." Cade opened the door. "Come in, ladies."

"Good evening, Cade." Bea stepped inside, followed by her sister. "Meg, are you ready to leave? We want to finish writing the invitations after supper. Jay promised Miss Mary will add her guests to the list by Monday."

"I have these few dishes to wash." Meg raised her eyebrows at Cade. "What else did you want me to do this evening?"

"Have fun." He took the wet dishcloth from her hands. "I'll take care of the rest."

He understood her need to share as much of the wedding preparations as possible. He was a treasure. "Thank you." She picked up her basket.

"Cade, Jay said to tell you we'll go on a picnic after church on Sunday." Bea tilted her head. "Please say you'll come. It will be something fun for Blanche's sons to do after their long travel. They arrive tomorrow morning."

Cade quirked an eyebrow at Meg.

"Oh, yes, please come." She put her hand on his and looked up into his eyes.

"I'll bring bread for sandwiches."

Meg couldn't keep a smile from her face. She'd never been on a picnic with Cade. This promised to be fun.

~

*C*ade followed Jay's landau to his favorite spot on the James River, by the Falls for the picnic. Cade was glad that Blanche's sons wanted to ride with him. Little Joe and Donald had climbed in and out of his seat to hide inside the walled wagon no less than a dozen times.

Cade didn't mind. It was pleasant to have their company on the drive that had already taken thirty minutes.

Meg turned from her place in Trudy's landau. She smiled and waved at him and then turned back around.

A smile tugged at his lips. She was sweet to think of him. He wished she sat beside him. It would seem more as if he escorted her.

But he didn't. He wasn't her beau. He'd best remember that important fact.

Mary Nickson also rode with them. The two older women were trying to catch up on five months of news that likely excluded Meg. She probably didn't mind, for hadn't she done the same with her cousins?

"Mr. Yancey?" Seven-year-old Little Joe stuck his head, thick with wavy brown hair, out of the back.

"What is it?"

"How much farther? I'm hungry."

"Me too." Blond-haired Donald, a year younger than his brother, climbed into the seat beside Cade.

"Another ten or fifteen minutes." Cade wasn't certain of the exact location. He looked over as Little Joe wiggled into the seat beside his brother. "I reckon you can have a biscuit from my basket, if you promise to eat a sandwich when we get there."

"From the basket back there?" Little Joe pointed to the opening.

"That's the one."

"I done had one." Little Joe's face turned crimson.

So that was what had kept the boys entertained. Cade tried

to smother a laugh. "It would have been nicer to ask before helping yourself."

"I 'spect so." The boy's head went down. "Don't tell my ma, will you?"

Cade paused as if considering the request. "How about you, Donald? Did you eat a biscuit?"

"They smelled too good."

A laugh burst from him. Meg wasn't the only one to turn and look at him. He smiled and waved. "Yep, I reckon they did."

"How about Mama?" Little Joe persisted.

"I'll give her one too." Cade winked at him.

Their faces cleared.

Cade laughed again. He wasn't much used to children. If this was any indication, he'd have enjoyed fatherhood.

His smile died. *Don't think of Little Cade. Not now. Enjoy the afternoon with Meg's family.*

This was the only family he'd ever have...and that was only until Meg's heart was ready to court some worthy man her age.

$\sim$

$\mathcal{M}$eg stayed with Cade throughout the afternoon as much as possible. Sadness seemed to emanate from his eyes. After his laughter on the drive over, she wondered at its cause. Had she said something to upset him? She'd ask on the drive back, for he was driving her home.

Everyone strolled by the Falls of the James River. It was a beautiful place, made more so by the leaves changing color. Blanche hadn't been to the spot, which were more rapids than waterfalls, in many years. The boys threw sticks and leaves into the swift river and watched the current snatch their treasures away.

Blanche was a pleasant companion, and Meg saw that Bea was pleased with her future sister-in-law. Not surprising, for

Blanche was friendly and sweet-natured. She was perhaps thirty, a patient mother of active boys, and as gracious as Aunt Trudy. Blanche shared the same color of green eyes as Jay though was much shorter than her tall brother. She wore her brown hair in a braid and pinned around her head like a crown. Meg imagined the woman never met a stranger or suffered for lack of conversation.

No wonder Jay was crazy about his sister.

"This bread is delicious." Blanche, who sat with her legs tucked under her on a blue quilt, took another bite of her ham sandwich. "Why, it makes the whole sandwich a treat. Where did you get it, Jay?"

"Cade brought it. He's a baker."

"A baker?" Her eyes widened. "Perhaps you can teach me to bake bread like this before I return to Chattanooga."

"I bake many loaves six days a week." Cade grinned. "Come by one morning, and I'll give you a lesson."

Meg tried to keep a pleasant look on her face. After that first disastrous attempt at breadmaking, Cade had never offered to teach her how to make bread again, and here he was, making that offer to an almost complete stranger. Was Meg such an inept baker that she wasn't worth the trouble?

"I will be happy to come, if there's time." Blanche smiled at Bea. "Wedding preparations come first."

"Thank you, dearest Blanche." She squeezed her future sister-in-law's hand. "I hope you will come shopping with me. There is much to do."

Meg wished she didn't have to work every day the shops were open, for she enjoyed shopping as well.

"Well, Mr. Yancey, I may have to come and simply purchase bread from you for our journey home."

"That's fine. Rye bread is my specialty."

"And it's my personal favorite." Blanche's mouth formed into an 'O' shape. "My dear Joe loves rye bread. He hasn't eaten it since our local baker moved North last year."

"I'll be pleased to bake him some, with my compliments." Cade's voice trailed away as he stared down at his sandwich.

Concern replaced Meg's resentment, for the friendly atmosphere didn't ease the sadness in Cade's eyes.

~

"*I* want to ride with Mr. Yancey." Donald tugged on his mother's hand. "Please, Mama?"

"Mr. Yancey isn't going back to Mrs. Weston's house." Blanche gave Jay a harried look.

"That's right, Donald." Jay rubbed a gentle hand over his nephew's blond hair. "Perhaps next time."

Cade glanced at Meg, wondering if she'd mind the delay. She seemed to read his thoughts and gave him a smiling nod. "Well, maybe I will just take these two boys to Mrs. Weston's house and then take Miss Meg here home from there. What do you say?"

The boys jumped up and down. "Please, Mama?"

"If you're certain." She glanced at Cade.

"It will be a pleasure, ma'am."

"Such formality." Trudy tsk-tsk'd at them. "We're to be family. You may all refer to me as 'Aunt Trudy' and the rest by our given names. Does that suit everyone?"

Though he wasn't to be a member of the family, Cade nodded with the rest. He glanced at Meg, who blushed. He'd sure like to be family to them someday.

What was he thinking? He sighed. It was all this talk of weddings, he supposed.

~

*M*eg waved to the boys from Cade's wagon seat when they made it to Trudy's porch with their mother. "How those boys played in the sunshine all day and still have energy to run back and forth in a bouncing vehicle is beyond me."

"Bouncing because they were in it. Old Sam here may never be the same." Cade chuckled as his horse plodded along. "It was a good day."

"I can't remember when I've had such fun." Meg giggled. "Of course, the boys added to the liveliness of the picnic."

"That they did." The corners of his mouth turned up as he dodged a cart.

Meg looked at horseback riders, wagons, and carriages on the streets. Groups of soldiers smoked on street corners. Women talked on the sidewalk and children played in side yards, making plenty of noise. Hardly the place for a quiet conversation, yet she had to know something. "Cade, I noticed you seemed upset when you arrived at the Falls."

He tensed. "It was nothing."

"Did the boys do something wrong?"

He shook his head.

"Did I hurt your feelings?"

"No."

"Then what was it?"

"I reckon…Little Cade was on my mind."

"Ah." Jay's nephews reminded Cade of all he'd lost. There were no words of comfort. She tucked her hand into his arm, where it stayed until the wagon stopped in front of her boarding house.

"I wish…" The words died on her lips.

"I know." He patted her hand and then jumped down. He hurried around the wagon, pausing to rub Old Sam's mane. Then he was at her side.

He extended his arms to her. She placed her hands on his shoulders, her eyes never leaving his, even when her feet touched the ground.

Her hands fell from his shoulders. "Thank you for the ride home." She smiled up at him.

"My pleasure." He stepped back. "Thanks for sharing your wonderful family with me."

Her heart melted.

She watched him drive away in the approaching twilight.

How did that man always know what to say?

CHAPTER 26

*S*unday, October twenty-sixth.

Meg could hardly believe the day was here. Bea was to be married this afternoon. Uncle Hiram had been in Richmond a week. Bea's ecstatic father beamed with pride at every mention of escorting his daughter down the aisle of St. John's Church.

Meg sat in the service that morning with Cade and Blanche's family. Blanche's husband, Joe, had arrived Friday, having left two days later than he intended. Joe was to perform the wedding ceremony.

No one staying at Aunt Trudy's attended church, for Bea believed grooms shouldn't see their brides the day of the wedding until the ceremony began. For that matter, Jay and his mother weren't there either.

Meg considered the notion of bad luck to be nonsense, but it was probably best this way. She doubted her cousin could have sat still for a sermon. She'd been nervous the night before, too, when Meg and Cade attended the family dinner in the couple's honor. After supper, a lot of fuss had been made over placing all the dining tables in the parlor. Uncle Hiram paid for the cost of everything and had wanted all eighty guests to partake of the wedding meal. Unfortunately, only half of that number could be seated, even with moving everything to the parlor. Trudy had warned Bea of the problem before the invitations were sent, so it was merely a matter of arranging the furniture to accommodate the dinner guests the night before. The children were to dine in the family parlor, which also helped the seating arrangements.

Last night had been fun. It had been Meg's first opportunity to enjoy a private conversation with Uncle Hiram since he'd arrived. They'd talked about her job and her decision to move to the boarding house. Sandwiched throughout those topics were questions about Cade. It was only natural her closest male relative was curious about her escort. Later, when Jay and Cade drank coffee in front of a low fire burning in the large fireplace, Hiram and Bea's uncles, Isaac and Michael, had joined them. They soon left the parlor and didn't return for nearly an hour. Meg had been glad for Jay's opportunity to talk with the men in the family—and especially happy their conversation included Cade.

He never forced his presence on anyone. Not only that, even when engrossed in conversation, his eyes often sought hers across the room as if seeking assurance she didn't need him.

Her hands clutched the hymnal in her lap. She needed him now. There was much to do before the wedding. She went over the list in her mind...change into her beautiful new gown, pin up her auburn hair so that it fell in a profusion of curls that Thomas used to favor and she hoped Cade would admire as well, arrange orange blossoms in Bea's hair—

"Are you all right?" Cade whispered during the closing hymn.

"I fear Bea's nerves have affected me."

"Me too." Whispering, Blanche leaned toward her. "So much to do before we can get back here for the wedding. Half-past one on a Sunday." She threw up her hands. "What was my brother thinking?"

"That he'd not have to beg for a day off from Tredegar Iron-works to wed his bride." Cade whispered.

The music ended. There was no time to say more.

The pastor prayed a final prayer and dismissed the congregation.

"Pardon my rush, but I must get these boys ready. See you back here in a couple of hours." Blanche ushered her sons out of the pew. Her thin husband pocketed his spectacles and, with a smiling shrug, scurried after her.

"At least there's no need to worry about eating since the meal will be after the wedding." Meg took Cade's arm and nearly pulled him out of the church. "I'm changing my dress at Aunt Trudy's, so I will meet you back here at the church."

"Want me to walk with you now?"

"No, I'll walk fast. I have lots of nervous energy."

"Runs in the family." Cade grinned at her.

She laughed. "It seems so." She hurried down the sidewalk, grateful for Cade. His sense of humor coupled with his solid presence calmed her.

She'd need to hang on to that sense of peace for she feared Bea would be a mass of jitters.

~

*C*ade sat next to Meg in the church, which was silent except for the couple who held hands, staring into one another's eyes as guests looked on.

Jay—wearing a black coat and cravat, white shirt, and burgundy vest—had been as nervous as any groom when Cade found him waiting in the back of the church. He paced back and forth and told Cade that he worried he'd stumble over the vows or some other foolish thing. Cade reminded him that he'd be the happiest man at the reception.

Now, Bea stood with Jay, a radiant bride in a white silk dress with a lacy bodice. A ring of orange blossoms cascaded like a waterfall down her blond curls. She had never looked more beautiful to Cade as she smiled up at her groom.

Still, the bride didn't hold a candle to the woman at his side. He stole another glance at Meg, whose smiling attention was riveted on her cousin. The dark green of her silk dress enhanced the sheen of her auburn hair and made her eyes the color of grass after a good hard rain. Her beauty took his breath away. How privileged he was to escort her to this wedding and the reception to follow.

As Bea began to speak her vows, Meg suddenly turned her head and met Cade's eyes. Whatever she saw—admiration, love, adoration—made her gasp.

Heat crept up his face. He'd forgotten himself. He was here to support the bride and groom's nuptials, not drink in his companion's beauty.

Cade shifted his focus back to the couple, who clasped one another's hands as they were bound in holy matrimony. How blessed they were to have found one another. They had committed to one another despite the obstacle that they supported different sides of the conflict, tough to overcome in the midst of war. Cade was glad they respected one another's opinions and beliefs.

He bowed his head to pray for the couple when Joe asked for prayer.

Difficult days came to all marriages. He prayed this couple would face those trials together.

Perhaps someday Meg would hold his hand in front of a congreg—

No. Best leave that dream alone. Just as he'd been alone for six years.

~

"Your sister is a beautiful bride." Meg tugged her shawl over her shoulders against a nip in the air. She stood in the garden with Annie following the wedding luncheon. Eighty guests milled around the garden and in Aunt Trudy's two parlors. Children played among the trees. Her gaze skimmed the crowd for Cade until she spotted him talking with Joe, Uncle Hiram, and Annie's uncles, Michael and Isaac. He caught her eye and smiled. Good. Cade seemed content to listen and observe.

"Aye, that she is." Annie smiled a little sadly. "At least that's how my John would say it."

"I'm sorry he didn't make it to the wedding." Meg's heart ached for Annie, who missed her Irish husband terribly. "Are you all right?"

"I'm strong, but I miss him." Tears shone in her eyes but didn't fall. "My apologies. It's been an emotional day. I cried when Bea said her vows."

"I cried during the ceremony as well." Meg squeezed her hand. "We've all been so focused on keeping Bea's nerves from overtaking her that I hadn't given a thought to your troubles."

"And so you shouldn't." Smiling, Annie turned to look at her sister. The newlyweds talked with several of Jay's friends gathered under a magnolia tree. "Today is Bea's day. I'm happy for my sister."

It thrilled Meg that Bea wore happiness like a cloak. The nervous energy had passed. Her only responsibility now was to enjoy her guests.

Meg's gaze traveled back to Cade, who gestured with his hands as he talked to Joe. Meg had glimpsed loneliness and hunger in him during the ceremony. And what appeared to be love.

She didn't know what to think, what to feel. Something held

her back from giving her heart permission to love him. It wasn't memories of Thomas, who wouldn't have wanted her to live her life alone. What was the problem?

It scared her to think how important Cade had become to her in a few months. Was she ready to fall in love again?

"Oh, there you are." Blanche joined them. "What a busy day. Joe had the most important job, as he married the happy couple, so the job of chasing the boys around fell to me. It's been pleasant to catch up with old friends. But I wanted more time with my brother and new sister."

"Rest assured that Bea loves you already." Annie patted her arm.

"And I adore her." Tears welled up in Blanche's eyes. "Had I searched the land myself for a perfect mate for my brother, I could scarcely have chosen more wisely. I am happy for them."

Elizabeth Van Lew strolled over. Blanche had been introduced to her as a child but hadn't seen her since her marriage. They exchanged pleasantries.

"Miss Elizabeth, Blanche has come to us from Chattanooga." Meg knew Elizabeth would pounce on the opportunity to learn whatever Blanche would inadvertently reveal.

"A far journey." Elizabeth wrapped her shawl closer around her arms. "I trust you didn't suffer delays in your travel."

"Given our current environment, nothing to complain of." Blanche accepted a glass of milk punch from a tray Clara offered. "Thank you. My throat is parched."

Each of the ladies accepted a glass with murmured thanks.

"When will you return home?" Annie sipped hers.

"Tuesday." She sighed. "I had hoped for another week, but Joe worries about Union troops in Tennessee. He believes it best not to tarry."

"Have there been big battles recently?" Meg was ashamed that nearly a month had passed since she sent letters to Ina.

Now that the wedding was over, she'd refocus her efforts to gathering information.

"Not certain I know the recent news. There's been fighting in various regions of my state. What the newspapers term as 'skirmishes.' I don't like the word. Soldiers still die in even those short clashes." Blanche shifted from one foot to another. "Our troops occupied our town beginning this spring. They began to build forts and batteries close to the Tennessee River."

Meg had accompanied Mary, Blanche's mother, to Chattanooga in May and had seen them. Descriptions had been sent to Ina. "For that reason, your mother felt it wiser to stay with you."

"I don't know why. Forts surround Richmond." Blanche glanced at her mother, who sat in the garden with Trudy and other women.

"True." Elizabeth ran a finger of the rim of her glass. "Tell me, do you feel safer with the soldiers occupying your town?"

"I'm not certain I do." Blanche's brow furrowed. "Soldiers drilling and milling about the businesses and homes of our community only serve to remind me of war. I fear the soldiers' presence will bring the Union army to our very doorstep."

Meg feared Blanche was right. Armies on the other side discovered which troops and approximate numbers camped in particular areas, thanks, in part, to local spies. She didn't know whether to rejoice in that or feel guilty for passing along details of the fort she'd seen near the Tennessee River.

"Oh, you're all here." Bea gave her sister a side hug. "Isn't this the most glorious day?"

"It is." Meg glanced at overcast skies. The morning's gentle breeze had turned chilly. None of that mattered to the bride.

Annie laughed. "Am I to assume you're not speaking of the weather?"

"The weather? Sister dear, it could *snow* and I'd scarcely notice."

They all laughed.

"I will love living in the South. Blanche, you must return to Richmond soon." Bea clasped her sister-in-law's hand.

"Well, as to that, the war may dictate what we do." She stared down into her empty glass.

"What do you mean?" Elizabeth leaned closer as a breeze caught the fringes of her blue shawl.

"Should Chattanooga be overcome by the enemy, Joe has agreed to accompany me and the boys back here to Richmond." She raised her gaze to rest on Bea. "Jay has offered your home as a refuge in such a circumstance. I hope you do not mind."

"Of course not." Bea hugged her. "You must come to us whenever you fear for your safety."

"Thank you." Blanche returned her hug. "Now I know we will be sisters."

Meg exchanged a glance with Elizabeth. This could be a premonition on Blanche's part. Or it might be that the situation in Tennessee grew worse for the Confederacy.

Either way, it seemed good news for the Union.

CHAPTER 27

"Father had a long discussion today with all his siblings and their spouses," Annie confided once Meg was safely inside Trudy's carriage from the rain the next evening when she picked her up after work.

"They needed to talk while they're all together." Meg recalled when Aunt Trudy learned that her brother, Isaac, had cheated his siblings from their inheritance. He had modified his father's will shortly before his death so that the plantation's two thousand acres went entirely to him.

"True." Annie sighed. "What Uncle Isaac did is ugly. Greedy. And hurtful."

"Was anything resolved?"

Annie nodded. "My father determined to bring up the matter with his brother *after* the wedding. He didn't want anything to mar Bea's special day. Had Father not known of his brother's remorse, today's confrontation might have been more forceful."

"I can only imagine." Meg recalled the battle that had wrecked a good portion of Isaac's tobacco crop. He'd been both sorrowful and angry over his ruined crops, which he saw as his punishment for robbing his siblings.

"Yes, I prayed while the siblings talked." She twisted her hands. "Father confronted him. Uncle Isaac offered to give my father and Aunt Trudy a hundred acres each. Aunt Victoria and Uncle Michael discussed the matter alone and decided to release any rights to her childhood home."

"I imagine the original will entitled your father to more acreage?"

"It did, but Father wants to put the ugliness behind him." Annie held up her palms with a shrug. "Besides, Aunt Trudy's desire is to build a home on the land to be near family. And Father doesn't want to live as a planter. Even if he moves here, he'll either establish his own bank or return to being a lawyer. That was his original profession."

"I had forgotten that." It seemed that the family had emerged from the conflict intact, though Isaac still profited from his misdeeds.

"No one will press charges as long as Uncle Isaac makes the promised changes. I believe he will." Annie pressed her forehead against the side of the carriage. "I'd prefer Father stay up North, especially since Bea lives in Richmond now."

"Bea said she had dreamed of living on that plantation as a child."

"I did as well." Annie looked out the moving carriage into rain-drenched streets. "Father built a life with Mother in Washington City. Now that she's gone, he may decide to move south after the hostilities end."

"I will have many homes to visit to see you all, won't I?" Meg patted her arm, hoping to lighten her cousin's sadness.

"As to that, I suppose John and I will be following the railroad west anyway." Her face brightened in anticipation. "Working with the railroad is his chosen career."

"Your families will be spread throughout the country. Family visits will require planning." Meg smiled a little sadly.

She had only her cousin's families to visit—and Aunt Trudy, for the dear woman had welcomed Meg with open arms. "Decide now that we'll make lots of long trips to see one another."

"What about you, Meg?" Annie studied her. "Where will you live? I'll want to see you as well."

Where indeed?

All of the sudden, Cade's face popped into her mind.

It was a good thing the carriage halted in front of Trudy's home, for Meg didn't know how to answer Annie's question.

~

*M*eg climbed into Bea's carriage at dawn on Wednesday morning. "Oh, Annie, I can't believe you must leave today."

Tears trailed down Annie's cheeks. "If John were waiting for me at home, it would be easier to leave."

Bea hugged her sister close. "We have a few more minutes. Father and Aunt Trudy will meet us at the depot."

"It's not goodbye yet." Annie swiped at her wet cheeks with a dainty pink handkerchief. "You were a beautiful bride. I'm thrilled I was here for it."

"I'd have waited on you, dear sister, make no mistake." Bea blew her nose. "We'll see one another soon. Let's see what's happening in the war at Christmas."

"It's October twenty-ninth. Christmas is less than two months away." Annie sniffed. "That's not so long."

"True." Meg leaned forward. "You'll see one another often. And your children will be more than cousins—they'll be the best of friends."

"They will. We'll make certain of it." A sob escaped Bea. "I hate saying goodbye."

"But you already have plans to gather for Christmas. I hope

you can come here, Annie." Meg clasped her hand. "I won't be able to leave my job for a long visit."

"Will you continue to write letters for your contact up North?" Bea studied her.

"Bea," Meg gasped, "you promised."

"She told me." Annie covered Meg's hand with hers. "I'm proud of you."

"I know I promised to keep it to myself, but Annie supports the Union with her whole heart." Bea flushed. "I didn't think you'd mind."

"Did you tell anyone else?" Meg didn't know what to think. She'd told Bea about her spying activities in confidence, trusting her not to say anything. "Not...your father?" Meg feared her uncle was involved in *something* to support the Confederacy but didn't know what. Rose Greenhow, the Confederate spy from Washington City, had told Trudy, Bea, and Meg bluntly that Hiram supplied her with information for the Confederacy.

"No." Bea straightened. "I'd never tell Father—nor anyone else. Not even Jay knows."

"That's good, since he has his own secrets at Tredegar." Meg leaned forward. "Promise me, both of you, that you'll not speak of my activities to anyone. Not even your spouses."

"I promise." Annie stared out the window. "Seems everyone has secrets in this war."

"Thank you." Meg wondered at the sadness in her eyes. Did Annie suspect her father? "And you, Bea? This is important. Remember the spy they hanged in April?"

Her eyes widened with fear. "I promise. Not even Jay will know."

"This must remain a secret between the three of us." It was almost a relief that Annie also knew. The three of them shared a close bond already. This knowledge tightened it. "Possibly for all time, for we don't know the outcome of the war nor the ramifications for spies on either side."

They were all silent for a moment. Dawn's early light seeped into the carriage, highlighting the fear, sorrow, and sheer dread of not knowing the future on the sisters' faces.

"How long do you intend to stay in Richmond?" Annie blew her nose.

"At least until the war ends." Sorrow from the imminent parting seeped into Meg's heart. She forced herself to smile. "I have family here. And my job at the bakery means a lot to me."

"As does the baker?" Bea tilted her head.

"He does." Meg smoothed her dress in the semi-darkness. "Thomas was very dear to me, as you both know. Yet there's something about Cade that draws me." It was those secret overnight trips that troubled her. She must learn about them before trusting him with her heart. And she'd have to trust him with the truth about her former job though it placed her in further danger of joining her friend, Hattie Lawton, in a Richmond prison.

Annie and Bea looked at one another. "Father approves of him. He's ready with an answer when Cade approaches him for permission."

"There's been no proposal. Nor even a true courtship. Such plans are premature." What if nothing came of it? After all, Cade had never professed to love her. Yet that kiss—

"You're blushing." Bea giggled. "I knew you had feelings for him."

"Yes, we discussed it often." Annie grinned. "We've decided he's the perfect man for you, dearest Meg."

"Now you need to figure it out," Bea added.

"I'm coming for the wedding." Annie, eyebrows raised, tilted her chin in an impish angle.

Meg's eyes widened. They seemed to have it all decided. When the sisters began to laugh, Meg couldn't help joining in.

Even in the midst of her sorrow over Annie's departure, her heart lightened.

It was good to know her family approved.

~

*C*ade looked up as Meg carried a plate of individual cake slices into the kitchen on a crisp mid-November day. He'd already locked up and it was nearly dark these days at closing time.

"We're not selling as many sweet baked goods." Meg frowned at the half-filled plate.

"Noticed that." A dozen pieces of cinnamon cake, one of his best sellers through the summer and early fall, were left on the plate. "Happened about the same time we stopped selling pies and shut down the café tables. Maybe we should have kept the café open."

"I don't think folks have enough money to splurge on sugary desserts."

"Cost of supplies have gone up, so I had to raise my prices too." He rubbed his jaw. "Any bread left?"

"No. Biscuits and rolls all sold by one o'clock." She started washing plates and utensils.

"Corn muffins are gone." She'd been reserved with him since the wedding. No, it had started after her out-of-town family left Richmond. She was still friendly enough. It was little things he missed...like not holding onto his arm as they strolled to church or her choosing to sit in an armchair in Trudy's parlor instead of beside him on the sofa. "I believe you're right. Folks haven't been as interested in desserts."

"Why don't we test it out tomorrow? You normally make rye bread on Fridays. Make some rye rolls too."

Her idea had merit. "Make extra biscuits, say four dozen more. I'll bake extra muffins and egg rolls. How about the apple fritters?"

"Those are my favorite."

"I know. And you've become quite good at making them. In fact, it's the tastiest thing you make."

"Oh, thank you." Her green eyes softened.

He grinned. "Let's do the same number of fritters with the other changes I suggested for the next two days." He hoped it would make a difference in the cash box. He didn't want to raise prices again. Meg was right—most folks were feeling the pinch of higher priced goods. He usually waited to count the money until Meg went home. He didn't want her to worry about the dwindling balances.

Sales of rolls and biscuits did even better than the higher priced loaves of bread in the next two days.

"Meg, you are a genius." Cade grinned. "The extra biscuits, rolls, and muffins all sold both days. Did anyone ask for cake?"

"One man." Meg carried towel-lined empty baskets into the kitchen. "Both days."

"Same fellow?" After turning down the lanterns, he followed her with a stack of empty plates.

"Yes." She laughed. "Our daily customers are pleased with the changes."

"It's the cheaper, individual servings of bread-type goods that sell best."

"Want to see if it made a difference in how much cash we made?" She met his eyes squarely.

"I'm curious." He gave a slight shake of his head. "I didn't know you noticed we'd been earning less money."

"I sell most of the baked goods. The number of bills inside the cash box has dwindled somewhat." She touched his hand. "I want you to succeed, Cade."

His heart melted at the admission. She did care, at least about the bakery.

She looked away. "I'll fetch the box." She disappeared into the dark front room and was back quickly. "Will you count it now?"

Cade opened the lid and did just that. "Nine dollars more than yesterday. And yesterday was an improvement on Thursday's till." He grinned. "Thanks for the suggestion."

"My pleasure."

"In fact, you've made lots of suggestions that have helped the bakery since you started." He took a step closer. "Seems like my life changed for the better that June day I hired you."

"Mine too." She didn't look away.

The atmosphere suddenly became charged as if with electricity. He caressed her face.

She backed away. Looking every which way except at him. "Why, it's getting dark. I believe we'll need to light another lantern or two."

Her rejection stung, but hadn't he asked for it? He knew she didn't return his love. "Since it's dark, I will walk you home and clean later."

She didn't budge. "Supper isn't served at my boarding house for another three quarters of an hour, and it's a ten-minute walk. Let's wait on that for a bit. I have something to say."

Meg must have sensed he'd wanted to kiss her again. Cade steeled himself to hear the reasons for her rejection—as if he didn't already understand why a common man like himself didn't appeal to such an extraordinary woman.

"Cade, there's something you need to know about my past." Head tilted, she gave him a direct look.

His heart pounded. What secret had she hidden from him? "If you think it best."

"Shall we sit?"

Cade took the chair opposite of hers at the work table that doubled as a dining table.

Meg took a deep breath. "Have you heard of Allan Pinkerton?"

"The detective? Wasn't that Union spy who was hung in April connected with Pinkerton's agency?"

"Yes, Timothy Webster." Her shoulders straightened. "I knew him a little."

"How?" Cade shifted in his seat. *Please say you didn't work with him.*

"I worked at the Pinkerton National Detective Agency with him." She studied his expression. "I met him there, though I didn't work directly with him on any cases."

Cade's heartbeat accelerated. "Perhaps that was Divine intervention, since he was hung for spying. Aren't there three others connected with Webster still in Richmond prisons?"

"Yes." She wrung her hands. "Hattie Lawton, Pryce Lewis, and John Scully. Though I've had no contact with them in months, I pray for them often. Hattie, my friend, warned me to stay away. Soon after I saw her, she was arrested. I never met the others."

"Are you in Richmond because you work for Pinkerton?" Meg was in serious danger if anyone discovered her connection with them. Cade rubbed his hands across his sweaty brow.

"Pinkerton released me from his employ in December, two months before I came to Richmond. He said he didn't need me any longer." She studied her folded hands resting on the table. "That was after I moved to Washington City at his request in the fall. Bea and Annie had invited me to live with them for the duration of the war. I sold my Chicago home. There was nothing to keep me there anyway."

"What did you do in the Union capital?"

"My job was to interview female fugitive slaves, female prisoners, and Southern women who came to the Union army for help. Most were ready to share their story."

"How do you know they told the truth? That they weren't sent by the Confederates to mislead us?"

"I gave the information to Allan. Efforts were usually made to verify the details before the army acted upon it. I'm not certain if Allan did that or a staff of Union soldiers. Allan didn't explain the process. He kept my name out of it, which I appreciated. I never needed any of the glory."

Cade understood about wanting to keep her name out of the reports. He didn't spy or work with the Underground Railroad in search of glory either.

"Lots of good information comes to the Union army through fugitives, Confederate prisoners, and Confederate soldiers who flee to the North desiring to fight for the Union."

"I did notice you possess great skills of observation. " He shook his head in wonder. "You are amazing, Meg. What a courageous woman you are."

"Thank you. That means a lot to me coming from such a brave man as yourself." Her smile was tremulous. "Now, is there something you want to tell me about..." She looked toward the window.

Footsteps on the walk outside snapped him to reality. *Please be Paul.*

Four raps on the back door. His heart sank.

Meg's lips pressed together in a grimace. "Want me to wait in the front room?"

He nodded. "My apologies."

Oh, boy. Even Evelyn hadn't known about his family's Underground Railroad activities until after their marriage. How was he to explain this to Meg?

CHAPTER 28

*M*eg turned up the lantern in the front room, frustrated at the delay in their conversation. Cade had wanted to kiss her. She'd stopped him, knowing that big secrets between them jeopardized their future together.

She grabbed the broom from the corner. Might as well sweep while she waited.

Light footsteps on the stairs to Cade's living quarters halted her sweeping. Three, maybe four, people.

They must not be strangers for him to invite them upstairs so quickly. It had to be something to do with their community of Unionists.

She hadn't learned any news worthy of a letter carrier fee since Bea's wedding three weeks before. Meg had sent a letter to Ina through regular mail using the flag of truce to inform her Northern contact that Meg was alive and well. There was simply nothing to report.

She stared at a creaking floorboard overhead. How long should she wait?

It wasn't fair for him to leave her wondering about his guests. She and Cade worked together. Now that it grew dark so early, Cade insisted that she be gone an hour or so during the afternoon to deliver her letters to Mrs. Jordan in the daylight. He now knew her biggest secret, that she had been a Pinkerton scout. Because three of her past fellow scouts still resided in a Richmond jail, Meg had no doubt she'd be there too if the connection became known to city authorities. General Clayton's security force seemed to arrest folks on the slightest suspicion.

So now Cade knew the danger she faced. Why not bare his soul to her? Hadn't she proved herself capable of guarding secrets?

Meg swept the dirt through the kitchen and out the back door. A glance at the clock on a side table showed a quarter to six. Cade hadn't descended the stairs to talk with her.

She found a scrap of paper and a pencil. After penning a quick note, she donned her warm cloak and stepped out the back door into the brisk breeze.

~

*A*ware that his conversations with the fugitives—a father, a nearly-adult son, and the boy's uncle—had lasted longer than he intended, Cade ran down the stairs. He must escort Meg home and then return to prepare supper for himself and the runaways before heading out that evening.

"Meg?" She must be waiting for him in the front. He hurried to find one lantern's glow barely illuminated the room.

Meg was not there.

His glance bounced off the empty hook by the door where her cloak had been. Where was she?

A note laid next to a pencil on the empty table where she'd spilled her heart less than an hour before. He snatched it up.

Cade, I will see you Monday morning. Meg

He ran his hands through his hair. She didn't want to see

him tomorrow. That actually worked in his favor because the men upstairs were skittish. Their owner—his teeth gritted at the word, even in his thoughts—had sent the sheriff after them, and they didn't believe the lawman to be far behind.

They insisted on leaving for the next safe haven tonight. After learning of the lawman in hot pursuit, Cade agreed. The men were bound and determined to get to Freedom's Fortress— Fort Monroe—as soon as possible. They'd learned of Lincoln's Emancipation Proclamation that was to become law on January first. Their excitement at approaching freedom was matched by their fear of capture before arriving at their chosen destination.

This unexpected trip meant he didn't have an hour to spare tonight for explanations to Meg, even if there was a private parlor in the boarding house available for such confessions. He didn't know what to tell her anyway. He'd buried this secret too many years to release it easily.

Cade opened the cellar door and climbed down the stairs in search of the ham he'd baked last evening. He needed something quick for his hungry guests. A slab of ham sandwiched between bread slices made a hearty meal.

Danger had been his companion many times over the years. Tonight he had best keep his wits about him and pray the sheriff remained in Richmond to search its streets after they left the capital in their dust.

~

*M*eg was sorry that Bea and Jay had plans to dine with friends after church the next day, though it had benefits of a quieter meal. Since Mary, Jay's mother, suffered from a cold and didn't attend services, only Aunt Trudy and Meg carried their coffee after lunch to the cozy upstairs parlor.

"It's November sixteenth already. How the seasons fly past."

Trudy set her cup on a table and tugged her chair closer to the fireplace. "A blazing fire warms up the gloom of a fall day, don't you agree?"

"Nothing like a cozy fire on a cold day." Meg situated her chair caddy-cornered to Trudy's.

"Harold will drive you home. Where was Cade today?"

"He didn't tell me." Meg suspected he was back home after an overnight excursion. Her thoughts darkened. A secret mission—too secret to divulge to the woman he'd escorted around the city for months.

"Oh?" Trudy waited.

"I will see him at the bakery tomorrow." Meg wasn't so upset that she forgot Trudy's Southern loyalties. She didn't know what Cade had done last night, but it surely had something to do with the war.

"Is there some trouble between you?" Trudy studied her.

"No." It was true. They simply wouldn't get beyond the present barrier until he unburdened himself to her.

"You've been in a thoughtful mood today. I wonder if there is something on your mind?"

"My apologies." Meg bit her lip. "I didn't mean to be poor company."

"Not at all, my dear." Trudy stared into the fire. "I merely had the impression that your quiet reserve wasn't only that you missed Bea this afternoon."

Meg gave a short laugh. "You're very observant. I suppose I am thinking of Cade." And wondering if he trusted her.

A log shifted on the fire, shooting sparks up the chimney.

"I can scarcely believe this is our first moment alone since your return," Trudy said.

"So it is. Bea's wedding carried us all along like a whirlwind, didn't it?" Meg laughed.

"I'll say." Trudy smilingly shook her head. "I believe I'm just now rested up from the activity."

"Bea's happy. That's reward enough for our hard work."

"Indeed." Trudy drummed her fingers against the chair arm. "My dear, I'm wondering if you recall my last letter."

"I do." Meg cupped her hands around her half-filled cup of coffee. "I want to tell you what happened with my brother-in-law." She explained that Lance had been following her at least a week before revealing his presence. She gave a brief summary of his threats and the men who helped her but not that Lance had tried to kidnap her, nor of what he'd planned to do.

"My dear, this is terrible. I should have stayed in Richmond with you to protect you from this criminal."

"He has shown his true colors and I would not put it past him to try to get at me through my family. You must watch for him." Meg sipped her coffee and forced herself to swallow the cold beverage. She set the cup on the table.

"I will, to be sure." Twin spots of red brightened Trudy's cheeks. "I will warn Harold never to admit him to my home. That will be enough. But, my dear, the fear that man forced you to endure—"

"Is behind me." Meg stared into the blaze. "Cade brought me here after it was all over. Clara is a treasure. So is Harold."

"No argument from me." A soft smile lit her eyes.

"I cried. I prayed. Then I talked to Cade. Our conversation mended my heart." She looked over at Trudy. "I don't believe he will mind me telling you something he said."

"I'll treat it in the strictest of confidence."

"Aunt Trudy, he's a widower."

"What?" She touched her lips. "I didn't know. When did it happen?"

"Six years ago." Meg, recalling his agony, wrung her hands. "That's not the worst of it. His wife Evelyn died in childbirth, shortly after she named their son." Tears caked the back of her throat. "Little Cade was born too early. He lived only a few hours." A tear spilled over.

Trudy hugged her and then retained hold of her hand as she sat. "His sorrow breaks your heart."

"I'd have to be made of stone not to be moved by his grief."

"And you are far from that, for you are one of the most compassionate, caring women I know."

"Thank you." The fervently-spoken praise touched Meg's heart. "Cade's still such a lonely man."

"Perhaps not quite as lonely as he once was." A smile tugged at Trudy's lips as she released Meg's hand.

She looked up. "You mean…because of me?"

"Precisely."

"I do have reason to believe he has feelings for me." Remembering their passionate embrace, her face flamed. It had nearly happened again last evening. "Yet he's keeping something from me."

"A secret?" Trudy's chin lifted.

Meg nodded miserably.

"Let me ask you a couple of questions."

Meg motioned for her to continue.

"Do you believe Cade to be trustworthy?"

"Oh, yes." He'd proved that to her with Lance—and many times since with their Unionist activities.

"Is he a man of integrity, principles, high morals? A Christian man?"

"Yes."

"That's how I see him as well." She walked to the fireplace and stared down into the flames. "My dear, there is a war going on. If he has a secret that needs to stay locked inside, do not force him to choose between keeping it or losing you."

"But I'm not—" Meg sputtered at the mere suggestion.

"I have a sense that you want to force him to make such a choice."

"But I didn't…that is to say…I wouldn't…" The words died on her lips. She had planned to do just as Trudy implied. "I mean, is that such a terrible thing? To want honesty between us?"

"Honesty in times of war may come at a high price." Trudy turned to face her. "Am I right?"

Meg's skin tingled. Aunt Trudy suspected she had something to hide. There was no condemnation in her eyes. Nor any questions about Meg's activities. There were many things that she must not discuss with a loyal Virginian, and Aunt Trudy, it seemed, recognized that reality. Accepted it. And loved her anyway. "You're correct," she whispered.

"Don't you recall that Bea and Jay faced this very dilemma earlier this year? Bea insisted on a tour of Tredegar Ironworks, on knowing the secrets Jay knew because of his job. He could not reveal them in good conscience. They both viewed it as a lack of trust. She thought he'd tell her his secrets if he loved her, even though she was loyal to the Union. He likely assumed she'd not insist on knowing if she loved him." Aunt Trudy gripped the mantle. "I feared they wouldn't overcome this obstacle. Mary wondered at it as well, for I corresponded with her regularly while she stayed in Chattanooga. We both spent much time on our knees before the Lord about their relationship."

Meg remembered the long conversations between herself and her cousin. She'd warned Bea that she could not hope to agree with Jay on every topic.

"They learned to accept their differing loyalties. Respect them, for I tell you truly"—she met Meg's eyes squarely—"they would not be happily married today otherwise."

Meg swallowed. Would she not be respecting Cade by demanding he share his secret with her?

Trudy resumed her seat. "Do you recall what I wrote about the prophet Elijah's dilemma in my letter?"

"It's one of my favorite sections of the Bible. I've reread those chapters twice since you referenced them in your letter."

"I find it fascinating that God came to Elijah, a broken man, in a whisper. Elijah was so shattered that he even asked God to take his life." Trudy gazed at the fire. "We have a wise God. He understands exactly what we need and how each of us responds in times of turmoil. Had He come to him in the fire, or the wind, or the earthquake, perhaps Elijah might have felt too battered by life to recognize His voice. Yet that gentle whisper penetrated to his soul."

Meg stared at the dying orange flames. After Thomas died, and then after Lance's revelations that summer, she'd been too battered to hold up her head. Cade, a man of faith who understood sorrow, had poured strength into her. God had ministered to her through Cade and Clara.

"I will pray for you, that God guides your steps." Trudy shifted so that she looked directly at Meg. "I hope you know you can come to me any time you need help. I will do all I can, that I will promise."

"Thank you." Meg's heart filled with gratitude. "I will remember."

CHAPTER 29

Cade awoke earlier than normal on Monday morning, filled with dread over questions he anticipated from Meg. She wasn't the only one who regularly faced danger, and everything in him cried out to protect her from increasing it through participation in the Underground Railroad.

He'd fallen into bed at ten o'clock in the morning yesterday after a tense night of travel. A sheriff stopped him a mile outside Richmond and demanded he step down from the wagon. He complied while the large man, wielding his weapon, climbed inside the walled portion of his wagon. His stomping boots reverberated the floorboards. Cade had prayed silently every second that none of the fugitives moved so much as a finger. Frustrated, the sheriff had leaped to the ground. Said he was after some runaways. He then described the very men who quaked with fear under the wagon's floorboards. Finally, he let Cade go but followed him for two hours.

He'd passed Isaac's lane and chosen a roundabout way to keep the sheriff from finding him again. Fearing the lawman held back just out of sight, Cade pulled off the road and hid in the woods for half an hour. Hearing nothing but crickets and a hoot owl, he finally pulled out from his hiding place. He took country lanes that weren't close to any station for the next two hours. Then he circled back around. When they finally made it to Isaac's an hour before dawn, Cade warned him to keep the men hidden for a week or two until that sheriff gave up or followed another trail out of Richmond.

Cade went home on a different road that added five miles to his route. Even then, he kept a sharp eye out for the lawman. He didn't stop at a closed mill for supplies, nor did he buy a load of wood, which was cheaper in the country. It seemed best that no one be able to say they saw him—should the sheriff stop and ask.

It had been tense, dangerous. A night that tied his stomach in knots.

Very similar to the ones lodged in his stomach right now.

Yesterday had been a long day, even with sleeping for five hours. He had alternately prayed and read scriptures until bedtime.

He still didn't know what to say to Meg. Something in her demeanor had warned him not to brush her curiosity aside, especially after what she had shared.

Give me the right words, Lord.

Two batches of bread were rising, and he was kneading a third when he heard light footsteps approaching the back door.

"Good morning, Meg." His heartbeat quickened at the sight of her smiling face. Why, that was the same bright, sunny look she gave him every morning. Almost the same, that was.

"Good morning." She exchanged her cloak for an apron. "The usual?"

"Same as Saturday."

"That's right. We altered our baking." A bowl clanged as she set it on her work table.

Had she really forgotten? "Meg, are you all right?"

In the middle of measuring flour into a cup, she looked up at him. "Better now, thank you."

What did that mean? "You left without saying goodbye Saturday. My apologies for being above stairs so long that—"

"No apology is necessary." She dumped flour into a bowl. A cloud of white dust puffed into her face. She waved it away. "Nor is an explanation about who knocked on the door."

His chest tightened at the mere mention of Saturday night's dangerous mission.

"I'll wait until you want to tell me about it."

He closed his eyes in gratitude. "Thank you."

"Have you learned anything to report to Paul?"

Cade was thankful for the switch of topics. "Not much since Major General Burnside assumed command of the Army of the Potomac." This bread was ready for its first rise. He put it in a crock and covered it. "Of course, the Union army knows about that. You?"

"Elizabeth hasn't given me any messages to forward since last month."

"We'll keep a sharp eye—and ear—out for anything new." Cade grinned.

She looked up from mixing biscuit dough with her hands and smiled. "That we will."

His heart lightened. She really had forgiven him for not baring his soul as she had. *Lord, show me the right time and the right way to tell her. And please, protect her from harm always.*

~

*C*ustomers complained of cold days as December arrived. Meg, who had endured cold Chicago winters, didn't mind her strolls in the Virginia climate. Delivering messages to Mrs. Jordan wasn't a chore when done in the middle of the afternoon, even on a dreary day. Not only did

Cade not mind that she'd left work for an hour to deliver letters, he all but insisted she do so.

Sales hadn't rebounded to match the café days, and Meg now feared they would not until the war ended. Prices of food in general had escalated. Flour now cost sixteen dollars a barrel. Milk was twenty-five cents a quart. Little wonder that Cade often made trips into the country to avoid paying sixteen dollars for a cord of wood. Unfortunately, higher costs forced Cade to increase prices again.

Wives of soldiers away at war had families to feed. Soldiers' wages didn't escalate with rising food cost. Many families struggled.

On the battlefields, December was beginning to make up for a quiet November. Customers were ready for something to happen, and it seemed like they might get their wish. Both armies were said to be at Fredericksburg.

Meg and Cade had supper together the first three evenings of the second week of December and then strolled about the city to hear what was being said about Lee's army.

January's Emancipation Proclamation was a topic of many overheard conversations, mostly bitter complaints. Since Lincoln was no longer their President, most didn't feel obligated to abide by his laws. That didn't prevent Richmond citizens from resenting them.

The couple learned nothing that seemed vital, yet the shared camaraderie of those strolls had Meg, her hand tucked into his arm, dreaming of a future together. Their relationship felt as if they had waltzed into a courtship without discussing it. Cade had escorted her to church the last three weeks and accompanied her to either Bea's or Aunt Trudy's home for meals. Bea had given her a knowing look the week before that set them both giggling like schoolgirls.

Bea was right. Meg was falling in love.

On Thursday morning, December eleventh, Meg carried a

heaping basket of warm muffins into the bakery. A distant rumble caught her attention as the front door opened.

"That wasn't thunder, was it?" A mother with a little boy and girl tugging on her skirt looked at Meg with resignation.

"Doubtful." Meg sympathized with the blond-haired woman perhaps Annie's age, for she was as tired of hearing the growl of cannons as anyone. "That battle is too far away to threaten Richmond."

The mother looked down at her son, who was too young to go to school. "But might be close enough to threaten my children's pa."

"I will pray for his safety." Meg shoved her hands into her wide apron pocket. "What is his name?"

"Jacob Farmer, and thank you for the prayers." The worry in her eyes wasn't eased by the semblance of a smile. "My name is Elaina Farmer. There are my children, Jake and Samantha."

"Pleased to meet you." Meg didn't recall this family coming to the bakery. "I'm Meg Brooks."

"Pleased to make your acquaintance." Her daughter tugged on her cloak, revealing the woman wore a patched wool dress. She put an arm around the child.

"How many are in your home?"

"Besides us, my ma and pa." A flush stole up Elaina's cheeks. "We're staying with them until Jacob comes home for good."

"That's very wise."

The children rested their fingertips on a table, their eyes raised to the baked goods on top.

"Didn't have much choice." Her eyes lowered to the display of rolls, muffins, and biscuits. "Our proprietor raised the rent on our house. Couldn't afford to pay it and feed my children at the same time."

"Prices have risen at an alarming rate." Mrs. Ferris had raised Meg's boarding house fee last month. Her salary still covered it, but she'd have to watch the number of letters she sent, for the money Elizabeth gave her to cover the fee was long gone. "Do you prefer corn muffins or biscuits?"

"Biscuits, especially if they're fresh from the oven." Elaina's troubled gaze settled on her children, who only had eyes for baked goods. "But I don't have money to spare for any. Jake here wanted to come in and look at the bread. It smells good in here. We all love the smell of yeasted bread."

"I agree. There's nothing more appetizing than bread baking in the oven." Meg smiled as she gathered up five biscuits. "Please take these for your supper as my gift. I'll buy them."

"That's right kind of you. These are so big too. What my pa calls 'cat heads' because of the generous size." She looked down at the hopeful faces of her children. "I shouldn't accept, but it means a lot to my young'uns."

"It means a lot to me too." Meg placed them in the woman's basket. "Mr. Yancey, the baker, bakes everything fresh daily. Sometimes we have a muffin or two left at closing time. We can't sell them the next day…"

Elaina's eyes brightened. "Don't like to see you throw out good food. Maybe I'll stop by sometimes at closing, just to see."

"Do that." The tension in Meg's stomach relaxed. Elaina understood she couldn't afford to buy baked goods for them daily. "I hope you enjoy the biscuits."

"We will." The young mother opened the door, always shut now to keep out the cold. "Thank you kindly."

"I'll pray for your husband."

Samantha, the little girl, released her mama's dress and ran to Meg. She wrapped her arms around Meg's legs. "T'ank you, baker lady." Then she followed her mother outside.

Tears sprang to Meg's eyes. She turned away from the door to hide them—and looked straight into Cade's blue eyes.

"Don't you dare put any money in the cash box for those biscuits. I'll bear the cost."

"No, please." She sniffed. It was uncanny how the man

sensed something important was happening. He also possessed a keen sense of hearing that helped on the fact-gathering strolls. "Allow me to give this gift."

"All right. We'll set something aside for her. I believe she'll return." He watched as Meg tucked a bill into the box. "You are a remarkable woman, you know that, Meg Brooks?"

"They're hungry." A tear trickled down her cheek.

He wiped it away tenderly.

Meg lifted her face to the gentle caress.

"How fortunate I am to have found you."

A flickering glow warmed her heart at the admiration in his eyes.

A distant roar snagged his attention to the window. "How long has that been going on?"

"A few minutes." Meg blew her nose. "Is that the direction of Fredericksburg?"

"Possibly."

A load of sadness descended over Meg for all the soldiers who'd die in whatever battle was brewing. She bowed her head and sent up a silent, fervent prayer that Jacob Farmer was not among them, that he'd come home to enjoy a long life with his little family.

CHAPTER 30

*B*attle sounds lasted a few hours. Cade fixed a quick supper for them while Meg cleaned up the bakery. Then, wearing the peach seeds upside down to show fellow Unionists they hoped to share information, they strolled to the center of the city.

Cade tugged his slouch hat over his ears against the chilly night air as he gazed over the crowded streets. Soldiers on horseback rode past in the direction of the Executive Mansion. Those men likely knew something about Lee's army the public didn't know.

"I'm glad to see the stars again." Meg stepped around several ladies standing outside a restaurant, possibly waiting for their husbands to fetch their vehicles from the stable across the street. "It's been so gloomy with the clouds of late."

"Stars are pretty." He paused to listen a moment. The ladies complained of rising prices. He needed war news. He looked at the sidewalk to hide his smile at how adept he and Meg had become at exchanging pleasantries while strolling so others didn't know their entire attention was focused on everything going on around them.

"Oh, let's see if the hat I want is still displayed in the milliner's window." Instead of looking at the hat shop, she stared at a crowded street corner near the square.

"Good idea." Cade followed her gaze to a handful of men and women surrounding a half-dozen soldiers. They strolled to stand outside the hat shop on the fringes of the conversation.

"I hear the armies are outside Fredericksburg." One man, smoking a cigar, spoke up.

"Yep, that's right." A soldier nodded.

Cade looked at his uniform sleeve. A corporal.

"That distant roar this morning wasn't thunder." Another man near the back, wearing a multi-layered cape, took a step closer.

"We all recognize shelling, don't we?"

Short barks of laughter followed the corporal's attempt at a joke.

"Was it a battle or a skirmish?" The caped man pressed the point.

"Not sure." The enlisted officer seemed to be the spokesperson for his buddies. "Might be that the big battle is yet to come."

"Not another Antietam?"

The cigar smoker voiced the fear that Cade shared.

The crowd digested that possibility in silence.

The corporal looked uneasily at his buddies.

Cade figured they'd all had a stomach full of fighting. Yet more was to come.

~

On Friday, customers speculated about yesterday's shelling. Late in the afternoon, Meg learned that the bombardment occurred while the Union troops tried to build a pontoon bridge across the Rappahannock River.

She told Cade after they closed.

"Anything else?" Eyes on hers, he leaned his hands on the work table.

"Only speculation about a coming battle."

"No rumbles of battle today."

Meg shook her head. "Nothing I'm aware of."

"Let's see if those soldiers are down by the square again." He grinned. "Care for an evening stroll after supper?"

"Why, I thought you'd never ask." Meg smiled, comforted to share these serious experiences with Cade.

∽

"*Miss* Elizabeth." Meg looked up from wiping up crumbs with a wet cloth the following morning. "I haven't seen you at the bakery for a while." There were no other customers, and the windows and door were closed.

"Good morning, Meg." Elizabeth Van Lew set her basket on a table and clasped her hands. "Let me know if anyone comes in."

"A cold draft sweeps through the room with them." Meg scanned the room empty of customers. "I will nod my head and speak to them immediately. What's the news?"

"Firstly, there's a distant roar of cannon. A battle at or near Fredericksburg seems to be in earnest."

A chill ran through Meg to think of the lives already lost or forever changed because of it. She rubbed her arms. "May it be the last battle to be fought in this war."

"Optimistic, for I fear there will be many more." Elizabeth sighed. "And there's another bit of news. Perhaps you recall the widow of Timothy Webster?"

"I do." Her friend, Hattie Lawton, had pretended to be Timothy's wife and took care of him when he was ill last winter. She kept up the pretense after his hanging and, as far as Meg knew, through the long months of her imprisonment in Castle Thunder, a Richmond prison. "What did you learn?"

"Mrs. Timothy Webster has been freed as part of a prisoner exchange for Confederate spy Belle Boyd." Elizabeth clapped her hands.

"What? Exchanged?" It was too much to take in. Meg had prayed for Hattie's release daily.

"Yes, it is truly amazing. I've longed for this day. She didn't deserve such treatment." Elizabeth gave her head a little shake. "After all, the poor woman's husband was killed in April. You remember. I saw you and Bea at the hanging."

"I remember." It had been a terrible day. She'd attended to lend whatever support to Timothy that her presence at his execution might bring. Bea had agreed to attend with her. They slipped away once he saw her in the crowd.

"Mrs. Webster has suffered enough."

"Indeed." Meg closed her eyes and thanked God silently for this deliverance. "You said that Mrs. Webster was part of the exchange for Belle Boyd. What of Pryce Lewis? And John Scully? I seem to recall a connection between those prisoners and Timothy Webster."

"Excellent memory." Elizabeth eyed her. "That's part of what makes you valuable to the Unionists. Yes, there was a connection. Sadly, both men are still in prison."

"Mrs. Webster is already gone from Richmond?"

"I believe so." Elizabeth smiled.

"Thank you for telling me. I'll pass it along." This news filled her with joy.

"Please do. I—"

A cold draft swept through the bakery. She nodded at Elizabeth to signal a customer. "Mrs. Simmons, how lovely to see you. What may I get for you?"

"You can finish with Miss Van Lew." The plump woman gestured to Elizabeth. "I am happy to wait."

"Three egg rolls are all I require." Elizabeth nodded her thanks to the woman.

Meg placed them in her basket and accepted payment with a smile. She was almost giddy with happiness.

Mrs. Simmons carried over a loaf of white bread as soon as the door closed behind Elizabeth. "Business must be slow. You seem very happy to sell this loaf of bread."

"A little slow, to be sure." Meg schooled her features to wipe away her smile. "Folks don't have as much money these days."

"Food and other goods are not as available either." Frowning, the woman paid for her purchase. "One wonders if these hostilities will end before we all starve to death."

"We must all pray for a speedy ending."

Mrs. Simmons pointed to her. "From your mouth to God's ears. Good day."

"Good day." Meg waited until she was gone and then locked the door behind her, even though it was barely noon. There was something she needed to tell Cade without interruption.

～

*C*ade looked up when Meg rushed into the kitchen. "Cade, the most wonderful news." She clutched his arm.

"What is it?" He wiped flour from his hands as he stared into her upturned face.

"My friend Hattie Lawton has been released from Castle Thunder." A sheen of tears brightened her eyes. She explained about the prisoner exchange. "To think she is finally free."

"Amazing." He picked her up and swung her around and around. Her arms were around his neck before he knew what had happened. Her laughter was a tonic to his spirit. "I'm happy for you *and* Hattie."

"Thank you. I knew you would be." Green eyes held his.

He set her down, uncertain if she understood what her nearness did to his breathing.

Her arms tightened around his neck. She drew him closer for a kiss that shook him to his core.

"Meg? Do you mean to say...?" He leaned his forehead against hers. She smelled of lilacs and spring and fresh yeasted bread.

"I just put my whole heart into a kiss I initiated." She tilted her head at a roguish angle. "Must I also be the first to say—?"

"I love you." He kissed her with all the fervor he'd held back, love that had begun about the time she'd insisted on mere friendship. "If you love me, please let me hear you say it."

"I love you, Cade." Her green eyes shone like jewels.

Groaning, he kissed her again, taking his time. He reveled in how perfectly she fit in his arms.

When he lifted his head, she was breathless.

"I didn't believe I'd find such happiness." She nestled against his chest.

"Nor I." He caressed her soft face and wondered if she felt his fast-beating heart. "Will you give me your uncle's direction?"

"Why do you want to know where Uncle Hiram lives?" She raised her eyes slowly to his face. The impish smile was back.

He couldn't resist another kiss. "I've got in mind to ask him a question."

"An excellent plan." She laughed with delight. "I have it on good authority that he'll say 'yes.'"

"Good." Loneliness that had lasted too many years melted from his heart.

A knock on the back door broke them apart. Two taps. "Are you open? I knocked at the front door first."

"It's a customer." Blushing, Meg threw her apron over her face. "I locked the front door."

A laugh escaped from his very soul. She'd wanted to share her good news with a kiss.

So this was what happiness felt like. He'd forgotten.

CHAPTER 31

ade locked the door promptly at closing time. "I'd like to take you to supper this evening." He turned to Meg, who was wiping down the display tables. "To celebrate our..." His neck grew hot with embarrassment. He hadn't proposed yet.

"Courtship?" She dimpled up at him.

His throat closed up at her sweet expression. He nodded.

"It's my pleasure to accept your kind invitation, sir." She curtsied.

He laughed at her mock formality.

"We've never gone to a restaurant together." She headed to the kitchen.

"I thought about suggesting it on many occasions." He followed. "You said you only wanted friendship."

"When did I...?" She frowned. "You mean last summer?"

"Yes." He began to wash the last few dishes.

"Thinking back, I believe our courtship really began with Bea's wedding."

"I thought I merely dreamed it."

"I did, too." She looked down at her green print gingham dress. "I'd like to change before supper."

"I'll walk you home and wait while you get ready. It's not the fanciest place." He wished he could afford to take her to the city's expensive restaurants. "Because of your relatives, I know you're accustomed to better—"

"Wherever we go is fine with me." She rubbed his arm. "I don't need an expensive supper. All I want is to spend an evening with you without spying."

"As to that, you heard the roar in the distance all day."

She nodded. "Difficult to ignore. All right, if it's not raining, we'll take a leisurely stroll back and see what we discover."

"That's my girl."

"Indeed, I am."

~

*M*eg, feeling festive in the green satin dress Bea and Annie gave as a birthday gift, studied the Bill of Fare at Nolan's Café. Cade's favorite restaurant boasted all kinds of seasonal game. Seafood wasn't to her taste, and she skimmed over the choices of lobster, crab, and scalloped or fried oysters. Her heel tapped at the cost, for she didn't want to choose the most expensive entrée. Roast turkey, pork steak, and veal cutlets were the same price as an omelet. Soup was about a third of the price of the meats, yet that didn't seem like a celebration dish.

"What looks good to you?" Cade tilted his menu toward the lit candle in the middle of the table.

"I'm uncertain." Prices had escalated since the last time she'd dined at a restaurant. Goodness, that had been seven months before, when she'd gone with Bea and Jay during their courtship. Jay, while not wealthy, made a comfortable living and was able to pay for such meals with ease. Though Meg hadn't discussed money matters with Cade, he had undoubtedly lost income when they stopped selling pies and cakes. Could he afford this expense? Indecision put her in quandary.

"Remember, this is a celebration."

She relaxed a little at his reminder. "I'm torn between veal cutlets and roast turkey." Even so, the price of a cup of coffee was a dollar and fifty cents. Outrageous—and tea wasn't much cheaper. Neither of them drank wine, thank goodness, for she'd have to work five weeks to purchase the cheapest Madeira...not that she was paying. She decided on coffee.

The waiter, dressed in a gray coat and cravat over a white shirt and patterned red vest, greeted them and took their order.

"Is beefsteak a favorite of yours?" Meg sat back and looked around the room. A comforting blaze in the large fireplace captivated her attention. Businessmen and soldiers occupied most of the dozen tables. Another couple was chaperoned by an older woman. Now that Cade officially courted her, they should be chaperoned. Aunt Trudy had been insistent on that with Bea last spring, and rightly so, to protect her reputation.

"I always order the beefsteak." He grinned. "And it tastes better when someone else fries it for me."

"I'll learn to make it for you." Surely at her age, enjoying the company of a good man in a public place was acceptable. And widows enjoyed more freedom than a young woman never wed.

"I'll teach you. Didn't you cook for Thomas?"

"I didn't know how to prepare meals when we married." She laughed. "After a few burned dinners, he hired a widow to cook for us. I wanted her to teach me. She was a pleasant woman but possessed no patience for such instruction. Then his parents moved in with us, and my mother-in-law took command of the kitchen."

"Did you mind?"

"Not at all. And Thomas was the happiest of men when eating his mama's cooking."

He chuckled. "No wonder you seem content to let me prepare our lunches."

"Guilty." She looked toward the door as more diners entered. Two couples together. Her uneasiness grew. "Cade, we should have invited Bea and Jay to dine with us."

He scanned the crowded room. "I'm sorry. I didn't think about a chaperone."

"Yes."

"It won't happen again."

When their food arrived, Cade asked a blessing.

As they ate, each talked of their childhood. She learned what he knew about his life in England. His family had a bakery in the county of Norfolk. The nearest city was Norwich. They boarded a ship for America before he learned to talk. He didn't remember anything from the country of his birth except clinging to his sobbing grandmother outside a quaint stone house.

Meg confessed that she'd always wanted brothers and sisters and figured that was one reason she felt so close to Bea and Annie.

When they were finished, Cade paid the bill without the slightest grimace. It rained harder, adding a bit of fog to the darkness. Any folks lingering on the streets stood beneath store awnings.

Meg huddled next to him under his umbrella on their brisk walk back to her boarding house, glad the weather provided an excuse to snuggle. She listened half-heartedly to conjectures from the few gathered, hungry for news about the day's fighting, but did not display her peach seed necklace. Tonight belonged to her and Cade.

Upon reaching her home, she didn't want their special evening to end. He accepted her invitation to sit with her near the sitting room fire to warm himself before walking home. There were four others with them. Meg introduced Cade to the ladies, though she barely knew more than their names. After greeting them, two women returned to their knitting. Another read a book while the last penned a letter.

Cade only stayed half an hour. "I have a letter to write."

"Yes, you do." She smiled at him.

"I'll be here in the morning to escort you to church." She walked with him to the porch and waved as he walked away, whistling. The happy sound broadened her smile. The lonely man was lonely no more.

Meg didn't think she could wait for Uncle Hiram's answer to tell her relatives of the upcoming proposal.

～

talkative

Cade finished his letter after midnight. After five attempts, he was finally satisfied. Turned out that he was no more loquacious on paper than in person.

"I want to tell everyone our news today at lunch."

The brisk air on the walk to church awoke him fully, but not as much as Meg's confession. "Should you? Nothing will be settled until I hear from your uncle." His umbrella, carried as a precaution against the gray overcast sky, thudded like a cane against the pavement with each step. "I'll mail my request tomorrow."

She blushed a beautiful rosy shade. "It will require all my control to wait until lunch. This is one occasion when I hope Bea hasn't invited other guests."

"Their home is decorated for Christmas?"

"Bea stopped in the bakery earlier this week. She was on an errand to the florist for some holly leaves to decorate the main parlor. With Mary's assistance, of course. Actually, I'm uncertain who will be assisting and who will be leading." She gave him a side glance. "Bea plans to replace the wallpaper in the dining room, parlor, and downstairs hall. Of course, she'll have to rehang all of Mary's needlepoint samplers in their former locations."

"There are many beautiful samplers throughout the home." Too many, in Cade's opinion, for one couldn't read the message on one without being distracted by its neighbor.

"Yes. She hopes displaying them will satisfy her mother-in-law. Bea likes pink but not as the dominant color in nearly every room."

"It will be expensive. Paper is growing scarce."

"Oh, Bea will wait until products are more available and prices drop to reasonable rates. If it lasts too long, no doubt Annie will send packages from Washington City." Meg raised her eyebrows. "Mr. Yancey, I believe you tried to distract me from my excitement."

"Reckon so." Chuckling, he patted the small gloved hand resting on his coat sleeve. "The church is up ahead."

"And Bea is waving from the walk outside." She clutched his arm. "Perhaps I can pull her aside and whisper our news before services."

"Neither of you will hear a word of the sermon."

But he spoke to himself. Meg was already hurrying to her cousin.

CHAPTER 32

*M*eg, meeting Bea's expectant blue eyes for the third time in as many minutes, felt it wise to end her cousin's agony. She looked around the dining table at Jay's and Bea's home. Guests ate the last bites of delicious, fragrant apple pie. A cozy fire in the fireplace warmed the day's chill away. Sprigs of holly decorated the mantle for the coming holiday.

Decorated for a celebration.

Aunt Trudy and Mary were as dear to her as her own family. The only other guests were Jay's friend Troy Hanson and Christina Wyatt, the woman Troy courted. The couple had grown close to Bea and Jay on their many outings together during the year.

She touched Cade's arm, who inclined his head toward her. She lifted her brows with a jerk of her head.

Trudy, catching the movement, fastened her gaze on them.

Cade cleared his throat and waited until all eyes were on him. "Everyone, Meg and I have a bit of news."

She squirmed in her seat. Perhaps he wanted to savor the moment, for he didn't seem to be in a hurry.

"We want you all to know that I've written to Meg's uncle Hiram about permission—"

"To propose to me." Meg could wait no longer. "I'm ready with my answer when he does."

Bea leaped to her feet with a squeal and rushed from her seat at the foot of the table to her cousin's side. "You know he will grant his permission." She hugged Meg. "I'm thrilled for you."

Trudy was right behind her. "Come here, my dear, where there's more room."

As Bea hugged Cade, Meg squeezed from her spot behind the table to the open area. "Did you guess our news?"

"I prayed it would come to pass." Trudy held her close in a motherly embrace. "I will pray God's blessing on your life together."

"Thank you." Tears welled in Meg's eyes. She refused to allow them to fall. This was a happy day, and even joyful tears, in her mind, weren't permitted.

"We will talk more." Trudy held out her hand to Cade, who clasped it. "You could hardly have found a more loyal, loving, kind, and intelligent woman. I'm happy to welcome you to the family."

"That means a great deal." Her graciousness seemed to touch Cade. "I'm grateful she will have me."

Jay kissed Meg's cheek. "I like to think Bea and I had some small part in this."

"How?" Meg's brow furrowed.

"Perhaps seeing our happiness these past weeks persuaded you to consider your own?" He quirked an eyebrow at her.

"It did indeed. Though I think Cade's character would have brought me around to it eventually." She smiled at the man who would be her husband.

Troy clasped her hand and then shook Cade's. "May I offer you the best of wishes for many years of happiness."

"As I do." Christina hugged Meg. Then the blonde leaned

closer. "I hope to share such news with you in the coming months," she whispered.

Meg clasped her hand. It seemed inappropriate to say more with Troy standing at Christina's side.

"My dear, I'm sure I wish you much happiness." Mary came next with a brief hug. "Who would have thought both you girls would find husbands in Richmond?"

"I assure you, marriage was the last thing on my mind when I arrived in February." Meg laughed.

"Do you consider it lucky to have arrived on Saint Valentines' Day?"

"Perhaps God was whispering in our ear that rainy day. I don't consider myself lucky. I believe the best description is 'blessed,' don't you agree?" Meg reached for Bea's hand.

"Blessed indeed." Bea squeezed her hand. "Now we have another wedding to plan."

~

*C*onversation centered on the news in the parlor afterward. Meg and Cade received many questions on topics that they had yet to discuss.

"Where will you live?" Mary's bright eyes were on the couple seated on the couch.

Cade shot a look at Meg. "In my living quarters above the bakery. Is that your preference?"

She gave a smiling nod.

"And will you continue working there?"

"Yes. I enjoy my job. Cade must be looking forward to our marriage." Meg sent him a teasing glance.

"Of course." His brow furrowed. "Why do you say so?"

"Because you'll save on my salary." She giggled.

Cade joined everyone's laughter. "An unforeseen benefit."

"So you'll be happy living in Richmond?" Mary asked.

"Ecstatic." She patted Cade's relaxed arm. "Wherever my husband is will be my home."

"I feel the same way." Bea turned adoring eyes on her husband.

Jay clasped her hand.

"When will you marry?" Christina's looped braids shifted as she tilted her head.

"It's too soon to speculate on a date." Meg looked up at Cade, who nodded. "Since we await Uncle Hiram's response." She knew Cade wouldn't feel comfortable setting a date until receiving her uncle's permission.

"My dear Meg, I'd like to move you back into my home until the wedding." Trudy set her tea cup aside. "Harold will drive you back and forth from the bakery."

Meg clasped her hands together in gratitude for the offer. Money was tight with the cost of renting, and she had many new expenses with the upcoming wedding.

"That's a splendid idea." Cade turned to her. "It takes care of the problem of a chaperone."

"Precisely." Trudy leaned forward. "And just think of the fun we will have in the coming weeks."

"I need no convincing." Meg knelt in front of her. "If you are certain you want me, I accept."

"My dear, I never wanted you to leave in the first place." Trudy patted her shoulder. "Let's move you today while we have these young men to carry your possessions."

"Great idea," Meg said.

"I'll help." Troy glanced at Christina, who nodded.

"I will help you pack your things." Bea stood.

"Thank you. I accept any and all assistance."

Cade cleared his throat with a grin.

"You, especially, Cade." She laughed and then ran through all that must be done that day in her mind. "I'll ask Mrs. Ferris to return a portion of the rent I paid yesterday for the coming week." Now that the decision was made, Meg was more than ready to move back.

"If she refuses," Trudy said, "let me know and I will refund it myself. I'm so pleased to have company again." She looked at Mary. "Shall we wait at my house for these young ones to return with Meg's possessions? So many hands will surely make short work of the task."

CHAPTER 33

*T*he next week flew and suddenly it was the Saturday before Christmas, which would arrive Thursday this year. Cade had followed Jay's advice and sent a telegram to Hiram Swanson on Wednesday to let him know his intentions and that a letter was coming, though the letter wasn't measurably longer than the telegram. Since there hadn't been an answer yet, Cade figured Hiram waited for the letter to respond.

Harold had picked up Meg from work at five o'clock every afternoon. Cade had been invited to supper three evenings, invitations he treasured. He now felt himself part of a family again—and this time it wasn't temporary.

A precious gift indeed.

Christmas meals weren't going to be the grand affairs of prewar days in Richmond. Not only were some foods scarce, many families didn't have the money to splurge on dinners.

Added to that was the cases of smallpox, all the more unfortunate because of the approaching holiday. There were Richmond homes that displayed white flags, signaling that a resident suffered from the smallpox that had been reported in the city, adding to the misfortunes that had seemed to settle over it.

As for himself, Cade anticipated the holiday in a way he hadn't in years. Paul had often invited him to dine with his family after Cade closed the bakery. He had enjoyed those meals with his friend's lively family, but this year was different. He belonged with Meg and her family.

"We have another order for Christmas Day." Meg carried a slip of paper from the front room at noon. "Two loaves of Graham bread and a dozen egg rolls for Mrs. Walters."

"I'll have to bake the bread on Christmas Eve." He added it to the list. "That makes twenty dozen egg rolls, eleven loaves of Graham bread, sixteen loaves of white bread, four loaves of brown bread, and twenty-three dozen buttermilk biscuits."

"As much as that?" Looking over his shoulder, Meg scanned the list. "Mrs. Peterson asked for two ginger cakes. Will you make those?"

He made a notation for the cakes. "Any other sweet baked goods?"

"I thought we weren't selling them." She shrugged, palms up. "Mrs. Peterson requested them specifically."

"My mother used to make all types of cakes and pies. Christmas plum pudding with sauce. Several types of macaroons." Just mentioning the baked goods brought the nostalgic memories back. He could almost smell them, fresh from the oven. "I stopped providing those when she died."

"Perhaps we can offer them again next year. Now that I'm living with Aunt Trudy, it's easier for me to ask Clara for baking lessons."

"Are you happy there?"

"What a blessing." Her eyes went heavenward. "It was an answered prayer I didn't realize I needed." She turned away. "I hear the floor creaking in the bakery."

Even with Meg's help, the baked goods already requested

made for a tall order...and all to be ready for Christmas morning. Biscuits would still be tasty if he baked them the evening before. Rolls were best when fresh.

All this was good for business, which had been lagging for a few weeks.

Meg came back. She had a strange look on her face.

"Another order?"

"Telegram." Shaking fingers held it out for him.

Here was his answer. If Hiram refused... Cade opened the note. Excitement welled up. "Hiram gives his whole-hearted approval."

"Bea told me not to fret." Meg raised a radiant face to his.

"I feel like dancing." He held out his arms. She slid into them as if she belonged there. He waltzed her around the kitchen.

"I didn't know you danced." She stared into his eyes.

"My mother taught me when I was a wee boy." He stopped. "I'm forgetting something."

"I believe so." She stepped back, hands demurely clasped at her waist.

"Margaret Brooks," Cade knelt on one knee, "will you do me the very great honor of becoming my wife?"

"I will."

He stood. Cupping her face, he kissed her for the first time since they'd declared their love for one another. Their kiss was full of promise and hope.

The front door of the bakery closed with a bang.

"Cade, we have a customer." Meg's arms slid away from his neck.

"We'd best wait on the kissing anyway. I care about your reputation too." He gave her cheek a gentle caress. "The next time we kiss in the bakery, we will be man and wife."

~

*C*ade didn't linger at Trudy's home after lunch the next day. He had to go over the baking supplies on hand to ensure there was enough for the special orders. He would close the bakery itself at noon on Christmas.

Darkness had fallen by the time he finished his inventory. A tad short on a few items needed this week. To save a trip out of the city, he'd buy more flour from a mill in the city if they had any to—

Four taps on the back door.

No, not tonight. Not with so much already on his plate.

He opened the door. Two fugitives, both around twenty. A man and wife, presumably, for she looked as if she were ready to deliver a child any day.

Cade's heart sank at the sight of the pregnant woman. Meg might know what to do if the woman went into labor, but she couldn't stay in the apartment because they weren't married yet. Trying to hide his consternation, he ushered them inside and pointed to the stairs. He carried the lantern up after them.

"You may rest on the couch. Can I get you anything?" Once inside his apartment, he lit another lantern. The woman seemed exhausted, cold. Their woolen clothing wasn't warm enough against the chill of the first day of winter.

"Food would be a kindness. We're thirsty, too." The man, slightly built with muscular arms, helped his wife sit awkwardly on the cushioned couch.

Cade opened the metal door on his heat stove. "Build up the fire for me, will you? I'll get us something to eat. My name's Cade."

"I'm Reuben. This is my wife, Bekah. Her time's not far off."

Reuben's words confirmed Cade's fears. "I'll fry up bacon for us to eat with the morning's biscuits and return as soon as possible." Cade took one of the lanterns back to the kitchen and began frying bacon, his thoughts in turmoil. He remembered

Evelyn teasing him about taking long walks to hurry the labor as they dreamed ahead of Little Cade's birth. If such exercise hurried the birthing, had the couple's long walk today escalated it?

He carried a plate of biscuits and bacon and a pitcher of water upstairs. Warmth from the heat stove reached him from the open doorway. He set the plates down on the small dining table. "Please join me."

After Cade asked a blessing on the simple meal, the couple ate as if starved. "What is it you want me to do?" Cade, his thoughts chaotic, studied Bekah but she didn't seem to be in labor. But how was he to help her if that happened? He must not call a doctor or a midwife.

"We're looking for someone to take us to Freedom's Fortress." Reuben exchanged a long look with his wife as he arranged bacon slices on a second biscuit. "Folks at the last station we went to said they couldn't help. Sent us to you."

Fort Monroe. Other fugitives had claimed that as their destination. Portions of the Underground Railroad led to the fort. He'd tell Isaac their destination, comforted that the conductor's would know how to help a woman in labor.

"I'm going to have my baby at Freedom's Fortress." The woman gave Cade a direct look.

"I'm no doctor, ma'am. Do you think your time is close?" He'd never ask such a thing under normal circumstances. His face heated to even pose the question.

"Real close." She fingered the condensation on her glass without looking at him.

"Two or three weeks, maybe?"

"I gotta a feeling the birthin's not far off, Mr. Cade." One hand went protectively to her swollen stomach. "Mama taught me to trust my feelings. I'm telling you I see myself holding my baby by this time next week at Freedom's Fortress."

"That fort's eighty miles from here." He didn't see how that was possible, if her time was as near as she feared. Under normal circumstances, his responsibility ended with escorting the couple to the next station—or, in a pinch, the one beyond it. Each leg of the journey on the Underground required at least a day. The number of miles on each portion of the trip varied. Isaac's house was nine miles, if he didn't have to travel side roads. The eighty-mile journey would require ten to fourteen days—and that was assuming the couple didn't have an extended stay at any stops along the way.

"If we try to walk that distance, I know we'll never make it on time. We hear the soldiers there won't turn us over to no sheriffs. We'll be safe there." Her brown eyes pleaded with him. "Please, help us. I'm asking you to get me to Freedom's Fortress."

Cade drew back. What she asked was unprecedented. And impossible. "I'm sorry, what you ask is too much. I will take you to the next station tonight, if you're up to it."

"Won't you take us to the fort yourself?" She sat as straight as her pregnant stomach allowed. "I ain't gonna have my baby until I get there."

"Why not?" He brushed crumbs from his shirt as he studied her set jaw.

"My baby's gonna be born on free soil. I'm determined on it."

"Don't you see, Mr. Cade?" Reuben's hand covered his wife's clenched fist. "It's our best hope to protect our baby. No one can stake any claim on our babe, 'cept us. Our child can't be stolen from us and sold down the river." His eyes darkened in torment. "Or us sold away from our child. Think how you'd feel if you had to live with such a fear."

Little Cade. Were he in the same position, he'd snatch any opportunity afforded him to protect his son.

"Please, mister. Our babe can be born free." Her face lit with what seemed to be hope. "It's something I've prayed for. Dreamed of."

"If Bekah's time wasn't so close, we wouldn't ask it of you." Reuben leaned across the table. "Folks at the last station said you was the one to take us. That it was the only way to get us to the fort in time."

Impossible not to admire the young couple's determination. A desire pressed through him to do everything he could to aid her.

"Before you decide, you should know there's a sheriff following us." Reuben's face tightened. "Think we lost him this morning, though. He probably figures we're headed north, so we may not see him."

"Thanks for the warning." Cade sighed. Another obstacle to overcome, though not the biggest. "Let me ponder all this. In the meantime, you can rest on the bed in the middle room." He pointed. "There are no windows, so you should be safe to take the lantern with you since there's no one in the bakery at this hour. We'll find you both a change of clothes and coats later."

While they made slow progress to the bedroom, Cade took the empty plates downstairs.

Bekah's request for him to take her all the way to Fort Monroe threw him in a quandary. Even if he did take a week or longer away from his job—which he couldn't, not with all the special orders—he'd need a woman along to help Bekah.

Especially if she went into labor on the bumpy wagon ride.

And Cade had serious doubts about the wisdom of hiding her in the hidden compartment. It was too small and too uncomfortable for a woman in her condition.

Why hadn't the former station master just sent them on to Isaac's house, who had a wife?

Unlike Cade, though he'd soon be married. He wouldn't subject Meg to the risks involved in such a trip. Soldiers of both armies had fought at Fredericksburg, a Confederate win that had bolstered the hopes of Richmond's citizens. Lately, they'd been singing the praises of Generals Lee and Stonewall

Jackson. Their victory elevated the generals almost to hero status.

Where were the armies now? It didn't seem that much was happening after Fredericksburg's battle, as his strolls about the city had confirmed last week. He'd visit Paul to discover what he knew about troop locations and plan his route accordingly.

Trudy had invited him, her brother's family, and Jay's family to Christmas supper. He'd miss that if he took this couple to Freedom's Fortress, as Bekah called it. A disappointment but a minor one in comparison with other struggles.

The biggest was that closing the bakery might shift him into the focus of General Clayton's deputies, for they'd wonder where Cade had gone. They were a suspicious lot, for good reasons.

Money for the special orders—cash he needed to replenish supplies—would be lost, along with income from increased sales this week.

Not good.

What a can of worms.

The dishes were draining on a towel, and he had no idea what to tell the soon-to-be parents.

Little Cade, never far from his thoughts, leaped to the fore-front. He would have done *anything* to protect him, just as Reuben and Bekah would do for their child.

Oh, boy. What was he to do?

CHAPTER 34

"Mr. Cade requests a private conversation with Miss Meg." Harold entered the family parlor after seven that evening.

"Cade is back so soon?" Meg rose from penning some ideas for her wedding to be held at St. John's Church.

"Perhaps he finished planning his Christmas baking earlier than he thought." Trudy looked up from knitting. "You can talk in the downstairs parlor. Bring him up when you've finished your conversation."

Meg lifted her skirts and nearly ran down the stairs. Cade wasn't an impulsive man. Something must be amiss.

"Sorry for disrupting your evening." His brown hair appeared darker from the rain that flattened it to his head. "I didn't know what else to do."

"Please, sit by the fire." Meg turned to Harold, who waited by the door. "Will you build up the fire for us? And then, I believe we'll need a nice hot cup of coffee or tea, whichever is quicker to prepare."

"I drove my wagon over." Cade rubbed his wet hands

together. "Old Sam is standing out in the rain. Let me take him around to the stable." He strode for the door.

"I'll see to your horse and wagon, Mr. Cade." Harold put another log on the burning embers. "This fire is just about to catch hold." Flames licked around the small log. He added another. "There now. I'll go tend the rest of the tasks and bring you that tea." He went out and left the door ajar.

Cade closed it.

Meg raised her eyebrows. "What's amiss?"

"I didn't want to tell you this way." He extended his hands to the fire.

She stiffened. "Tell me what's troubling you. I'll do whatever I can to help."

"It's a secret I've kept so long. My mama insisted it was the only way to keep us safe."

Here it was. The secret he'd held so tight.

"No way to avoid it." His fingertips on the mantle turned white. "Remember the knocks on the door? The strangers who knocked a stack of books over in my living quarters?" He gazed at the growing flames.

"Yes," she whispered. Not a cat after all, as he had hinted at weeks before.

"Meg, I'm a conductor on the Underground Railroad."

"What?" Of all the things she'd expected to hear... "I had no idea. I'm so proud of you." Everything fell into place. His strong stance against slavery. His hints that he protected her by not sharing his secret. He really was a hero.

"I'm in danger if anyone discovers it."

"Of course." She stared at his slumped back. "You can't believe I'd betray you."

"No."

"Why tell me tonight?"

"A married couple wait in my apartment." He explained about Bekah's baby. "Whatever I do must be done quickly. I'm no judge of these things, yet my gut tells me that baby will be born in the next few days."

"You and I will take her." As soon as she uttered the words, Meg knew it was the right decision.

"I can't close the bakery so long without arousing suspicion." He ran his hands through his hair. "And you and I aren't married. There will be overnight stays…"

"That is a problem."

A knock on the door preceded Clara with a tea tray.

"Thank you, Clara." Meg gave Cade a cup when Clara shut the door upon exiting the room.

"I have all these special orders for Christmas Day." The beverage was half gone in one swallow. "This comes at the worse time possible."

"Let's talk to Aunt Trudy."

His head snapped down as he stared at her. "I can't tell anyone. It's the only way to stay safe."

"We must." Meg's conviction they were meant to help this couple intensified. The trip came with dangerous risks. So did telling others of the dilemma. "You trust me. You must also trust Aunt Trudy." She straightened her back. "A woman who hates slavery as you do."

He studied her expression. "I don't know what she can do." He rubbed his hands on his wet face. "Since you're so set on it—"

"Good." This sign of his trust did more to convince her of the rightness of her decision to marry him than anything he'd done. "She's upstairs. Let's take our tea with us."

∼

*B*etween them, Cade and Meg explained their dilemma. He waited anxiously for her to call the guards on them or to tell them what they considered doing was foolhardy in the extreme.

She did neither.

She sat, hands folded, staring at the fire. Finally, she stood. "I must see Clara and Harold before we talk further."

"No." Fear swept over Cade. He leaped to his feet. "Please don't betray my secret." Telling her had been a mistake. His mother had warned him.

"That's not my intention." Her eyes met his squarely. "But I must enlist their aid. It's up to them if they are willing. I won't promise them for tasks without consulting them."

"But what—"

"Pray, give me a moment." Trudy swept from the room.

"What will she ask them to do?" Cade ran a hand through his damp hair. At least it wasn't dripping anymore and Harold had taken his soggy hat and coat upon his arrival. Raindrops no longer rapped on the window pane, a promising sign the rain had slowed.

Meg's troubled gaze followed his to the hallway. "She has an idea. She's already praying for guidance."

"I pray before every trip." Cade paced the room. "Prayers for protection. I ask for the right words to say when I'm stopped."

"Does that happen often?"

"Far more than I like. Soldiers are curious when I travel at night. Folks living in the area know that's my custom because I've done it for years."

"Years?" She gulped.

"Yes, my father built the hidden room when I was a child. Slavery in Richmond appalled all of us. Mama taught me it wasn't normal. I've always hated cruelty. When my father grew untrustworthy, Mama involved me in the Underground Railroad." His pace increased. "That's when I learned our home was a station."

"You were a child?"

"Seven."

She gasped. "You say your father wasn't to be trusted?"

"That's a story for another day." He didn't want to go down that road tonight. He must focus on the problem at hand. "Suffice it to say, he wasn't a nice man when he drank."

"I wondered..."

"It's all settled." Trudy swept into the room. "Well, perhaps not all. Let's sit together."

~

*M*eg, with an anxious look at Cade, clasped her hands in a prayerful pose.

"Clara has offered to bake all your special orders," Trudy said.

"She hasn't seen the list." Cade sat on the edge of the chair beside Meg's.

"She'll need it as soon as possible."

Hope stirred in Meg. Her aunt had a plan.

"Clara will also bake some items from here each morning and take them over to the bakery when the shop opens. Harold will drive her, and Mabel will help her bake biscuits and such in the bakery's kitchen." Trudy turned to Meg. "I believe Bea is the best one to sell the items. Will you go over tonight to ask her if she's willing?"

"Certainly." She glanced at the mantle clock. "It's a little late to be calling..."

"It will be close to half past eight when you arrive, not too late to visit your cousin."

"I don't want Bea and Jay to know what I'm doing." Cade crossed his arms.

"All they need to know is that you, Meg, and I will be away a week or so." Trudy rubbed her knuckles. "You can tell her we're helping a family in need at Christmas. We'll naturally want that kept quiet, for the Bible tells us our good deeds should be done in secret. Tell her and Jay but not Mary. Keep everything from Mary."

"Agreed." Meg's stomach tensed. Mary still grumbled that Jay had granted their slaves freedom after her husband's death.

"Begging your pardon, Miss Trudy," Cade said, "but this trip isn't going to be a comfortable one." Cade raised miserable eyes to hers. "My wagon has no seats—"

"My carriage does." She smiled at him.

"There's no place to hide Reuben and Bekah in a carriage."

"No one will expect fugitives to ride openly in a carriage."

"True." Meg perked up. "We can treat them as free blacks who work for you."

"I don't intend to say anything about it, one way or the other, unless forced to do so." Trudy lifted her chin. "Then I will merely say that Reuben and Bekah serve me—and I'll make certain they do something for me such as fetch me a dipper of water, or help me into the carriage."

"That's brilliant," Meg said. "And I'll support you."

"I'll drive the carriage," Cade said. "Perhaps Reuben can be our driver when we approach picket lines."

"An inspired idea." Trudy clapped her hands. "We must leave in the morning."

"I normally travel at night."

"My dear, that's when you pose as a baker replenishing his supplies at mills. Tomorrow you will have your fiancée and her aunt with you. We're traveling to visit family at Christmas." She patted Meg's hand. "We'll stop at my brother's plantation on our return trip."

"You have it all figured out." Meg laughed.

"Not quite." Cade sighed. "Will you ask Harold to feed and

water my horse while I'm gone?"

"Yes, but I believe it best you leave the horse and wagon here."

He shook his head. "I'll need it to get Reuben and Bekah here in the morning."

"Why don't you fetch them tonight?" Meg asked. "Drive them straight into Aunt Trudy's stable, and no one will be wiser."

"They can sleep inside the walled wagon and sneak into the carriage from the barn." Cade's heel tapped against the rug. "I'll feel better with them being close to you ladies in case the baby comes during the night."

"You both have errands to accomplish before curfew. And we must all pack for our trip." Trudy rose. "Meg, I'll ask Harold to drive you so that Cade can return quickly. At least the rain has slowed."

"You have a knack for this, Aunt Trudy." Meg hugged her. "Have you considered spying?"

"No." Trudy tilted her head. "I believe this family has enough of those."

CHAPTER 35

*C*ade made it home at a quarter to nine. He stabled Old Sam, who looked around for his rubdown. "Night's not over, old boy." He smoothed his hand over the horse's wet mane. "Not for any of us."

He strode toward the back of the house, concerned at the light from the kitchen. Looked like a candle flickered inside. What were they doing downstairs?

Inside, he looked around. No one. Nor were his runaways in the bakery with its two large, uncurtained windows, thank goodness.

He ran upstairs. The couple sat at the table, eating the rest of the biscuits.

"We wondered where you were." Reuben stood with an uneasy glance at his wife. "Bekah was hungry again."

He refrained from reminding them he'd warned them not to go downstairs and to keep out of sight. "We're leaving in a few minutes." He explained the plan.

"You're taking us to Freedom's Fortress?" Bekah's brown eyes glowed. "I knew you was a good man when I laid eyes on you."

"Several others must work to be able to accomplish it. Now, let's find you each a new set of clothes and a coat. New shoes too, if any fit you."

They followed him to the bedroom. "That's right kind of you," said Reuben.

Cade lifted the hidden latch, and the door sprang open. "Pick out whatever you need for one set of clothes. Might be wise if you leave yours behind for the next folks. That way no one will identify you because of what you're wearing."

"Is there another turban for my hair?" Bekah held up a calico print dress.

"In that box." Cade pointed to the corner. "Reuben, select a new hat from the one next to it."

"Obliged to you."

He left them alone, shutting the bedroom door behind him, and packed a valise for himself. Then he ran downstairs for the list of Christmas orders. They hadn't discussed overnight stays. Trudy wasn't the type to sleep under a tree, as Cade often did on his overnight excursions.

No, they'd find an inn. Several nights at various inns—that was not an expense he'd planned for. All the money he had was set aside to buy supplies and a wedding ring for Meg. He had his mother's ring, a pretty gold band engraved with orange blossoms. He wondered if Meg would like that instead of a new, inexpensive one.

If this trip proved too costly, he might be unable to offer her a choice.

That was a problem for another day. He strode to the middle door and knocked on it. They must leave soon if Cade was to walk back by curfew.

Then it struck him—the fugitives didn't have passes to exit Richmond. Nor did the rest of them have permission to go over ten miles out of the city.

A stumbling block, to be sure. Could Paul help? He'd reveal

to Paul that he was smuggling runaways out of Richmond without mentioning his connection with the Underground Railroad.

It promised to be a long night.

~

our soldiers standing guard on picket duty stopped them within two miles of Richmond the next morning. Paul had forged free papers for Reuben and Bekah as well as passes last night, surprising Cade with his skill. What else was Paul capable of?

All the documents worked. Though the couple had been questioned each time, they were allowed to travel on. Outside the ten-mile radius of Richmond, things might be tricky because no one had passes. Though they shouldn't need passes unless stopped by soldiers. According to Paul, there weren't any known Confederate camps along his route. Cade prayed he was right.

At Trudy's suggestion, Cade had told the soldiers they traveled to Williamsburg, which he hoped to reach the next day. Trudy's team was younger and stronger than old Sam, so it was possible. And it was true, since they traveled to Fort Monroe by way of Williamsburg.

The next obstacle was the Chickahominy River. Cade had studied his maps into the night to determine the best place to cross. A bridge beyond White Oak Swamp seemed best. They'd be well past it by noon. A battle had been fought near it in June. In fact, he'd observed signs of battle a mile back in the broken trees, ravaged fields, and bullet-ridden buildings at Seven Pines. The wilderness they passed through must bear witness to soldiers marching toward the fighting.

"Did you say you'd teach me to drive the carriage?"

Cade gave a start. At his side, Reuben had been silent so long that he'd nearly forgotten his presence. "Sorry. I was planning the route in my head." He slowed the team. "You've never driven a team?"

"Nah." He studied the way the reins wound around Cade's fingers. "A pony cart is all, and I was a boy then. I work in tobacco fields."

"Don't know anything about growing tobacco."

"Wish I didn't." Reuben frowned. "I want to try my hand at blacksmithing. Just never got a chance."

"When we reach our destination"—Cade studied the surrounding fields but no one was around—"watch for opportunities to learn the trade."

"I will."

"Even learning to be a driver can be a new job for you." Cade grinned. "Let's start your first lesson."

~

"Can we stop and rest a bit?"

Bekah's eyes had been closed for an hour. Meg had assumed she slept. Not knowing their location, she exchanged a look with Aunt Trudy.

"It's wooded through here." Trudy peered out the window. "Perhaps this is a good place to get out and walk."

Meg stood to rap on the ceiling.

The carriage jolted to a bumpy halt.

"What is it?" Cade's voice, softer than Meg expected.

"We all need to get out and walk a few minutes." Especially Bekah, whose hands now cradled her belly over every bump.

"The road passes over a creek in another hundred yards. We'll stop there."

The carriage swayed as the wheels started again.

"We shall all be sick if this keeps up." Trudy's hand pressed against her flat stomach.

269

"I'll mention it to Cade."

Groaning, Bekah shifted on the thin leather seat.

"Bekah, are you hurting? Is it the baby?" Trudy leaned forward.

"No, he's not coming yet." She rubbed her lower back. "It's my back. Can't seem to get comfortable."

The carriage veered onto the grass and came to a halt.

Cade opened the door. "The icy water ought to be refreshing." He helped Trudy down the two steps.

Trudy walked over to the creek, a rushing brook after the previous day's rain.

Cade extended his hand to Meg, smiling up into her eyes.

"We're all getting a bit nauseated with the jerky stops and starts," Meg whispered. "Is it the road?"

"The driver." Cade grinned. "I'm teaching Reuben. He's getting the knack of it though. Not easy to learn to drive on a two-horse team and carriage."

"I gathered as much." She looked over her shoulder and watched Reuben lift his wife from the vehicle. "Bekah needs to rest outside in the bracing air." Meg shivered. "It's grown colder."

He squinted at the sky. "It'll be warmer again once we leave the woods. Be glad the rainstorm was yesterday."

"I am." She shivered again. "Will you retrieve the basket? There are cups inside."

"Keep your wits about you, even in a forest." Cade's voice was barely a whisper as he leaned into the vehicle. "We may have plenty to tell Paul later."

CHAPTER 36

our pickets at the bridge ahead. Not heavily guarded. Cade had figured there'd be guards at the bridge over the Chickahominy.

"Can you take over, Mr. Cade?" Reuben's hands shook on the reins.

"Nothing to worry about." Cade spoke softly while accepting them. "This close to Richmond, our passes should be enough to satisfy them."

"Halt." A musket-bearing soldier held up his gray-clad arm. No markings on the sleeve. A private. Two of the guards rested their muskets on their shoulders with a bored expression. One sat on a stump, whittling.

"Good morning." Cade brought the team to a smooth stop. "It will soon be Christmas."

"I've got picket duty that day too." The fellow frowned as the others watched. One spat tobacco juice on the grass. "Where are you folks from?"

"Richmond." Cade forced his shoulders to relax. The soldiers seemed more bored than alert.

"He your slave?" The soldier eyed Reuben.

"My driver."

"Why'd he give you the reins a minute ago?" The guard pointed at Reuben.

"We take turns."

"Where you bound?"

"Williamsburg." It was true, at least, initially.

"Got passes?"

Cade handed over his and Reuben's passes.

"Who's in the carriage?"

"My betrothed, her aunt, and his wife." Cade watched from the corner of his eye as the soldier peered inside.

"Henry, I'm gonna go make us some lunch." The tobacco-chewer strode to the trees. "I'm like to starve."

The soldier turned from the window. "They ain't the ones we're looking for, Henry. Let 'em go."

Cade's heart skipped a beat. Had someone asked them to search for the married couple this far from Richmond? No way to be certain without asking, which he had no intention of doing.

"Get on outta here." Henry slapped the horse closest to him on the neck. The horse's sudden lurch forward forced Cade to catch hold of his seat to prevent a fall.

The soldiers laughed.

One slapped his knee. "Good one, Henry. I get the next one."

Cade allowed the team to maintain a trot for the next mile. Then, aware the swaying carriage might play havoc on passengers' stomachs, he slowed to a comfortable pace. "Those fellas didn't recognize you."

"Must be the slouch hat." Reuben touched his brown coat. "New clothes too."

"Small details make a difference. No matter what happens, stay calm. Never let them know you're afraid." He guided the team onto a side road to the right. "This runs near the river.

Here's the reins. If we don't see more pickets, we'll look for a clearing to eat lunch. I'm like to starve."

Reuben grinned. "Lot of that going around."

~

*M*eg had watched out the window for an hour. It was getting dark and they hadn't passed an inn all afternoon. "We may have to travel farther than we'd like to find a place to stay."

Bekah opened her eyes and looked outside.

Meg listened to the sound of Cade singing "O God, Our Help" in beautiful baritone. She marveled at the soothing timber of his voice. How had she not known he possessed such talent?

"Is your back hurting?" Trudy asked.

"Reckon it is." The open fields seemed to hold Bekah spell-bound, for she didn't shift her eyes. "I don't care about that. All I care about is being one more mile away from the plantation and one mile closer to Freedom's Fortress." She tilted her head, listening. "That's a right pretty song. I never heard it before."

Meg told her its name. "I've heard Cade sing at church, where he doesn't sing loudly enough to call attention to himself."

"We shall ask him to sing for us sometimes. Mary plays the pianoforte." Trudy lifted the corner of the shade and peered into the twilight.

"Let's do that." Meg wanted to hear more too. For now, she wanted to know a bit about the mother-to-be who had been silent much of the day. "Where did you live?"

"Near as me and Reuben can figure it, the plantation is close to the North Carolina and Virginia line. I ain't sure exactly which one lays claim to it."

"Did you work in the fields?"

"In the house. Reuben worked the tobacco field. Things were

rougher for him because the women of the house weren't harsh with me."

Meg waited to see if Bekah wanted to say more. The pregnant woman reverted to her former silence.

"How did you learn about Freedom's Fortress?" Trudy asked.

Her eyes lit up. "Some folks visiting my mistress told her about it and I heard everything. I told Reuben, who wanted to learn more. I kept listening every time anyone talked about it. They said that the President up North wants to free the slaves in the South." She looked at Trudy. "Is that true? I mean, I saw your slaves. You treated them good."

"Those men and women are not slaves. I pay them to work for me." Trudy spoke gently. "They're free to come and go as they please. Free to find another job if they wish."

"Sounds like heaven." She gazed outside. "That's what I want."

"Fort Monroe—the place you call Freedom's Fortress— accepts fugitives like yourself, called contraband of war." It thrilled Meg that there were such havens in the South. "That's a term used so that Union soldiers can protect you and people like you from being returned to your former plantation."

Bekah's eyes softened in gratitude. "I never heard it told just that way, but I understood the gist of it already. That's why I want my baby born on free soil." She rubbed her bulging stomach. "I believe this little one is a boy. I want my son born free, right from the start."

Tears blurred Meg's vision. "We'll do everything in our power to make certain it happens that way."

~

"*Amazing Love! How can it be? That, Thou, my God, shouldst die for me?*"

Cade stopped singing at the welcome sight of a two-story

inn. He pulled into the empty yard. It was fully dark at seven o'clock. He didn't know this area of Virginia and had despaired of finding rooms for them.

Mary and Joseph had understood his dilemma, for they'd had that same trouble over eighteen hundred years ago.

"Reuben, let's pray the owners of this inn extend a welcome." Cade set the brake.

"Bekah's prayers'd do more good than mine. Her prayers got us this far."

"There's no doubt that the Lord's ear bends toward the faithful." Cade placed a hand on his shoulder. "The Creator's hand is on you too, my friend." He jumped down and then opened the door. "Finally found an inn. No other wagons or carriages here, so I reckon they'll have rooms."

"Yes, please try it." Trudy tugged the shawl covering her coat closer about her. "Two rooms, I think. One for the women, one for the men."

No need to talk about free papers if the pair appeared to be working for them. He figured that was wise. "I'll talk to them."

"Cade, remember…"

He felt his face flush at Trudy's reminder. She had given him money to pay for their lodging all the way to the fort. It embarrassed him that his funds didn't stretch enough to foot the expense for the whole trip. "I will. Thank you." His voice was gruffer than he liked. It humiliated him to have Meg guess at the arrangement.

He strode inside to talk to the proprietors, a gray-haired couple more than happy to welcome guests.

"Yes, we have two rooms." The old man dusted off a ledger on the table. "All six rooms are clean, if you need more."

He considered renting an extra one for the married couple, but such a detail would be remembered should a marshal come looking for them. "Just the two for five people. And supper and breakfast, please."

"Well, now"—the man smiled at his wife—"that will cost extra."

"I'm prepared to pay." Cade was glad they hadn't found anything sooner. These innkeepers, it seemed, could use the money. A lot of folks could these days. "How much?"

He quoted a price twice what Cade had expected. He paid it without complaint. "When will dinner be served?"

"In three quarters of an hour."

"We'll be ready. I'd like to stable my team."

"Of course." The man flushed. "My son used to take care of the horses. He's off fighting the war."

"I can manage." Cade smiled to alleviate the man's embarrassment over an inability to see to the task. "Is the stable behind the inn?"

"Yes, sir. Now I just need your name."

"Caden Jackson." He'd use his middle name as his last name for the hotel. It was another layer of protection for them should anyone be searching for the fugitives this far from Richmond.

CHAPTER 37

$\mathcal{M}$eg studied the few houses built around a crossroad as they passed them the following afternoon. Cade had brought a map of Virginia, published before the war. Much had changed since then.

Bullet holes in barns, homes, and the village's lone inn bore witness to fighting. Trees and bushes weren't destroyed, so it must have been a small skirmish. Lots of activity had happened between the coast and Richmond in the spring. Meg considered the countless lives that might have been saved had the Union army captured the Confederate capital, for Confederate surrender couldn't be far behind the fall of Richmond.

Not that she wanted her family to suffer. Far from it. Yet this war must end—the battles as well as slavery.

As the silent woman at her side also desired with an intensity that surpassed Meg's.

Every part of Meg's being wanted to get Bekah and Reuben to safety before the baby was born.

Trudy napped on the seat opposite. Bekah leaned against the side of the carriage with her eyes closed, one hand rubbing her belly.

Cade said they'd arrive in Williamsburg around supper time. Aunt Trudy knew of a couple of inns there with dining rooms. There were also taverns that served hot meals if no rooms were available.

Meg hoped for Bekah's sake that they would have at least a dozen hours of rest before mounting the carriage that became less comfortable every passing hour. Cade also wanted to rest the horses as long as possible.

A battle had been fought in Williamsburg in May, with the Confederates abandoning the city after the day's long and bloody battle. She hoped the city had recovered and that businesses were open.

Bekah shifted with a soft moan.

"Bekah, are you all right?" Meg touched her shoulder.

"What? Are we in Williamsburg?" She rubbed her eyes.

"Not yet. Sorry I woke you. I thought the baby…" Meg wished she had worked alongside Thomas with his patients more often. She'd never helped him deliver a baby, something she regretted. She whispered another silent prayer that they would find lodgings near a midwife or doctor, for the baby's time wasn't far off. Surely there were doctors at the fort. *God, please help us reach Fort Monroe before the baby is born. It matters so much to Bekah and Reuben.*

"I'm praying for him to stay in there." She patted her belly. "Is it Christmas yet?"

"Christmas is in two days." Meg rifled through the picnic basket of dwindling supplies for a bottle of water. She gave it to Bekah.

"Obliged to you." Bekah took a long drink. "I have a feeling we better get to Freedom's Fortress by Christmas."

"Have labor pains started?" Trudy asked, fully awake.

"Not yet." Concern darkened her features. "We'll get there by Christmas, won't we?"

"What if the men drive a little faster tomorrow?" A twinge of anxiety welled inside of Meg. They were well over half way to Fort Monroe. Cade had slowed when they complained of the jarring motion. Truthfully, it was less obvious who was driving now, which spoke to Reuben's increasing skill.

"I think we'd better go faster tomorrow," Bekah said.

"Agreed." Trudy glanced at the open basket. "We'll replenish our food before leaving Williamsburg. Our inn or a restaurant will suffice if we arrive after shops close. Offering to pay extra will help both the shopkeepers and us."

"Eating takes my mind off the baby." Bekah leaned over to look inside. "I don't want too much though."

"There's a bit of cheese." Meg pushed aside the dishes and towels. "And three crackers."

"I can't eat the last of the food." Bekah shrank into the corner.

"Of course you can, my dear." Trudy gave her a gentle smile. "We'll buy more."

"No one except my family has been so good to me." Bekah accepted the food. "I don't know why you all are doing this for me and Reuben."

"Perhaps we want to put right the wrong that's been done you"—Trudy met the mother-to-be's eyes with a steady gaze —"by doing all we can for your baby."

"So he's born on free soil." Bekah's glance darted between her companions.

"A worthy cause." Meg spoke softly.

"My son will be someone important." Bekah sandwiched the cheese in between two crackers.

"He will." Tears glistened in Trudy's eyes. "And my greatest hope for him is that he learns that he's cherished by his Savior."

"Miss Trudy, you don't need to worry about that one." Bekah's face glowed. "I'll teach him all about that myself, just like my mama taught me."

~

*C*ade drew Meg aside after breakfast at dawn in the inn's dining room. The rest of their group went back to their rooms for last minute preparations before leaving. "It's good we had a nice long rest here in Williamsburg last night, but we have another thirty-five miles to travel. We'll get there tomorrow."

"So far? Have you studied the map?"

"Last night and again this morning. I know the way. We'll likely see more pickets today. Union guards." He dealt so often with Southern pickets that it unnerved him to speak with Northern ones. Their Richmond passes had no value here. The forged documents proving Reuben and Bekah were free citizens weighed on his conscience. He wanted to convince the married couple to burn the dishonest documents. Not a matter he could discuss in a Southern inn because the conversation could be overheard.

"Because spring battles drove the Confederate troops from the area." Her voice dropped to a whisper.

Cade nodded. His gaze swept the room. General conversation was loud enough that no one could easily overhear, unless they shared his keen hearing. Best change the topic. "We slowed down to keep you ladies as comfortable as possible. Do you think you all can tolerate a faster pace?"

"Bekah wants to be there by Christmas." She walked with him to the inn's front door. "She has a feeling her son will be born tomorrow."

"A son?" How could a woman know such a thing until the baby was born? Unless her name was Mary and an angel told her. Well, it was the Christmas season.

"Just a feeling she has." Meg wrapped a shawl more snugly around her as a guest entered the inn, allowing a blast of cold air inside. "Not to mention that it's a cold morning. I think we should try to get there tonight."

"Christmas Eve night." He smiled down at her.

"Our first Christmas together."

That beautiful smile melted his heart. This morning it also smote him because he could only pray he wasn't leading his betrothed and her beloved aunt into a hornet's nest.

CHAPTER 38

"Halt."

"Good morning to you." Cade stopped for the third time that morning for Union guards, four of them. He was headed toward a forest. Beyond that was a creek where he planned to stop for lunch, unless they discovered a village with a restaurant. "My name is Cade Yancey." Now that they were in Union territory, he felt it safe to give his name. Reuben and Bekah didn't need to fear these soldiers would turn them over to a Southern marshal.

"What's your destination?"

"Fort Monroe." Cade glanced at the spokesman's sleeve. Chevron stripes of a corporal. The other three were privates. They all held rifles resting against their shoulders.

"What's your business at the fort?"

A new question. How was he supposed to answer truthfully when Reuben and Bekah had free papers with them? Why had he allowed Paul to talk him into taking those forgeries? Of course, the papers had allowed the couple safe passage through Richmond. Perhaps his conscience was too sensitive about the matter.

The corporal, a man probably in his twenties, frowned.

Best tell him the truth quickly, or they'd all be turned out on the road and led to the next higher authority to tell their story.

Reuben straightened beside him. "We come for our freedom."

The corporal looked at his comrades.

"This man, Reuben, and his wife, Bekah, seek the freedom of Fort Monroe." The truth felt good on his lips. "Their baby is expected to be born any day."

The corporal strode to the carriage and peered inside. "Who are you ladies?"

"I am Gertrude Weston and this is my niece, Margaret Brooks."

Cade hoped Trudy wouldn't mention her Richmond home unless asked. He figured it was a can of worms they didn't need to open. Though he was on the same side as these soldiers, his worry for the couple wouldn't ease until they were safely at their destination. Since he wasn't invited to get down, Cade shifted in his seat to watch the enlisted officer. The others stayed near the edge of the trees, where a trail likely led to a cabin or an army camp.

"Bekah?"

"That's me." Her voice sounded almost timid.

Cade didn't blame her, for it was undoubtedly the first time she'd spoken to a Union soldier.

"I am Corporal Ryan. Your child is expected any day?"

"Yessir, Mr. Corporal Ryan." Her voice strengthened, as if sensing an ally. "My baby's going to be born on free land."

Cade's whole body tensed. *Please, be her ally.*

"From what I see, your child may share our Savior's birthday." He touched his hat. "I wish you tidings of the day, ladies." He strode back to the front. "Reuben, Fort Monroe isn't large enough to hold all those like you and your wife. The Great

Contraband Camp has been established for freedom-seekers such as yourselves."

"The Great Contraband Camp?"

"Yes, former slaves started a camp two or three miles from Fort Monroe at the city of Hampton."

"Hampton?" Cade raised his brows. "I thought Confederate soldiers burned that city."

Reuben stiffened at his side.

"They did. Then they left it. New buildings have gone up. There's a goodly number of folks there."

"You say they'll find safety at the Great Contraband Camp?" Cade liked the sound of this place. The young parents could start their family life in an established community.

"Yep. As safe as you and me."

None of them were completely safe until the war ended.

"You know the way to Hampton?"

"It's on the way to Fort Monroe," Cade said.

"Good luck to you folks." He stepped back.

"Much obliged." Cade tipped his hat and drove off.

"That sounds like a good place for us to settle, don't it?" Reuben drummed his hands against his legs.

"Sounds promising." Cade shared the young man's excitement. He could barely wait to stop for lunch and talk to everyone about the good news.

"It's a place we can belong."

Cade's heart skipped a beat. A place to belong, what they all needed. He whispered a silent prayer that the safe haven the couple sought also gave them a home.

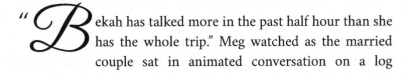

"*B*ekah has talked more in the past half hour than she has the whole trip." Meg watched as the married couple sat in animated conversation on a log several yards from the bridge where she stood with Cade. This spot over a six-foot wide creek was peaceful with very few travelers on the dirt road. A few homes dotted the countryside, and it comforted her to be in a community.

"She and Reuben are making plans for the future. Too bad Aunt Trudy preferred to sit in the carriage to eat lunch." He glanced back at the carriage beside the road.

"She's unaccustomed to the cold and has been coughing this morning." Meg looked at Bekah. "And I believe Bekah is starting to feel the pains of childbirth." A couple of groans that morning had been accompanied by a pained expression. "How much farther?"

"Less than ten miles." He shook his head in wonder. "Can you believe what the corporal told us about the camp? Reuben said he wants his family to live there."

"I'm excited for them." Meg relaxed against the wooden rail. "We're far enough from Richmond that I doubt we'll see anyone searching for them."

"Too many soldiers. That danger is behind us."

Bekah gasped and grabbed her stomach. Reuben looked at her, eyes widened in alarm.

"I'd best hitch up the team." Cade straightened. "I wanted to give the horses a long rest but I don't believe that's an option."

Meg rushed to the log where the mother-to-be clutched her swollen belly. "Bekah, shall we see if there's a doctor or midwife in the village we just passed?"

"No going back." She panted. "Just ask Mr. Cade to get us to the camp right quick. Folks there will help me birth my baby."

Reuben raised her to her feet. "We're still in Virginia. Won't be safe until we reach the camp."

They were set on reaching camp first, even though Bekah was in labor. Meg prayed the baby was in agreement. "I'll try to prepare a comfortable place where you can rest your head."

"And my back." She rubbed her lower back. "I can't get comfortable. My apologies for being a burden."

"Not a burden at all. Can you walk?"

"Slow like." She took a step, secure with her husband's arm around her waist.

"Very good. I'll run ahead to prepare the seat."

Cade walked the horses to the carriage.

She rushed over to him. "Her pains have started. They don't want to search for a midwife. Labor *can* take hours. No way to know when the baby will be born."

"I'd best hurry then."

"The ride will be painful for Bekah. Take it as easily—and as quickly—as you can. Pray for all of them."

"I've scarcely stopped praying since meeting them."

"Good." She climbed into the carriage. "Aunt Trudy, Bekah's labor has begun. She insists on getting to the camp."

"Then let's make her as comfortable as possible." Coughing, she splayed her fingers over her throat and chest. "There are towels in my trunk. Will you ask one of the men to climb up and retrieve them?"

Reuben's tense face as he neared the carriage with his wife told Meg the man needed something to occupy his hands. She asked him to tend to the task.

She spread a wool blanket over the seat while Bekah leaned against the carriage. Icy breezes swept through the open door. Each of the men had a blanket to protect them from the chill. Another cocooned Trudy in its warmth. Bekah would lie on the blanket Meg had been using as a lap quilt and cover herself with the only blanket left.

It would be a chilly ride. What mattered more was that they reached the camp in time for the baby's birth and that Trudy didn't get any sicker.

Lord, please get us to the camp in time for this baby's birth.

CHAPTER 39

*D*arkness fell quickly on this early winter's day, as Cade had known it would. They'd stopped for every labor pain, for the jolting of the carriage increased Bekah's agony. Of course, this slowed their progress. They'd also stopped for a half hour's rest when the pain got too much. Cade feared they couldn't go on, but Bekah insisted they continue— and fast.

Cade peered ahead. The smell of salt water from the Chesapeake Bay grew stronger with each turn of the wheel. Pickets had stopped them a quarter hour before and, after seeing Bekah's face, sent them on their way. They should be within a mile of the camp now. *Please, God, ready a doctor or a midwife to help her immediately upon arrival.*

Reuben took a turn driving as the sun sank into the trees. The poor man was as jittery as a June bug. Sweat actually trickled down his face, even though the temperature was cold enough to freeze puddles on the side of the dirt road.

Perhaps a song would soothe their spirits. One came to him that fit the Christmas Eve night as well as the young mother-to-be.

"Silent night, holy night, All is calm, all is bright;

"'Round yon virgin mother and Child! Holy infant so tender and mild,

"Sleep in Heavenly peace, Sleep in Heavenly peace."

Buildings up ahead. Could this be the Grand Contraband Camp? The smell of wood smoke filled his nostrils.

He sang the second verse as they plodded closer.

Bekah cried out.

Reuben relaxed his hold on the reins, and the horses sped up to a trot.

"Silent night, holy night, Son of God—"

"That's Mr. Cade singing."

Cade stiffened at the familiar voice. There was movement among the ramshackle buildings ahead. He recognized the boy's voice yet couldn't remember—

"You know that man, son?" a man said.

"Pa, he helped me and Max get to you. He's the singing baker man."

"George, is that you?" Cade touched Reuben's arm and motioned for him to stop.

"Yep, it's me, Mr. Cade." The ten-year-old stepped into the glow of the carriage's lantern light. "Me and Max made it to Freedom's Fortress, just like we told you we would. And we found our pa."

"I haven't heard such good news in a long time." Cade tore off the blanket from his shoulders and leaped down. "I'm happy to see you."

"You helped my boys." A man extended his hand. "I'm beholden to you."

"It was my privilege. I prayed they'd find you." He gave the man's hand a hearty shake. "I need help, if you can." Cade peered at the crowd gathering behind George's family. Some men held candles. In its glow, Cade read both mistrust and curiosity. The

Good Lord had gone before him to pave the way for this evening in sending young George to the camp months before.

"What is it?" George's father eyed him.

Bekah cried out from the carriage.

"We need a midwife. Fast." Cade turned and saw Meg looking through the window. She looked terrified. "Reuben and his wife Bekah seek the shelter of the Grand Contraband Camp, and their baby will very soon need it too."

Reuben climbed inside the carriage. "I need help."

George called to the crowd behind him, "Send for Aggie!"

Men rushed around the carriage as Cade held the reins of the tired horses. Men's voices filled the air.

"Let's make a pallet with our arms."

"Link arms to make it stronger."

"She's on it."

"Why, she ain't much heavier than a sack of flour."

A woman ran into the throng. "Let me at her."

The men parted. The gale that parted the Red Sea couldn't have been mightier.

"I'm Aggie." The black woman held Bekah's hand as she glanced at her bulging stomach. "I'm a midwife."

"Did I make it to free land?"

"Yep. You're safe here."

"Then I can have my baby in peace." The tension eased from Bekah's voice.

"That you can."

The men carrying Bekah followed Aggie down a dark lane between cottages.

Cade wanted to help but realized they didn't need his aid.

Meg suddenly stood at his side.

George, the boy's father, turned back. "You folks might as well go on to Freedom's Fortress. They'll have a place for you to stay."

"But we want to help." Meg took a step forward.

"We'll be just fine. Thanks just the same. Come back tomorrow and see the babe." He pointed to his left. "Just follow that road to the bridge over Hampton Creek. When that road ends, turn left and follow the road onto the island where the fort is."

"You want me to give you their possessions?" Cade glanced at the valises and bags tied to the carriage.

"Bring them tomorrow."

"Mr. Cade?" A boy tugged on his sleeve.

"Max?" Cade lowered on one knee to look the boy in the eye.

"Thanks for helping me find my pa." Max threw himself into Cade's arms.

He hugged him close. All the sacrifices, every single one, was worth this moment. "It was my pleasure, Max."

The boy dashed after the crowd.

A tear blurred Cade's last view of the child. He brushed it away.

"My boy told me about the baker man who sang to them." George stared at him. "Max never talked until he found me, and he still don't say much. Reckon he just needed to thank one of the people who helped him on his way." He strode after his son.

"I never heard Max say a word the whole time he was with me," Cade said.

"You made an impression." Meg's gloved fingers curled around Cade's. "A baker man who sings to soothe the fears of his passengers. I believe I understand how they might feel."

"We made it to the camp. I can't take it all in." He pressed a palm to his eye. "We got them here. In time for the baby's birth."

"My hero." Leaning her head against his chest, she smiled up into his eyes.

"Hardly a word that describes me." The soldiers were the real heroes. He simply did what he could.

"Oh, yes, that description suits you perfectly. Didn't you hear that little boy? Sounds like a hero to me."

He gave her a quick kiss. "You always know the right words to say. Now, I think we'd best get your aunt to shelter, for the night air grows colder."

CHAPTER 40

$\mathcal{M}$eg didn't worry overmuch when Union pickets stopped them again before they reached Fort Monroe. They had been through so much already the past few days that this last stop almost seemed anticlimactic.

Trudy coughed in her sleep. Her flushed cheeks concerned Meg, who feared a cold had turned into something worse.

She positioned a blanket around Trudy's shoulders. "Not too much longer," she whispered.

When there was no response, Meg pushed aside the shade to peer at the Union camp to the right of their carriage. Candle-light and lanterns gave a dim glow to long wooden buildings and tents arranged in rows about the field. She had been at the fort in February, when her cousin Will was exchanged and sent South under a Flag of Truce. Annie, Bea, and even Uncle Hiram had been beside themselves with sorrow over the parting. Will was a lieutenant in the Confederate army, and Meg didn't doubt he'd returned to the fighting.

The carriage finally started again. Cade must have satisfied the guards' curiosity, for they headed toward the fort. She had advised him to drive straight to the Sherwood Inn for accommodations. She prayed they had two rooms available, for none of them was in shape to travel elsewhere on Christmas Eve.

She had only been at the fort for a day yet remembered a church. Surely, they would have services in the morning.

For tonight, she'd expend the last of her energy on making Aunt Trudy as comfortable as possible.

~

*C*ade paid for two rooms for three nights. He worried about Trudy, who hadn't been herself since morning. If she suffered from a fever, which he suspected, three days' stay wouldn't be long enough. The Sherwood Inn was costly for a simple baker, but Trudy's plans had made all this possible.

He carried the trunk and valises to their rooms while Meg helped Trudy settle into a chair and remove her coat.

"Thank you for carrying our bags upstairs, dear boy." Trudy's voice sounded hoarse, as if her throat pained her. "Is there a dining room?"

"It's open for guests for another hour." Cade glanced around the comfortable room with two beds, two chairs, a chest, desk, two lamps, and a pitcher and bowl. The ladies should be content here. "Feels good to reach a destination."

"Indeed." Trudy coughed into an embroidered handkerchief.

"The hotel attendant offered to send for the doctor." A good idea, in Cade's opinion.

"Perhaps that's best, don't you think, Aunt Trudy?" Meg cast an anxious look at him. "It was very cold in the carriage."

"I don't mind telling you that a leisurely day or two in bed appeals to me more than it should on Christmas." She moved to sit on the bed. "Yes, please send for the doctor. I'm likely merely suffering from the cold. My feet feel like blocks of ice."

"Mine too." Meg sat beside her.

She coughed again. "Perhaps I will ask the staff for a dinner tray in my room. I suddenly feel rather spent."

"I'll do that and ask for a doctor too." He placed a reassuring hand on Meg's shoulder. "Be back shortly."

A quarter of an hour later, he escorted Dr. Bennet to Trudy's room and waited in the hall for them, staring at the floral pattern on the rug. He itched to get back to the bakery. Clara was even now baking for tomorrow's special orders.

His job—and he hadn't even given it a thought until reaching the fort.

"Mr. Yancey." The gray-bearded doctor exited the room, closing the door behind him. "Mrs. Weston has a fever. It would be best if she has a good three to five days of bed rest and another two days of taking it easy before leaving for home."

A week. "I see." Cade rubbed his jaw. That meant they'd not leave here until January first at the earliest. Would Clara continue to bake and keep his doors open? He'd send a telegram with his request. He owed her, Mabel, and Bea a bonus. Thankfully, Trudy had given him enough with some bills to spare for the extra days of lodging.

"Mrs. Weston says you'll travel back to her home in Richmond." Dr. Bennett studied him. "One wonders about her loyalties while staying outside a Union fort."

"She's a Southerner who hates slavery." Cade hoped that satisfied him. "And Mrs. Brooks, my betrothed, is from Chicago. Both of us support the Union."

"Good to know. What brought you here?"

Cade explained.

The doctor clapped him on the back. "A trip like that takes courage."

Cade figured it did. For all of them. "What do I owe you?"

"Only two dollars for the medicine. No charge for the visit."

"Oh, but—"

"It's my thank-you for bringing a married couple to the

contraband camp to have their baby." He grinned as he pocketed the bills. "And it's Christmas Eve."

"Is there a church here? We'd like to attend services in the morning."

"You can likely see St. Mary Star of the Sea from the inn's veranda. The Chapel of the Centurion, where my family attends, is a Protestant church open to all denominations. It's close enough to walk."

"We may see you there, then."

"Merry Christmas."

"Merry Christmas." Cade knocked on Meg's door. His stomach rumbled in anticipation of their meal.

CHAPTER 41

*M*eg strolled to the Chapel of the Centurion on Christmas Day with her gloved hand resting on her betrothed's sleeve. The sun shone as they exchanged greetings of the day with passing soldiers and families.

"That sea breeze feels bracing, even in the sunshine." She drank in the beauty of gentle waves approaching the shore.

"Was your aunt sleeping when you returned from our breakfast?"

She nodded. "I hope she awakens before her oatmeal and tea grow cold."

"The medicine makes her sleep?"

"Hard to tell. Dr. Bennett said it might, but Aunt Trudy's exhaustion may have something to do with it." Meg admired the two-story wooden homes they passed.

"What about the ride home? Will she be all right?"

"I believe so. Bekah had two of our blankets yesterday. We'll bundle blankets around Aunt Trudy, especially her feet. She's not old nor an invalid. It was a combination of the stress, worry, and exhaustion that made her vulnerable, I think." She hugged his arm. "Thanks for paying the maid to sit with her while we're at church. Isabel seemed happy to make the extra money."

"Good. We'll ask her to stay again when we go visit Reuben and Bekah."

"I'm eager to see the baby." She looked up at the Gothic-style wooden church. "And here we are. Let's celebrate the birth of another baby."

～

*C*ade sat elbow to elbow with a stranger in the crowded church. Attending church on Christmas morning with soldiers in uniform heightened the patriotic feelings that had consumed him since they'd arrived. The organ and the carpeted aisle made him feel at home. Or had that been due to the greetings and handshakes he'd received outside?

Beyond the pastor's head was a beautiful stained glass image of the Roman centurion, Cornelius, who was said to have been the first soldier to become a Christian.

This was the first Christmas in years where Cade had sat beside the woman he loved. For little, he'd marry Meg while they waited for Aunt Trudy's health to improve, right here at this fort that had become a symbol of freedom to fugitives.

He sat straight up, knocking against the soldier beside him. He whispered an apology and then met Meg's eyes.

She raised her brows.

Cade patted her hand and returned his attention to the pastor's sermon.

They had Uncle Hiram's approval. Indeed, the whole family approved of their upcoming marriage.

Would the pastor agree to perform the ceremony?

What about Meg?

His spirits deflated. He recalled her excitement at Bea's wedding and her beautiful green dress, which he wanted her to wear for their own wedding. Chances were slim that it was in her valise.

She'd also want at least some of her family in attendance.

But, oh, what a perfect place to marry the woman he loved.

~

*M*eg sat beside Cade in the carriage as they pulled up to the street corner where they'd left Reuben and Bekah the evening before.

"Mr. Cade." Reuben pushed himself upright from where he leaned against a wooden building. "Miss Meg. I thought you'd come today."

"How is Bekah?" Meg kept her eyes trained on his happy face while Cade lifted her to the ground.

"She's a sight happier today than yesterday." He chuckled. "Our son was born in the middle of the night."

"Reckon we had more time than we'd figured." Cade laughed with him.

"Reckon so. Want to see him?"

"Please." Meg's feet bounced against the dirt road.

"We brought your bags and a few other things. What shall I do with my team and carriage?"

"There's a stable on the left." He pointed. "They'll be pleased for your business."

"I'll be grateful for the service."

Meg waited outside while the men talked with the owner. Charred remains of tree stumps and buildings retained the odor of the flames that had destroyed Hampton. Some new buildings looked as if they'd been built in a day or two. Others were stronger homes that would stand the high winds of the Chesapeake Bay and Hampton Roads waterways.

She looked back at the sound of male voices.

"Let's get you folks over to our new home."

Meg gasped as much at the words as at the pride on Reuben's face. "You already have a home?"

"Yep. The family that built it left for the North last week." His smile lit up his face. Toting half-filled sacks, he pointed straight ahead with his other hand. "They abandoned it and we was the next ones to come and need a home."

"I'm happy for you." Cade switched a bag to his left hand to shake Reuben's hand. "You own a home."

"I can't rightly take it all in." Reuben gave his head a little shake as they strolled past folks in yards and on porches. "So much has happened since we run off. Now I'm a father. I got my own home. I can drive a two-horse team. I'll be looking for a chance to learn blacksmithing, but meantime, some fellas offered to teach me to fish with them. They sell to the soldiers."

"A fine profession."

It thrilled Meg to learn of Reuben's opportunities. His family's lives were forever altered.

Reuben knocked on a door of an unpainted two-story home. "They're here, Bekah. Are you ready for 'em?"

"One minute," Bekah called.

"I'll be right back." Reuben stepped inside and closed the door.

"Home looks sturdy." Cade mounted two steps to the porch. Bounced a little. Rubbed his fingers over the side of the house. "This one will last."

"For more than one reason." Meg smiled at him.

"A firm foundation."

Reuben opened the door wide. "Come in, folks. Bekah says to come meet Benjamin Yancey."

"Yancey?" Cade froze, the sack in his hand swinging.

"Hope you don't mind us taking your name as ours." He stared at the spotless floor. "We figured you all done so much for us—"

"I'm honored." Stepping inside, Cade clasped Meg's hand. "Thank you."

Bekah sat in front of a cozy fire on a spindle-backed chair, holding her precious baby.

The expression of joy on her face filled Meg's heart with a kaleidoscope of emotions, for their sacrifice had been worth the cost. She rushed across the room and knelt beside her. "Oh, Bekah, he's perfect." Benjamin's chubby brown cheeks and a smattering of dark hair brought tears to her eyes. They had all labored for this child.

"That he is." Bekah stared down at him with such love that a tear spilled down Meg's face.

"And he was born on free land, just like you determined him to be."

"Determined do be the proper word for how I felt." Bekah touched his face with her finger. "I hoped he'd be awake for your visit."

"Please don't awaken him on our account."

"All right. Where's Miss Trudy?"

"She's feeling poorly." Meg stood. "She'll be good as new in about a week. Do you have everything you need?"

"Oh, yes." Bekah's face lit up. "The family left us a bed and a dining room table and chairs."

"And a few clothes, blankets, towels, and such." Reuben smiled as he stared at his baby. "We're invited for Christmas dinner with our new neighbors, and I'll fish for our supper tomorrow."

"Looks like you're in the right place." Meg reached for the sack Cade held. "We have a few things you'll need for the baby."

"Why, I never..." Bekah opened the bag. "Nappies. Two little nightgowns. I sure will need these. And a knitted blanket."

"The nappies and nightgowns are from Clara, who works for my aunt. The sack with a dozen biscuits and a pound of coffee is from Cade and me." A little sack of coffee was all the inn agreed to sell them. No doubt it was a welcome gift anyway.

"Well, I do declare. Coffee beans." Bekah scooped a handful and sniffed them. "Don't smell as good until they're roasted. We'll roast some and take them to Christmas supper."

Her pleasure in the gifts filled Meg with the joy of the season. "The yellow blanket is from Aunt Trudy. It's big enough for a school boy."

"He'll be that size one day. I'll double it around him so he'll be extra warm." She smiled at her guests. "Tell her thank you from me."

CHAPTER 42

"I'm happy for them." Meg sat beside Cade on the journey back to the fort.

"Amazing how things have changed for their family."

"We had a part in that." She snuggled closer.

They drove in contented silence for a few minutes.

"I need to talk to the guards about extending our passes for the fort. Last night I thought we'd leave in three days."

"Guards at the camp?"

"Yes. That's why we were stopped so long on the last step of our journey."

"I confess I was too tired to notice."

"I believe the only reason we're allowed to go onto the fort—not inside the moated military section, but outside it—is our reason for coming here."

"Bringing Reuben and Bekah to safety?"

"Exactly. Otherwise, we'd already be on our return trip. I'm not certain your aunt's illness would have mattered."

"They must watch for Confederate spies."

"And they do. I had to tell them of my Unionist ties in Richmond." He glanced at her. "Yours too. I asked them to keep that secret. Don't know if they will."

"You did what you had to do. We may have to find another way to serve the Union."

He grimaced. "Maybe not. If they only talk about Unionists being in Richmond…"

"Authorities there know of Union supporters."

"That's why Clayton's security force is so active."

"I wish we were already married, for now that little Benjamin is born this feels almost like a wedding trip." She surveyed Hampton Roads, the waterway beyond the camp. Hampton Roads led past Fort Monroe, which sat on land that jutted out with the Chesapeake Bay on its left. It was a beautiful area. Union soldiers were in the camp ahead and all around the fort, which was surrounded by a moat. Patriotism coursed through her simply to be here, so far from her home in the Confederate capital.

"About that."

She raised her eyebrows. "What?"

"We'll be here a week or so while Aunt Trudy recovers." His ruddy cheeks flushed a darker shade. "How do you feel about asking the pastor to wed us while we're here?"

"Can we?" She bounced in the seat, causing the horses to neigh in protest. "This place already inspires me. It was here that General Butler paved the way to save the fugitive slaves by declaring them contraband of war."

"Seems a fitting place for us to wed."

"Only Aunt Trudy is here to witness it." Her hopes for a romantic ceremony by the bay crumbled.

"We can send a telegram to Annie in Washington City. She's within a day's journey."

"They can come by ship or railroad. Or even in a carriage as we did." Hope revived. "Bea and Jay can't come."

He shook his head sadly. "Bea waits on our bakery customers

for us and Jay's job binds him to the ironworks nearly seven days a week."

"Bea will be crushed to miss it." Disappointment welled up that her cousin had no way to attend. "Yet I believe she'd be thrilled for the wedding to be held in such a symbolic setting."

"True." His blue eyes brightened. "Why don't we have the wedding on January first?"

"It's perfect. That's when the Emancipation Proclamation is supposed to become law." Meg clapped her hands. "It also allows Annie and Uncle Hiram time to make arrangements."

"And for your aunt to recover."

Another snag presented itself. "Will the pastor agree to perform the ceremony? You're not a soldier."

Cade sighed. "He may refuse."

She clasped his hand. "Let's speak with him tomorrow. Until then, we'll pray."

"Depend upon it."

~

*D*rummers beat a rhythmic call in what felt to Cade like the middle of the night. He'd managed to fall asleep again about the time a bugler played reveille. Cade opened one blurry eye. Full darkness in the room. It wasn't even dawn. He planned to escort Meg down to breakfast at seven o'clock. He rolled over and fell back asleep.

Buglers and drums awoke him again. An officer shouted orders in the distance.

Cade fished his pocket watch from his coat and held it to the window where the eastern horizon was lightening. Six o'clock. He yawned. At least that was a more reasonable hour.

Then he chuckled to himself. Were he at the bakery, he'd have fires lit in the ovens by five. Meg was right. Now that

Bekah and Reuben were safely at the contraband settlement, this was beginning to feel like a holiday.

When he knocked on Meg's door an hour later, it surprised him to see Trudy emerge before his fiancée. "Are you much improved?"

"Enough to prefer to eat breakfast with the other guests." Her red cheeks and nose indicated that she still suffered a cold.

Meg followed her into the hall. "She has promised to take a nap later."

"Very good." Cade extended an arm to each woman, pleased to see Trudy up and about.

"Shall we tell her our plans at breakfast?" Meg squeezed his arm.

"Indeed you must." Trudy smiled. "I missed celebrating our Savior's birth yesterday. I don't wish to miss anything else."

"Then we shall." Cade grinned at his betrothed. They had decided to tell her before they spoke to the pastor anyway in case Trudy had strong objections.

Trudy's playful requests for hints set Meg to giggling, and it was a happy trio who filled their plates from bowls on the sideboard in the half-filled dining room.

After Cade asked God's blessing on their meal, Trudy gave Meg an expectant look. "Well, my dear, will you please put me out of my misery?"

Meg laughingly explained that they wanted to marry in the Chapel of the Centurion and planned to speak to the pastor later that morning.

"I understand why you want your wedding in such a place, but have you considered your cousins' disappointment?" Trudy, sprinkling a bit of salt from the bowl in the middle of the table onto her scrambled eggs, darted a glance at both.

"We hope Annie, John, and Hiram will be able to come." Cade looked at Meg, who filled in the gaps.

"It could work." Trudy buttered a muffin. "Is my illness the only reason we're allowed to remain here?"

Cade explained his belief they'd been allowed to stay because of the couple they'd escorted to the Contraband Camp.

"Then perhaps the pastor will agree. This is a military fort so I'm uncertain of the rules for civilians. I see families here"—her gaze swept the dining room—"but they are likely related to soldiers on the fort."

Cade's spirits sank. He hadn't realized how high his hopes had grown. He couldn't argue with Trudy's observations that most of the folks here were soldiers. Perhaps his candid conversations at the military camp and with the doctor would help, as news about strangers always traveled fast in the South.

At least the officers at the camp had extended passes for the three of them through January second.

～

*A*fter a leisurely breakfast, Trudy was ready for another dose of medicine, hot tea, and her bed—in that order. Meg got her settled, and then she and Cade talked with the maid they'd hired to sit with her and learned that security had relaxed a bit after the armies had left the area.

The fort bustled with activity an hour later as Meg and Cade strolled to the church. They stopped to observe a parade of soldiers in uniform. It stirred a feeling of pride that these men served the Union.

Soldiers strode past, sometimes exchanging greetings, sometimes merely tipping their hats.

"Mr. Yancey. Mrs. Brooks." Dr. Bennet walked toward them, leaning on his cane. "I was just coming to check on my patient."

"Good morning. " Meg smiled. "She just took a dose of medicine and is likely asleep."

"Then I shall stop later. Where are you off to?"

"The church. We hope to see the pastor." Cade explained their errand as the doctor fell into step beside them.

"Pastor Jones tends to be a suspicious sort. May I speak with him first on your behalf?"

"Of course. We'd appreciate it." Meg clasped her gloved hands together.

Cade added, "Obliged to you."

"Why don't you stroll along the shore while I go to the church. Give me half an hour." Dr. Bennet strode away without waiting for an answer.

Meg's anticipation withered as they headed toward the calm waters. The doctor expected to require so long to convince the pastor? It didn't bode well.

"We mustn't get our hopes up." Cade gently squeezed her gloved hand as it nestled on his arm. "Our wedding will be just as meaningful at St. John's Church."

Richmond. What a disappointment that would now be.

She couldn't believe how quickly her heart had latched onto the dream of marrying Cade here by the bay.

The wind nipped at her face. They walked without speaking for a while. Meg tried to memorize the whole scene—the gentle swell of waves, sailing ships bobbing on the horizon, the horse-drawn railroad, the octagonal stone tower lighthouse, and even the captured city of Norfolk to the south on the other side of Hampton Roads.

"The doctor is waving to us." Cade's voice brought her back to reality, and they hurried toward him. "He's smiling."

When they gained his side, the doctor said, "Pastor Jones is agreeable." He tipped his stovepipe hat at them. "You may meet him at the church."

Meg forgot propriety and threw her arms around Cade's neck. Then her cheeks flamed as the doctor chuckled.

"Please invite my wife and myself to the ceremony." He smiled kindly. "We shall be most happy to celebrate with you."

CHAPTER 43

"*A*nnie!" Meg rushed to her cousin's side as soon as her feet touched the dock.

Annie hugged her and then held her at arm's length. "How good it is to see you."

"We took a boat just like this one in February to this very fort." Meg admired the tall white sails of the ship out in the water. They'd moved from it to a rowboat to reach shore.

"Who'd have guessed I'd return to attend your wedding?" Annie asked.

"Uncle Hiram, how good of you to make the trip." Meg hugged him. "May I ask the favor of you giving me away?"

He kissed her cheek. "My dear, there was never any doubt."

An officer stepped forward. "Ye didn't forget meself, did you?" The tall Irishman grinned at Meg.

"I'll not forget my cousin's husband." She hugged him and drew back to peer at his shoulder straps. "What's this? Are you a first lieutenant now, John?"

"Aye." His green eyes shone with pride. "Just last month."

"I'm proud of you." She turned to her fiancé and waited until he'd finished greeting her uncle. "John, I want you to meet Cade Yancey. He's to be my husband."

"Aye. So he is." John, though about six-feet tall himself, looked up a little as he shook Cade's hand. "'Tis a pleasure to meet you. Annie has much good to say of you."

"Pleasure's mine. You're a hero in our eyes. Thank you for serving our country."

"'Tis a word that describes you as well." John put his hands on his hips. "I heard what you did."

Cade flushed crimson.

"That's what I tell him." Meg spoke softly. He was a true hero in her eyes.

"I agree." Annie smiled at him as a second rowboat approached with bags, boxes, and trunks. "Where are we staying?" She took Meg's arm, and they walked toward the hotel while the men lagged behind to see to the trunks. "And is Aunt Trudy recovered?"

"Much improved." Meg's legs did a little skip of their own volition. "She'll be at the wedding tomorrow. And we're staying at the Sherwood Inn. We were on and off the fort so quickly last time that I doubt you know where it is."

"Don't remember much about that day except Will's resigned face as he waved from the ship. And Father's tormented eyes." Annie shook her head. "We're here for the happiest of reasons this time. Do we need passes?"

"Cade will accompany Uncle Hiram and John to the army camp, but a lieutenant will encounter no problems obtaining them. When is he due back with his regiment?"

"January third." Her sigh came from deep within. "He'll leave on Thursday from here. I hate our goodbyes."

"Will you go with us to Richmond then?"

"Yes, John agrees, and I miss Bea. I sent her a telegram that I'll see her in a week. She's devastated to be apart from you on your big day."

"I know." A twinge of sadness washed over Meg. "But this place is so meaningful to us. It's the perfect place to marry. I just wish I'd brought the green dress I wore to Bea's wedding. I think Cade liked it."

"I'm certain of it." Annie laughed. "However, I brought you a dress. Our dressmaker employed two additional workers to stitch it up in time. I hope you like it."

Meg's heart skipped a beat at her cousin's thoughtfulness. "What color is it?"

"A deep blue, the color of the bay when you look down from the ship. Not dark exactly but...you'll see once we have our trunk. You'll be a beauty in it." She grinned. "Cade will like it too."

∞

*A*fter supper that evening, they all gathered in the inn's parlor. The day had been a whirlwind of activity. Cade marveled anew at the family he was blessed to join.

"Do you all know that Cade sings?" Trudy kept her eyes on her knitting.

Her latest endeavor looked like a big blue swirly square to Cade, but he knew it would be wondrous when completed.

"He sang to us while traveling. Very soothing." Trudy smiled at him.

"Do sing for us." Annie tugged on his arm.

His face felt like it'd been lit by the lantern on the table beside him. "It ain't nothing."

"It comforted me when I was afraid." Meg tilted her head.

Cade liked hearing that. He'd sing to her often in the coming years.

"Won't you sing for us?" Trudy lifted her eyes from her needles.

"All right." He figured he was the host of this gathering and should entertain his and Meg's guests. "How about a Christmas hymn?"

Enthusiastic nods encouraged him. He sang "It Came Upon a Midnight Clear."

Their applause embarrassed him.

"Do you know 'O Holy Night'?" Meg's eyes shone with love as she looked up at him.

"One stanza only. It's my favorite Christmas song." He could barely think when she looked at him that way. "Do you know more?"

"I do." Her gaze swept the room, empty except for their family. "I'll write it down for you." She left the parlor.

"She must really want you to sing it." Hiram relaxed against the cushioned chair.

"While she's gone, can you sing another?" John leaned forward, his elbows on his knees. He suggested "O Come, All Ye Faithful."

"Sing with me," he invited. He began the song, and they all sang with him. Others entered the parlor and joined in. After another song, all the seats were filled. "Joy to the World" was truly joyful with additional voices. It surprised him how comfortable he felt leading strangers in song. Perhaps all those lonely overnight trips with no eyes on him had trained him to concentrate more on the song's message than the singer.

"Here it is." Meg hurried into the room and sat on the sofa beside him. "All I know is these three stanzas. Will you sing it?"

He read over the words. His eyes widened when he reached the third stanza. No wonder he didn't know it. "I believe I'll stand for this one. It's not an easy song to sing."

Meg gave him an encouraging nod.

"O holy night! the stars are brightly shining;
It is the night of the dear Savior's birth.
Long lay the world in sin and error pining,
Till He appeared and the soul felt its worth.

A thrill of hope—the weary world rejoices,
For yonder breaks a new and glorious morn!
Fall on your knees! O hear the angel voices!
O night divine, O night when Christ was born!
O night, O holy night, O night divine."

Cade wondered at how his voice strengthened with the rapt looks on each listener's face as he sang the second stanza. Meg stared up at him with clasped hands, as if supporting his every note. All gazed at him as if the words transported them from the parlor to the manger to the Savior's throne.

Movement at the door caught his eye. Officers and privates entered the now crowded room while others peered inside from the hall. He took a deep breath and put his heart and soul into the last verse.

"Truly He taught us to love one another;
His law is love and His gospel is peace.
Chains shall He break, for the slave is our brother,
And in His name all oppression shall cease.
Sweet hymns of joy in grateful chorus raise we;
Let all within us praise His holy name.
Christ is the Lord! O praise His name forever!
His pow'r and glory evermore proclaim!
His pow'r and glory evermore proclaim!"

As the last note faded, there was absolute silence. Then thunderous applause overwhelmed him. Folks leaped to their feet and began thumping one another on the back.

Tears trickled down Trudy's face.

Annie's mouth was shaped in a big "O" as she tore her eyes from Cade to Meg.

Hiram, rubbing his hands together, looked as if a bolt of lightning had struck him. Cade never thought to see the savvy businessman so moved by a simple song.

Meg placed an arm around Trudy, who wept into an

embroidered handkerchief, and stared at Cade with so much love in her eyes that he felt humbled.

After all, he had done naught but put his whole heart into the message of a song.

John shook his hand. "Me wonders if that's the first time that particular stanza has been sung in Virginia. Bravo, me friend. They've heard it now."

CHAPTER 44

*T*oday was the day. As Meg stood in a lovely blue dress in the back of the church with her fingertips resting on Uncle Hiram's arm, she marveled that the rest of the country would remember this as the day the Emancipation Proclamation took effect.

She'd always remember it first as the day she married the finest man alive, the man who waited for her beside the altar with Pastor Jones, John, and Annie.

Lord, help me be the wife he deserves. He's known much sorrow in his life.

Her eyes lifted to the stained glass where a Roman soldier was depicted above the podium. Several officers and soldiers who'd heard Cade sing the previous evening shifted in their seats when Aunt Trudy turned a smiling face to look at her.

The organ began to play.

"Are you ready?" Uncle Hiram whispered.

Tears glistened that her father wasn't the one asking, that her mother didn't sit in the front pew. She willed the tears away, for this was a happy occasion.

"Never more so." She gave him a radiant smile and turned her face to the man who waited for her with that wonderful big heart in his eyes.

Cade Yancey. The baker man who sang.

Did you enjoy this book? We hope so!
Would you take a quick minute to leave a review where you purchased the book?
It doesn't have to be long. Just a sentence or two telling what you liked about the story!

Receive a FREE ebook and get updates when new Wild Heart books release: https://wildheartbooks.org/newsletter

Book 1: *Avenue of Betrayal*

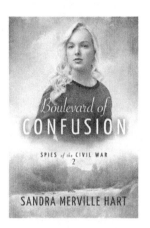

Book 2: *Boulevard of Confusion*

Book 3: *Byway to Danger*

ABOUT THE AUTHOR

Sandra Merville Hart, award-winning and Amazon bestselling author of inspirational historical romances, loves to discover little-known yet fascinating facts from American history to include in her stories. Her desire is to transport her readers back in time. She is also a blogger, speaker, and conference teacher. Connect with Sandra on her blog, https://sandramervillehart.wordpress.com/.

ACKNOWLEDGMENTS

I will always be grateful to my agent, Joyce Hart, for her perseverance, guidance, and friendship for the past several years. I've learned that agents suffer along with authors the sting of rejection and I'm grateful that she shares the joy of seeing this Civil War book series published.

I've learned much from Robin Patchen, who is an amazing and gifted editor. I'm thrilled to work with her, Misty Beller, and the team at Wild Heart Books, who have been both professional and gracious to me. I look forward to working with them on the next series!

As always, historical novels require much careful study to add authenticity. My research trips to Richmond museums, cemeteries, battlefields, and other locations were incredibly insightful. My husband and I also traveled to Fort Monroe, which is an amazing place. In fact, I was so inspired by the historic fort that I knew it must play a pivotal role in my story.

The Historic St. John's Church where Patrick Henry gave his famous "Give me liberty or give me death" speech is part of my story. I had a wonderful and educational visit to this Richmond church. The staff there were extremely helpful, taking time to answer my questions and explain the church's history. What an inspiration to be in a location steeped in history. Thanks for the warm welcome by the entire staff.

I missed a few family events while writing this book. Thanks to family and friends for their understanding and continued support.

Thank you, Lord, for giving me the story.

AUTHOR'S NOTE

I learned much about the spying that happened during those turbulent years of the American Civil War while researching this "Spies of the Civil War" series. History reports a surprising amount of spying happened in the capital cities of Washington DC (largely known then as Washington City) and Richmond, Virginia, which was the Confederate capital.

After all my research, I'm convinced that much of the spying never made it into the history books. Spies kept their activities hidden to protect themselves and their loved ones. Of course, Northern spies received praise after the war ended. Southern spies received scorn, so they were more likely to bury their secrets from the pages of history.

In our story, Meg is a former Pinkerton detective, often called "scouts" in those days. It was dangerous work. One Pinkerton scout, Timothy Webster, was hanged in Richmond. (His death touches *Boulevard of Confusion*, Book 2 of this series, as part of the story.) Other scouts spent months in Richmond prisons, so Meg's fear of discovery is valid. Much has been written about Allan Pinkerton and his agents. Pinkerton's agents were loyal to the Union and were active in several southern cities, including Richmond. They were a courageous group that changed their names, professions, and style of clothing to fit the parts they played in order to discover secrets of the Confederacy.

Miss Elizabeth Van Lew, a wealthy Richmond resident and Union spy during the Civil War, lived in a mansion across from St. John's Church, which she attended. On June 26, 1862, Elizabeth, Eliza Carrington, and an unnamed female visited John Minor Botts's farm, where they listened to a nearby battle. Because history refrained from naming her, I chose Meg, the heroine of our story, as that third woman who observed the Battle of Mechanicsville, which marked the beginning of the Seven Days' Campaign. In *Byway to Danger*, Elizabeth sometimes supplies Meg with information to pass to Washington City (as Washington DC was then called) via her letter carrier. Historically, Elizabeth was aloof from her neighbors and careful with her secretive spying activities. She often worked independently from other Richmond Unionists.

Civilians of the North and South were able to send letters to loved ones in the opposing states by using a "Flag of Truce." These letters were often read by officials before reaching its intended audience. For this reason, folks with secret information paid letter carriers to deliver mail directly to the recipient across the Mason-Dixon line. Timothy Webster, the Pinkerton spy who was hanged, was a letter carrier. His charge was $1.50 per letter so I used that as the rate Meg paid.

General Clayton in my story was loosely inspired by General John Henry Winder, the man tasked with enforcing martial law in Richmond. History records him as a stern, gruff officer.

St. John's Church in Richmond where Patrick Henry gave his famous "Give me liberty or give me death" speech is another historic location in this series. The church's history and its current staff inspired me during a research trip. Some characters in *Boulevard of Confusion* (Book 2) and *Byway to Danger* (Book 3) attend this church and both books contain scenes with this location.

I visited the impressive Fort Monroe in Virginia as part of my research. Constructed from 1819 – 1836, its rich history inspired me, leading me to include it in two books of this series. This important fort on the Chesapeake Bay was under Union control throughout the Civil War. It was at Fort Monroe that Union Major General Benjamin Butler refused to return three fugitive slaves to the South. Virginia had seceded from the Union and Butler wasn't bound to comply with the request. Instead, by declaring them "contraband of war", Butler protected them and all who would flee slavery onto Northern soil. Fort Monroe became a symbol of freedom and many called it Freedom's Fortress. A moat surrounded Fort Monroe and there were homes, churches, and a few businesses outside the fort.

The two churches mentioned in the story, St. Mary Star of the Sea and Chapel of the Centurion, were outside the fort in 1862. I wasn't able to venture inside the Chapel of the Centurion where Meg and Cade visited, but I did find a few clues about the sanctuary that were included in the story. Also, Sherwood Inn was an actual inn outside Fort Monroe. I couldn't find details about the inside of the two-story inn, yet imagined they provided meals for guests in a dining room and at least one parlor for gatherings, as this was a common practice at that time.

Freedom's Fortress became a powerful symbol for enslaved people. Soon after General Butler declared the three slaves as contraband of war, hundreds of men, women, and children arrived, seeking the fort's safety. When the fort couldn't accommodate so many, the Grand Contraband Camp was established in nearby Hampton, which Confederate soldiers had burned before fleeing. On those charred remains, the nation's first self-contained black community was built about three miles from Fort Monroe by the autumn of 1861. Over ten thousand former enslaved people eventually made the camp their home.

I chose to end the story on Fort Monroe, where so many important historical events have taken place over the years. President Abraham Lincoln officially issued the Emancipation Proclamation on January 1, 1863. From other research, I knew that the proclamation was read before crowds and at celebrations on that day, but found no records it was also read at Fort Monroe. I thought it fitting in my story to celebrate the event through a Christmas song, sung by a heroic baker man.

I hope you enjoyed this story set in Richmond in the second half of 1862. I invite you to read the whole series. Please watch for "Second Chances" series, which starts a dozen years after the Civil War's end. It begins with *A Not so Convenient Marriage*, where a spinster teacher desires to help a family recover from tragedy and dreams of finding love with her schoolgirl crush.

Sandra Merville Hart

If you love historical romance, check out the other Wild Heart books!

Marisol ~ Spanish Rose by Elva Cobb Martin

Escaping to the New World is her only option...Rescuing her will wrap the chains of the Inquisition around his neck.

Marisol Valentin flees Spain after murdering the nobleman who molested her. She ends up for sale on the indentured servants' block at Charles Town harbor—dirty, angry, and with child. Her hopes are shattered, but she must find a refuge for herself and the child she carries. Can this new land offer her the grace, love, and security she craves? Or must she escape again to her only living relative in Cartagena?

Captain Ethan Becket, once a Charles Town minister, now sails the seas as a privateer, grieving his deceased wife. But when he takes captive a ship full of indentured servants, he's intrigued by the woman whose manners seem much more refined than the average Spanish serving girl. Perfect to become governess for his young son. But when he sets out on a quest to find his captured sister, said to be in Cartagena, little does he expect his new Spanish governess to stow away on his ship with her six-month-old son. Yet her offer of help to free his sister is too tempting to pass up. And her beauty, both inside and out, is too attractive for his heart to protect itself against—until he learns she is a wanted murderess.

As their paths intertwine on a journey filled with danger, intrigue, and romance, only love and the grace of God can overcome the past and ignite a new beginning for Marisol and Ethan.

~

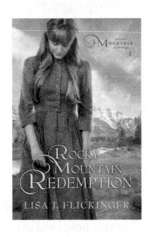

Rocky Mountain Redemption by Lisa J. Flickinger

A Rocky Mountain logging camp may be just the place to find herself.

To escape the devastation caused by the breaking of her wedding engagement, Isabelle Franklin joins her aunt in the Rocky Mountains to feed a camp of lumberjacks cutting on the slopes of Cougar Ridge. If only she could out run the lingering nightmares.

Charles Bailey, camp foreman and Stony Creek's itinerant pastor, develops a reputation to match his new nickname — Preach. However, an inner battle ensues when the details of his rough history threaten to overcome the beliefs of his young faith.

Amid the hazards of camp life, the unlikely friendship growing between the two surprises Isabelle. She's drawn to Preach's brute strength and gentle nature as he leads the ragtag crew toiling for Pollitt's Lumber. But when the ghosts from her past return to haunt her, the choices she will make change the course of her life forever—and that of the man she's come to love.

∾

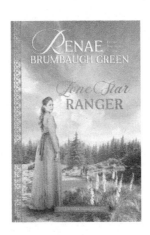

Lone Star Ranger by Renae Brumbaugh Green

Elizabeth Covington will get her man.

And she has just a week to prove her brother isn't the murderer Texas Ranger Rett Smith accuses him of being. She'll show the good-looking lawman he's wrong, even if it means setting out on a risky race across Texas to catch the real killer.

Rett doesn't want to convict an innocent man. But he can't let the Boston beauty sway his senses to set a guilty man free. When Elizabeth follows him on a dangerous trek, the Ranger vows to keep her safe. But who will protect him from the woman whose conviction and courage leave him doubting everything—even his heart?

Made in the USA
Middletown, DE
24 July 2022

69875066R00189